THE
EXECUTIVE
GAME

Pearse Elliott

Pearse Elliott

First published in Northern Ireland in 2018
by Excalibur Press

Copyright © 2018 Pearse Elliott

ISBN: 978-1-910728-49-9

Formatting & layout by
Excalibur Press

Excalibur Press
Belfast, Northern Ireland

team@excaliburpress.co.uk
07982628911 | @ExcaliburPress
www.excaliburpress.co.uk

I would like to dedicate this book to my Mother and Father Sally and Paddy and all the Elliott family. My son Shane, and the two Genevieves. I would also like to dedicate this to all those who toil with a quill for a living.

Pearse Elliott

I would like to thank Larry Lamb and Felicity Blunt for their support in the writing of this book. And a very special mention to Tina Calder and Excalibur Press for having the bravery to publish it.

CHAPTER 1

Havana, 2000.

Move. That's what everything did in Havana. Animate, inanimate. From the blonde palm fronds that acted as corrals for salsa parties, to the soggy potato frites hopping to the vibes of the Afro Cuban music on the bonnet of a dark green Chrysler that lay abandoned in a liquid mess of congregated filth at the corner of the black street. O'Neill moved with the languid grace of a boxer towards the awry knot of rickshaw men, smoking and drinking rum, waiting on tourists coming from the jazz pits, and city cabarets. The rickshaw men were the portals to the illicit in Havana, where a man could acquire most natural vices. Their raucous banter and fiery cigarette buds, O'Neill's beacons to these vices.

The throb of music smouldered in the close night, the sounds of salsa - Weedos, maracas, and drums, his soundtrack. O'Neill loved the omniscience of the music in Cuba; the music was tremors in the ground, currents on the air, some invisible and invincible virus that infected all. It had taken him some time to grow accustomed to the humidity, which for the first few weeks was an unseen and crushing force, that induced a man's body to a constantly uncomfortable state of sopping sweat but he had learned to pace himself, to keep movement to a minimum and his breathing slow. Everything in life was breath. He knew this from when he had boxed. And now as he reached the untidy unit of men he knew it was important to breathe slowly in the close heat. An older man in his fifties seemed to be in charge. The rickshaw man was out of shape, with a huge distended gut that leaked grotesque from under a too small child's Nike T shirt mangled with grease stains. An insurmountable barrier between his groin and torso. The rickshaw man smoked and coughed simultaneously. O'Neill got in the wicker rickshaw. The man moved slower than stone. His chest wheezed bronchial with every step and finished each wheeze with a high-pitched whistle. The malecon, the coastal sea wall that offered little resistance to the sea stretched before him an immense bending promenade of few lights and lots of people. People sashaying and hustling, smoking and drinking shin deep in shit and litter. The rickshaw man began his sales pitch.

"My name is John Rambo, here I am the big boss – You want chikka'?

Rambo removed a portfolio of photographs from underneath the rickshaw carriage, and handed them to O'Neill. Since he had been resident on the Island, O'Neill had encountered these catalogues. Most in the public transport service, even the government taxis that sat outside the hotels had their own personal collection of women and although the novelty had passed O'Neill couldn't help but leaf through all that was passed to him, with voyeuristic curiosity. O'Neill flicked through the grubby stained photographs of lot's of women in various states of nudity, black women, white women, Asiatic, and Latino. The only thing they shared was astounding beauty that seemed to wane with each turn of a page. The photographs were impersonal, the women with bored looks on their faces and the graphic images of their private places almost gynaecological. O'Neill handed the photographs back.

"No chikka Rambo." O'Neill said. The rickshaw man began his new sales pitch.

"Well how about some coca rock, from Bogotá my friend, or some nice mountain weed?" Rambo said labouring on the coastal road like an old ox on heavy plough, stopping at a battered lorry container that sold cheap beer and rum.

"Drinky for Rambo?"

O'Neill felt little pity for the man. He was a hustler, and a rogue but he possessed the information O'Neill wanted.

"One for Rambo then we move on."

He purchased the Cuban the drink, and had one himself and then delivered the ultimatum. "I want you to listen carefully Rambo, I don't want pussy, and I don't want coca, I want cigars – the best you can get from the good tobacco regions, Vegas, Pinar Del Rio province, and so forth. Montecristo, Cohibas, you get me quality cigars comprende?" O'Neill showed him a fan of U.S greenbacks, the fat man's eyes dancing on their receipt, like a crow plotting a theft.

"Comprende, I big boss, no problemo - cigars". "Rambo – you fuck me? I fuck you and all you own".

O'Neill left the rickshaw, paying the man five dollars for his time.

***

There were simple rules with cigars that forbade a sensible man being ripped off. The darker the colour the stronger the flavour. The best cigars were grown under cheesecloth to protect them from direct sunlight, and rolled on the inner part of a woman's thigh. O'Neill didn't know if it this was true but he liked the sound of it and kept the myth alive in his memory when he smelled and smoked them. Quality control was a simple squeeze of the cigar - if the cigar sprang back into shape quickly it was bona fide, if it didn't it was a rip off. That's all a man had to know with cigars; trust your tongue and touch and you couldn't go wrong.

It was late the next night, and another electricity blackout in the city, when he walked fast up the malecon wired for action. A gusty night with a stormy mane of clouds in the sky, moving fast over the sea. Night fishermen passed him wearing the huge inflated rubber inner tubes of cars on their heads like absurd sombreros. The first time he had seen them he had wondered what the purpose was, until he had watched the men float on the big tubes fishing by candlelight on the night surf like fallen stars on a black plain. O'Neill glanced to the opposite side of the malecon cautiously. A man always had the impression he was being followed in Havana, the strobe light shutter flashes of the silent storm revealed nothing but the salt decayed, antiquated once grand houses, their faded pastel colours of marine blues and ambient greens glowing in the tropical night.

He had travelled from Canada three months before, lured by the promise of a quick killing from contraband cigars and a Real IRA man's vouch. "The Coca Colas" they called themselves after Coca Cola's advertising catch phrase "Coke – The Real thing". The irony was not lost on his train of thought in Havana. Where America's number one consumer product was banned, and The Real IRA's demand for a thirty two socialist Republic for small farmers in Ireland was no more a flag of convenience for dirty deeds. The Real IRA had tried to recruit him back in Ireland, aware of his reputation as an operator, as a life taker with former micro Republican groups, whose campaigns were mostly spent in insidious feuds taking the lives of friends, as well as others. For a small period of time he had even contemplated his contact's offer, bored with the ceasefires and soporific inertia induced by a violence free Ireland. That was until they detonated that bomb and then O'Neill realised they were nothing but incompetent at best and left Ireland to earn a living in smuggling contraband. But this contact had provided him with the information of quick money and that was all at this stage of his life he wanted.

Time to do the business. He smiled to himself. "The business" that's what it was called everywhere, that's what anything could be called, from death to sex, and sex from his time in Havana seemed to be the number one pastime. The Cubans liked to fuck. Everybody liked to fuck, that was a no brainer but the Cubans would fuck everywhere, without the constraints of Western mentality, and bedrooms where attitudes instructed instincts, here he had come to realise instincts instructed attitudes, all they needed was the night, desire and area and it ignited him.

He headed at a quick pace up past the old bank now used as apartment blocks for hundreds of people to meet his contact. Two hundred yards further up the Malecon, the crumbling coast wall fanged by the sea. O'Neill passed a young couple - a pretty teenage mulatto girl wearing a bright summer dress who teased her lover on the Malecon's chipped wall as she feigned indifference to his nuzzles and rubs, a thick lipped young man in his twenties. She swayed as O'Neill stared and turned provocative allowing her buttocks to rest on her lover's lap.

O'Neill stopped mesmerised, and puffed hard on his cigar - sweat had saturated the end and he found great difficulty in tasting the tobacco. That and the distraction of the girl combined to make him toss it away. Her nipples were large as buttons and brown, they spiked through the slight summer dress, as she pressed her buttocks tight to her lover and grinded them succumbing to the music, O'Neill spat tobacco flakes from his mouth as her lover braced himself tight and aimed at her with his hips on the sea wall. Her lover kissed her on the shoulder and her body convulsed as the music got louder, and faster, the light of the tropical storm glowed a clearer image. She raised her beautiful face to the storm clad sky, revealing traces of her Asiatic, black, and Spanish heritage-high cheekbones, full mouth and a black silken mane of hair. She closed her eyes and hissed like a snake O'Neill watched her hands as they hurried behind her little cotton dress, firstly working expertly her lover's short's down, then hitching up her own skirt.

No underwear was the first thing he thought, no underwear and she didn't care, that wasn't as important to her as a cock in her pussy, the organ in her gland, not as important as the music, the night, the instinct over attitude. O'Neill took residence ten yards from where they frolicked on the wall, and in one fluid movement they were fucking. O'Neill thought he could document penetration to the very second, the second the beautiful girls' eyes flickered as fast as dragonflies wings.

The couple began to rock as one in undulating movement, a thread of saliva beamed from her lover's mouth falling onto her slender neck where it remained, glistening like a crystal necklace. The storm photo-flashed their ecstasy in silent strobe explosions of light igniting the vibrant night. O'Neill was diseased with envy, he felt rage swarm about him, inspiring him to tear her young lover off and slam him numb to the dirty rocks behind the old sea wall, and claim her for his own. An insect careered into O'Neill's head, interrupting his train of thought with its velocity. It was big enough to follow its descent to watch it crash to the dirty ground. It tried to recover by propelling its big diaphanous wings to a blur until he stepped on it cracking it into an inky smudge.

A policeman appeared from nowhere moving him on with his black eyes. Easy to tell he wasn't Cuban, from his fair appearance, his shaved blonde head chipped in scars and his suntanned muscular torso. O'Neill read the cop's face which was as pitted as the Cuban streets they stood on. He reeked of sweat and cigar but most of all of corruption, the corruption of power that seemed to infest Cuba. O'Neill headed across the road, away from the old sea wall. Crossing the busy two laned roads avoiding the old cars driven at high speeds and headed into the old streets of Havana.

Old Havana - a necropolis hive of fading grandeur. He turned into a side street past apartment blocks, their facades bruised with dirt and stained with condensation and peeling paint. Kid's clothes and leafy plants hung from nearly every scuffed balcony and he imagined he could see other things peering from their dark confines. Things he couldn't possibly understand. A man's mind could play tricks in Havana's night blackness, staring up at the cracked slat doors and reja iron grill barred windows that reminded O'Neill of jail.

The old city smells made him feel nauseous, the stench of

open sewers and the city as it rotted. It had taken him a long time to get used to it, again with his Western mentality. The third world was one hell of a place. A place he had cultivated a belligerent admiration for. People survived as best they could appreciating the simple things in life, the live music, sweet rum, the ubiquitous sex and all its sweetmeats. The odour of decay pervaded the olfactory system with every step, at the turn of every corner. Both acrid and organic as piss moored at every kerb of every street. He turned into the street where he was supposed to go nearly stepping on a worm ridden dog, all ribs and hip pins that roared a warning as it tugged on the entrails of an equally worm-ridden dead cat. O'Neill sidestepped the snarling cur stepping into a puddle of piss.

"Motherfucker" he spat at the dog, conscious now of his urine sopped foot.

It was a good word to have in foreign countries, almost every nationality understood it's meaning, a global word that conveyed all. He had picked it up in the States and had now coveted it dearly. The street was serpentine and obscured by a blanket of darkness. He walked up the middle avoiding the impenetrable sides. Halfway up he noticed an abandoned machete that lay on the roof of an old marine blue Chevy. The car bizarrely, made O'Neill incongruously think about an old American TV show. Every Motherfucker in Cuba had a machete, the way most yanks he had ever met had a gun, only you wouldn't find yanks leaving loaded guns around. Beside the machete lay the hacked off scalps of coconuts, O'Neill lifted it, tenderly running a calloused finger over it's serrated brown edge, certainly sharp enough for coconuts. He reached the end of the street where at the corner he discovered an impressive stone sign. The sign was in three languages

-English, Gaelic, and Spanish. He concentrated on the English text, which it proclaimed "The people of Cuba and Ireland two Island peoples whose struggle for hope is the same." This was the place.

The rickshaw man Rambo had arranged it earlier. He waited a little while, underneath the sign. The night loomed darker, with the regular event of a power cut apparent from the flickering streetlights.

After a while still plagued by the uncomfortable sensation of being watched, he saw a man emerge from a tall door frame of a derelict building to his left, beside a salt bitten wall with a vivid mural of Che Guevara smoking a cigar. The man was fringed by shadows but O'Neill could sense he was a warrior; white aged scars were scored on his lithe torso, the petty vandalism of knife fights. On his left hand was the faded green tattoo of a scorpion, in his right hand a large knife that flashed, making humming sounds as it cut the air. The man flaunted his knife skill at O'Neill, the way an arrogant gambler would a fan of cards, making the blade glint and blink as he flicked it in his hand. Within O'Neill's extensive experience, and extensive experience was as vital as blood to a heart in this game of illicit contraband, there was always the perception that the stranger was the weaker man. O'Neill had thought about all the different, and hairy situations he had been in, and an honest evaluation would be that eight times out of ten, people wanted the deal done, but sometimes depending on how desperate the other party was, there would be situations like this. Where the stranger unfamiliar with the terrain and area had two choices, like in the animal kingdom – fight or flight. O'Neill always chose the former. "Dollars amigo?" The Cuban asked.

"Cigars amigo," O'Neill answered.

The Cuban laughed at O'Neill's reply, a laugh of arrogance and confidence. "My fren - dollars." The Cuban repeated. "Cigars." O'Neill countered, neither backing down.

"Ok you win gringo"?" The Cuban conceded and moved stealthily ten feet to his left outside a derelict house where he removed a cigar box of Cohibas from the interior and pushed them along the filthy ground to O'Neill. O'Neill picked them up with his eyes locked on the Cuban. He inspected it flicking his eyes from the cigar box to the Cuban. It was a genuine Cohiba box all right, made from cedar wood that kept the cigars moist and the cigar bands seemed authentic too, but they were often easy to acquire pilfered from the local factories for the purpose of counterfeit. On closer inspection the quality of the texture was poor to the touch and this was confirmed when O'Neill sparked one up with his Zippo lighter, only to flick it away with contempt into the night after two puffs.

"No deal," O'Neill said.

"Dollars amigo!" The Cuban replied, an edge to his voice that qualified demand. O'Neill shook his head an emphatic no, and walked away keeping the Cuban in view as he did so.

The Cuban walked quickly to the centre of the street, thirty feet in front of O'Neill, in front of the mural of Che that overlooked proceedings like a billboard, cutting off O'Neill's exit. O'Neill looked behind him into the murky night and the dead end of a solid wall.

The Cuban moved with athleticism, like a dancer into the centre of the street, closer to O'Neill cocky at the knowledge of the dead end. It was a matter of good fortune with the machete O'Neill thought, a man needed it in the places O'Neill went, these dark places, with dead ends and only one way out. These dark places where havoc was the only indigenous species. O'Neill was glad to have the machete behind his back, but aware that the Cuban was cautious at the apparent lack of fear. O'Neill was more confident on seeing the Cuban in the light, not overconfident, confident - there was a difference. O'Neill had thirty pounds of muscle on him, most of it on his shoulders and arms but more importantly he had the machete to his knife - the equivalent of a magnum to a derringer. O'Neill stared at his combatant's eyes where he saw the dark places, places only the killers of men recognise and can only imagine the distant wrecks of other poor vessels they have plundered. No doubt about it the Cuban was a killer - like O'Neill. The Cuban lunged fast with the knife, raking the air where O'Neill had been, O'Neill leapt back startled by the Cuban's speed, saved only by his fighter's instinct. He retaliated with a low kick in an attempt to sweep the Cuban's feet - but the Cuban met his leg with a kick, O'Neill realised that the Cuban had tried to kick him on the kneecaps. He made a mental note of the Cuban's co. ordination commending him in his head, confirming for O'Neill that he faced a formidable adversary. There was silence except for their shallow excited breathing O'Neill with his experience as a boxer knew how crucial breathing was in judging opponents and judging by this the Cuban had plenty of oil left in the tank. The Cuban raced forward punching the air with the blade backing O'Neill up, before making a diagonal leap sure onto a porch trying for the advantage of high ground, aware now that O'Neill was not afraid, that the Irishman intended making a fight out of it.

"I'm going to fucking kill you motherfucker!"

O'Neill whispered it slow so that the man could see the hell in his eyes, calling his bluff. He had hidden most of the machete blade at his hip to give the impression that the blade was not so large. The Cuban bought the subterfuge and leapt from the porch driving his blade forward like a swordsman. O'Neill sidestepped, allowing the Cubans' momentum to take him past, then he hit the Cuban hard with the machete. The blade whizzed through the Cuban's right arm severing the Cuban's hand sending it flying into the night. Bizarrely and in shock the Cuban pursued his hand as a Mother would an errant child in doing so he offered up his life in the form off his back and vital organs. A man could show no mercy in a fight, he had to finish and finish was what O'Neill did. He almost chopped the man in two with a hacking two-handed blow. He shipped consistent heavy swipes to the torso, alternating sides as blood splattered O'Neill's face and upper body and the mural of Che as the knife fighter fell at O'Neill's feet.

O'Neill watched the man die below him in supplication, the Cuban's language universal and clear now in the slight mewling and whispered laments of the ruined that needed no translation and that all men understood. O'Neill stood over his victim sucking oxygen in great gulps, the adrenaline flushing through his system, euphoria in his veins, like electricity through cables. He left the scene the only way he could from the dead end street, his body slick with sweat and gore and walked as quickly as possible until he was a long way from the scene. It was important to walk, running attracted attention -witnesses. Running was panic. He took refuge in a derelict building that had a rusted sign which read "MOSCOW" above it's broken arch. He dragged a cigarette from the crumpled box he stored on his shoulder, under his ripped and blood stained Guinness T shirt, glad that it was black and that it camouflaged the new blood on it. He lit the cigarette grateful for the comfort as the smoke clouded his lungs.

Kill or be killed was the law of the jungle, wherever that jungle would be - Belfast, London, LA, Havana. He felt nothing, nothing but relief at being alive, and the comfort of his cigarette and the exorcism of violence. He sat bleeding and smoking as lightning silently stalked the grey sky above him. O'Neill was a man without a soul. He came to Cuba to risk his life amidst the sex, the dark rum, and salsa for the tobacco. A bad man -a man who had failed his species and defied his tribe, warrior, gladiator, killer.

This world was a feral place, where a man needed the primal tools to survive, like the machete, by now a great blood sopped weight in his hand, that revealed him as some great ancient primate that brawled for life with a predator, rooting and digging in the earth's scabrid muck for a tool that usurped the advantage over tooth and claw. Ireland and its bloody legacy had reared him. Before the machete, it had been a gun, and before the gun a bomb. He could kill without mercy and sleep in his bed at night, eat a meal, defecate - function. And that's what O'Neill did - function. Once he even dared to think it was political, but now he was resigned to the fact there was very few things political about killing, killing was blood and shit, terror and fear, killing was his life or his death, no more no less…

O'Neill had lived thirty-nine years of his life in Ireland - twelve in jails. The last five in different countries, forging a living in these dark places, where few men like to inhabit, or see. He had killed thirteen men in his life. And with the political notions came the romantic notions, socialist notions, the thirty-two county Republic of small farmers. It seemed preposterous to even think of it with a dead man's blood spotting the ground. He now knew it to be a lie, reminded in perpetuity by the Che Guevara tattoo on his right arm. The tattoo now tainted by a dead man's blood that gave Che a slightly vampiric visage. O'Neill had come a long way from the teenager who had gotten the tattoo. A soiled symbol of who he once was. O'Neill chugged on the cigarette and flicked the ash onto the blood on his arm where he used the ash to soak up the blood and obscure Che's disappointed eyes. He would have to get it removed soon. O'Neill did not know how he had ended up this way, all he knew was that a man was minted from the hell fires of life and a hard life made a hard man. He stubbed out the tan butt of the cigarette and watched the silent lightning freeze on the sky above him like diseased lung bracioles on an x ray.

Chapter 2

Mauritza posed on the dirty ruffled sheets as the man took photographs of her naked body with a Polaroid camera. The man then removed a freshly killed chicken from a bloodied white plastic bag and slashed it with a pearl-handled bowie knife in the abdomen, holding it over her and the old bed in the small room. The chicken was a banty cock. Yellow as a sunset with silver mirrored razor spurs still tied to its heels that caught her reflection on the bed, an ugly fucking chicken with even uglier green and grey innards, that spilled in grotesque loops close to her face.

A fighting cock from the ranch she thought. It was typical of The Caribe. Nothing went to waste with him, everything had a purpose. The chicken blood dropped slowly onto her breasts, bouncing off and adding new stains to the already stained crumpled sheets. She worried about Grace the Casa owner, giving her more work to do. She always had the room immaculate for Mauritza, rum on the cabinet and sometimes even pilfered soap in the toilet.

The Photographer was an Italian, in his thirties, olive skinned with a little goatee beard and thin glasses, a photographer The Caribe commissioned regularly for his women. Mauritza had little love for the Italians. She granted them a handsome nation, but she cared little for their spendthrift natures and their predilection for black women.

"You are a very beautiful woman," the Italian said.

Mauritza ignored his bullshit and shot daggers of contempt

with her beautiful differently colored, eyes, one jade green the other a nutty brown.

"In Milan you would be famous?"

"Italian just hurry it up and save your bullshit for fools."

"Beautiful women like you are as precious as jewels."

Mauritza felt her toes curl and smiled through her gritted teeth. The Italian was but another of The Caribe's minions, a man summoned when she had a client. The Italian used a simple Polaroid camera, he turned it sideways as if he were an expert, when taking the photographs, and strategically placed the sheets close to her torso accentuating the chicken blood that glistened on her naked body and the Casa de particular bedroom. The things she did? The room had the hum of sex still fresh in the air, the pot pourri spoor of expensive aftershave and stale sweat mustered to make her nauseous in the hard heat of the afternoon. The stench of the fat tourist she had fucked for money was hard to remove even with the rickety fans and open windows. The situation was simple, with the images captured on Polaroid's another minion selling flowers would approach the tourist, in this case an obese Canadian architect in his forties called Mel as he lounged in the pool at the Nacional hotel. The minion a trusted confidant of The Caribe, would then explain to him in clear English and certain terms that she had some photographs he must see and then she would quite calmly remove two Polaroid's from her flowers.

One would depict him leaving the cabaret with Mauritiza, the night before, the second the lurid and quite realistic image of the feigned dead Mauritiza in the blood dotted bed. The tourist would then be asked to make a donation of two thousand U.S. dollars to clear up the "situation". Nine times out of ten they obliged, horrified.

"Now my love play dead, stare with those beautiful eyes to a distant place."

The photograph slid from the camera like a tongue and the Italian waved it until it was dry. He looked closely at the photograph, impressed by the image he had captured.

"Very good, very good, you look like you are dead."

And Mauritza for the first time that afternoon spoke to the Italian with truth in her eyes and honour in her heart.

"That's because I am."

CHAPTER 3

The black 1954 Fleetwood Cadillac coasted at three miles per hour down the Prado street dappled with shadows. Street kids ran alongside watching their lengthening, distorted reflections in the ebony paintwork. The car was as immaculate as it was long complete with fishtail fins as sharp as the mirrored razor spurs that adorned the heels of his fighting cocks, ten front lights, and a shining chrome engine grill. The street kids knew this great car belonged to The Caribe. The man in the white suit, the master of the blades, the Devil with the cigar box. The street kids scrambled onto the snarling stone lions that lined the streets of the Prado district, as the Black Fleetwood pulled up outside a large lemon coloured Arabic styled house. The Caribe got out of the car in his white suit and a Panama hat, which shrouded his mahogany face. The Caribe was over six foot, well over it, and he had the gladiator physique of a heavyweight boxer. Once, a tourist had stopped him and asked him for his autograph, mistaking him for Cuba's famous super heavyweight boxer Felix Savon, but The Caribe was bigger than Savon, badder than Savon. Under his brilliant white suit jacket he wore nothing, a magnificent cleft of sculptured chest muscles rippled as he moved, a torso of dancing knots. Under his arm he carried a Romeo y Julieta large cedar cigar box capable of holding five hundred large cigars, that jingled with its cargo of metal as he walked. On the front of the box was an ornate painting of a young man proclaiming his love to a young damsel on a balcony.

The Caribe could trace his ancestors back to the fierce warriors who proved the only real resistance to the Spanish in Cuba. Through his veins raced the cannibal Carib blood that once ate other men's flesh.

The Caribe entered the slat-blinded house and strode through the room out back into a large courtyard, past a canary that suddenly stopped singing. There he was met by two policemen who bowed submissive, holding a young Cuban man in his twenties tightly by the arms. The young man's face was badly beaten, one of his eyes was swollen tight and blood trickled from his mouth. The young man thrashed like a fish in a net on recognition of The Caribe.

The Caribe set the cigar box down on a little oak coffee table that had been placed, on his prior instructions in the middle of the courtyard. He flicked open it's tiny intricate brass latch to reveal a set of knives, knives of every shape and description from Thailand, Africa, the Philippines all stainless steel which sent shimmering reflections creeping all over the courtyard.

The young man moved his head from side to side crying, his features crumpling seeking mercy.

"Senor I sorry, Senor I sorry."

The young man's voice keened with the desperation for exoneration. "Sorry like a snake senor." The Caribe's voice crackled with irony and wit. "I not know senor, I not know..." The Caribe noted that the young man repeated most things twice, which he found irritating. With languorous precision he removed his white suit jacket and hat and hung them on the bars of an open window, closing the wooden slat blinds. He turned, revealing the huge, impressive torso covered in fine scars and a green jailhouse tattoo of a serpent over his heart, and the muscles that flickered under his skin like live things.

"The Caribe is the only seller of cigars in Habana you know amigo…" He held the three men's gaze with his mighty frame; he then slipped on a knuckle knife with a curved blade that fitted like a ring on his index finger. The Caribe nodded to the policemen who released the young man. The Caribe pointed to the cigar box in the centre of the courtyard, with a gracious sweep of his arm pointed to the blades.

"You want a knife senor?"

The young man shook his head slowly a solemn and begging no, his features getting even more crumpled.

"Coward as well as a thief." The Caribe said.

The Caribe was sometimes baffled when men would not fight or even when they refused to flee, when they accepted their death almost graciously, when they whispered one of the two words "Please" or "No". The Caribe moved fast, in one balletic movement like a swordsman driving a rapier blade, he struck the young man once hard in the chest cavity piercing his heart and vital organs. He then withdrew the blade as the young man dropped to his knees and into the position a baby sleeps in gasping for air that would never come.

"You know now senor, you know now."

The Caribe crumpled twenty US dollars in his palm and let the money fall to the ground watching the policemen set upon it on their hands and knees, flagrantly enjoying the abuse of authority, for in Havana he was the authority, and left them to deal with the dead man. He walked powerfully from the house without his suit and hat on and entered his black Fleetwood and drove away at the same speed he arrived at.

O'Neill returned to the hotel Nacional the next morning after bathing in the dirty sea water to wash the hard blood off his body. On bathing he had discovered a small wound above his kidneys that wept a serum of pus. He was intrigued at how oblivious he was to it during the fight, and fearful of the subtlety of blades.

The Nacional was busy with a wedding party in progress. O'Neill watched as a young couple took their vows in the elegant grounds, in sun-bleached grass full of fallen mangoes, and two courting peacocks. A group of traditional Cuban musicians provided lush music, which filled the air with an elegant arrangement buoyed by the peacock's calls. O'Neill watched and he wondered what the attraction was - Marriage, or monogamy? Of love? He realised that within in his life he had no beliefs anymore, no belief in love, or revolution.

It was not as if he was impervious. He had been in love once. When he was younger and Ireland full of revolt. Meabh was her name, named after the famous Celtic warrior queen. They had met at a riot, her a left wing student with militant tendencies, him a brawler with nothing but murderous intentions. The smell of fresh petrol ripe on her clothes, a scarf masking her face. Her flashing, bambi lashed eyes betraying her gender, demanding his pistol to shoot at riot police. O'Neill demanding to know what organisation commander sanctioned him surrendering the weapon, her retort - "me". And from there on in he had been caught, caught by youth and common cause. He banished the thoughts because of the complications and because sometimes he was unsure of what his true feelings were. Another three troubadours approached him on the veranda blocking his entry to the foyer, an old man and two young pretty women wearing bright, traditional garb. He had been serenaded by many Trovas since he had arrived, now was not the time.

"Fuck off". In his best Belfast accent.

They soon parted, their mouths frozen in the deep breaths that were being primed to sing. O'Neill entered the elegant foyer of the old hotel, past marble columns and ornate crystal chandeliers, and the glass fronted miniature version of the hotel that took centre place in the foyer. O'Neill bunked the queue bustling with tourists at the information desk. He stayed at the hotel at the behest of a recently deceased man's credit card. In Ireland he had a contact that worked in the death records, and together on recent deaths they would apply for various credit cards. It was a lucrative scam that allowed him the privileges of luxury accommodation and that revealed it's true benefits in faraway places. He approached the concierge at the hotel desk, a wide-eyed butterscotch coloured man in his forties.

"Is there a Hotel Doctor?"

"Si Senor, room 411."

O'Neill walked up the foyer past the photographs that lined the walls and of past and present Hollywood stars, Spencer Tracy, Clark Gable. The only recent one he recognised was the man that acted in the first Batman film, but he didn't know his name. His side had begun to ache a dull distant throb that indicated that the wound was possibly becoming infected. O'Neill headed to the doctor's room which was simply a vacated hotel room on the fifth floor, the beds replaced by a desk and chairs, with an air conditioner that sounded like a chainsaw cutting a tree, and a standard eye sign that O'Neill could read from fifteen metres down to the dots. The Doctor was beautiful, in her twenties. O'Neill studied her the way an artist would a good painting. Her skin was alive and tanned silk by the sun, her mouth full and red as a pepper, with a fine mane of ebony tresses that she had to keep pushing away from her fine face.

"What happened?" The Doctor asked. "I walked into a door," O'Neill said.

She met his eyes with a proud, arrogant glance that shot caution. O'Neill noticed that her eyes were different colours, one the colour of an emerald the other as brown as tree bark.

"Well it looks like it's infected," she said, aware that his eyes were idling on her. He loved the way she spoke, the words clear but with the exotic pronunciation of far away places.

"Where are you from?" she asked. "Ireland."

"Irelandes, a long way from home." "The way I like it," O'Neill said.

She foraged in a wonky drawer for something that she knew was there, removing an old jar. She opened the stiff lid of the murky brown jar with a manly twist, into which she dunked a cotton wool pad before pressing it hard on the open wound. O'Neill recoiled a little on receipt of the stinging liquid solution. The Doctor tutted flirtatiously.

"A big strong boy like you." "Well am I going to live or what?"

"Some antibiotics, and salty water, will secure that. You have to watch those doors – they're very sharp."

"I will. What's your name?" "Doctor is my name."

"Well Doctor how would you like to go for a drink with me tonight in the hotel?"

In another country in another place this would be regarded as insulting for the Doctor, but this was Cuba, she looked at him with defiance and continued to tend his wound, concentrating on exerting pressure and applying the bandage. O'Neill was slightly thrown by the length of time it was taking for her to respond.

"No."

The words came with conviction and confidence. She feared but one man in her life; men were a commodity, an economy, nothing more. He shrugged his shoulders and headed for the door, she stopped him at the door with a hiss.

"But I will fuck you for a hundred U.S dollars. But not here in the hotel".

It was the ways things were done in Cuba everything back to front, upside down. From sex before courtship to the old fifties cars to the health and education system, nothing was spectacular but it worked. He liked it, the way the women didn't bullshit, kept it simple, how the people worshipped black religions here, the dark Saints, in a religion called Santeria, which consisted of African effigies, and lace. The Santeria followers had debunked the satanic influence of their practice to the same novelty as Christians worshipping a bearded man on a cross. This was Cuba.

The women in Havana had opened his eyes to all during his stay in Cuba, he had had numerous and consensual encounters instigated by women's gentle flirtation. He liked the way she used the word fuck, matter of fact without taboo or agenda. It was a business transaction, her body the sale. His desire would cost money. It almost reversed roles, she was a woman that spoke matter of fact, flippantly as if her proposition was the done thing and this time when she pressed the bandage on his wound he winced. The deal was struck and before he left he asked her where the steepest hill in Havana was, she told him she thought El Rincon, beside Verada, had a hill the street vendors called "The Hill Of Tears".

This suited his purpose just fine. O'Neill went to his room and ordered a hotel taxi from the queue outside. He got in and asked if the taxi man had a catalogue of women that he could look at. He explained to the fine-featured mulatto man that he had a preference for the larger woman. The man seemed to understand through hand signals and O'Neill's slow speech, what exactly he was looking for. He licked his forefinger and flicked fast through to the catalogue of whores until he reached the last page. On the last page there was a huge naked black woman who looked to O'Neill to be aboriginal in origin, but the taxi man explained her family had lived on the Island for a very long time and had come from the Polynesian

Islands. O'Neill asked to be brought to her. They cruised through the old districts and the cramped streets until they reached her address. They parked outside the battered shanty shack, constructed of old rotten boards and rusted tin. O'Neill rapped the tin door and was met by the huge woman whose name was Sandra. She brought O'Neill into the tiny, dirty room where her body odour was almost overpowering. O'Neill took a seat on a little plastic stool as the vast woman plopped on a smutty mattress where her business was conducted. O'Neill explained his terms of agreement and paid the large woman a hefty wad. He then took the woman in the cab to downtown Havana, where the heat was over a hundred and twenty degrees, and the tar on the road melting. There were only three rickshaw men standing at the corner, but one was Rambo.

O'Neill approached him like he had before; with a languid stride. Only both now knew what the consequences of that last meeting were.

"Rambo?"

The man engrossed in discussion with his two colleagues and unaware of the caller's identity said "Si Senor." Without turning, and then when he did and on recognition, he took a step back caught unawares unsure of where the situation would take him, a guilty look on his face. The Cuban as nervy as an animal before a storm, almost crouched in a defensive position, holding his chest, his breathing now a bronchial bark with the high pitched whistle more prominent.

"I have a friend, Sandra, who would love to see the top of The Hill of Tears."

O'Neill motioned to the waiting taxi, and Sandra with great difficulty got out of the taxi like she was chained, the taxi practically rising on her exit. The other rickshaw men burst out laughing, the large woman made her way with great difficulty towards them.

"Rambo shouldn't you be getting over there, and give that lady a hand?"

The Cuban looked to his sniggering colleagues and then to O'Neill, the killer of his friend, the back street jailbird and all round tough guy, found hacked to pieces in the barrio not three nights before.

"Si Senor" was all he said.

CHAPTER 4

O'Neill let the cold water of the shower blitz his skin. It was meant to be at least luke warm. Then realising that the only truly cold things in Cuba were beer and the rattling air conditioning. He felt the prospect of sex crackling in his veins. Porn never did it for him; there was no reality to it, the plastic pneumatic shapes, distorted genitalia. O'Neill loved the reality of sex, the crude overpowering smells, of cum and pussy. He liked bodies that were real; scars, and loose skin. Inside his room he turned on the old cranky TV set that gradually came to through fuzz and broken shapes that projected the inevitable repeats of Castro giving another speech, damming the yanks and praising the revolution. O'Neill had been in Havana three months now and he was amazed at how the old man with the beard and liver spots could speak for so long and so fucking much even in repeats! No wonder Che went to Bolivia.

O'Neill checked the case under the bed. He now had three thousand cigars, all top grade - Romeo y Julieta, Montecristo, some Caribas. He had a buyer in Key Largo who had agreed to give him forty dollars a hoagie. He would pack them in beeswax and cellophane, secrete them in olive oil and coffee to mask their scent and smuggle them into the states through British Colombia, a place called Kingsway the weakest immigration point he had found in the U.S. He had spent the last week in the Pinar Del Rio regions and in Havana gathering them up; the most he had spent on one cigar was eight dollars. It was a clear profit of around a hundred thousand U.S. dollars; and the penalties if caught were minimal compared to other contraband. O'Neill stretched out on the bed careful with his side, and took a thick Montecristo cigar out from the case, and lit it watching Castro and his old face damn the Yanks.

His wound felt better and he thought about the beautiful Doctor who had tended it, and fucking an intelligent educated woman, a woman that in the real world the world of mortgages and occupations, where Doctors were paid good, would've barely spoke to a wastrel like him.

***

O'Neill had arranged to meet her at a Jazz cafe called Cafe Guerto which was close to the Nacional in the hotel district. The building was modern for Havana, tall and well lit that rumbled with sound. It had a moat illuminated by underwater lights full of Terrapins, and a neon sign with the painting of a one eyed cat where the one eye of the cat flashed. A black muscled doorman as big as a polar bear stood over the front door growling at the hungry hustlers who stood just inches outside the designated property of the club, and the glare off lights, shrouded by the black of the night, fended off by the neon wash of the bright lights like jackals from flames, pestering the fat tourists entering with sharp hisses. Not jackals, snakes O'Neill thought prompted by the hisses as he entered matching the big doorman in his horn-locking stare. The interior of the jazz club was cold enough to make him cough, the air conditioning cranked to maximum. The entire place was adorned with mirrors. There were few people, mostly ubiquitous fat middle aged men with pretty senoritas, a couple of Cuban families awarded a night there by national coupons, an old cad in a cravat playing a piano with fingers as long as breadsticks and a group of musicians setting up.

O'Neill walked to the bar and ordered a daiquiri.

She came in late. He had expected that. A woman like that had no need to rush to meet men in this city. She was in a blood red dress that left little to the imagination; it swooped and clung to every curve on her voluptuous body like body paint. O'Neill watched as she hissed a welcome to the musicians on the stage. This was her regular, where she brought her prey. He loved the way Cubans hissed; a hiss meant approval, a hiss meant "Hello", "Goodbye", "Come here". Ancient and primitive, but as sexy as a woman talking about fucking. She lit a Marlboro cigarette and he ordered her a drink – whiskey, lots of ice.
"Hi Hirish".

It turned him on the way she talked; the tongue inflected an "h" on most words. O'Neill smiled as she hauled on her cigarette bloodying the butt with her lipstick.

"I talk too fast sometimes, so I'll try and talk slowly. You know about Ireland then?" She nodded her head slow.

"I love U2."

He smiled at her wit.

"I hate U2."

"You to?"

He gave her a second smile.

"I know very minute about Irelandes, for hiz' sample I know

that there has been a lot of political conflict, between the British and the Hirish".

"And the Irish against the Irish." O'Neill said. O'Neill bit the interior of his gum, it wasn't the subject he wanted to discuss on holiday, he thought the subject expired but somehow it was always there a belligerent grievance.

"So you're a Doctor. A good job being a doctor?"

"Not here in Huba", for hiz "sample in Huba" a fockin" hotel cleaner makes more money on tips than we do, that's why I must supplement my income."

She poked a finger at him as if he was a source, and he was. O'Neill always liked women who swore, Meabh had sworn. It was his language.

"Besides we have very small resources due to economic sanctions..."

"But still the knowledge of being able to save a person's life that's a fucking talent."

"As hiz taking it."

O'Neill looked at her, what did she know? How did she know? What did they call it a woman's intuition. Anyway it was one hell of a reply to what could have qualified as bullshit comment. The thought woke him to why was he trying to bullshit a whore anyway? O'Neill pointed at her with his baby finger.

"I like the way you talk."

She paused before answering, cracking ice on her sharp white teeth.

"Me too." She said.

O'Neill laughed. She was sharp. She accepted the compliment with a graceful smile. He lit a cigarette took a couple of puffs and passed it to her, she put it to her lips. He surveyed the scene, aware of the ambience - the tattered flames of candles wavering under the artificial air, the lush music, a lone couple dancing, expertly oblivious to the people in the room, their hips close and lips closer. Few places held allure for him. His nights in foreign destinations, and nefarious activities allowed little time for R&R.

"And you like my country?" Mauritza said.

O'Neill smiled. It was more smirk than smile but a smile some women liked, a smile that told them all they needed to know.

"I do now," O'Neill said.

O'Neill raised his glass and clinked it off hers before she had a choice in the matter, tonight he was going to enjoy himself, fuck he was paying enough for it. The band began to play rhythmic, and solemn music that gathered more dancers. It seemed to be a tune the interior population knew and liked.

"Slainte".

She quizzed him with her eyebrows.

"We say that in Ireland before a drink, and when we say goodbye."

"Slainte"

Sounded better on a Cuban tongue he thought.

"I'm O'Neill."

For a slight second he thought that she wasn't going to answer, or give him some bull shit porn star nickname like most hookers, lap dancers had but she answered with sensuality and deliberation.

"Mauritza."

It was her real name. He did not know how he knew, but he knew.

Mauritza did not know why she told him her real name, but somehow it felt ok to do so, a certain safety emanated from his physical presence that she liked. With the knife wound and the square jaw.

And the band played on. They got better with every clink of glass. The band picked up on the audience mood, erasing the solemn melancholy and introducing a more vibrant, and dance friendly, orchestral sound. Incredible music, music that wafted mellifluous, and tantalising, that captivated all. The Cuban people danced and swayed, mouthing the words to the songs like they were their own, the pretty senoritas leading the ungainly tourists. The tourists danced badly, their movements sluggish, like seals on land, trying to emulate the Cubans with little success. And how could they? O'Neill thought, these incredible people who all seemed overqualified for their lives of hardship. He watched as the band mingled among the patrons playing to each little group of drinker and eaters. Each time the band played a table, a member of the Cuban table would be assigned an instrument to complete a song, almost as perfectly as the band itself. O'Neill stared in disbelief as old men picked guitar strings impeccable, as children played trumpets, and finished off songs. This was a nation of genius, and yet a nation of failure, where doctors fucked patients to supplement incomes.

The band reached the bar, where Mauritiza and he stood; they knew each other - the band and her, O'Neill aware of furtive glances between her and the guitar player, surprised himself by a barb of jealously. They proceeded to pluck the notes of a song they knew she liked urging her on. She shook her head embarrassed, looking to the ground like an child at a parent's anniversary party. For the first time O'Neill could see who she was, girlish, her shyness overshadowed by necessity. The band rallied the crowd, who mustered, in support forcing her to do whatever it was the band knew she could do. Finally she gave in. Bucking her hair back from her face she was handed a trumpet, she held out a hand and O'Neill helped her onto the bar, trying to drag his eyes away from peering up her skirt. She towered above all her long legs lithe, and muscled like an athlete.

She took a breath, and then started to play with an intensity that startled him. Her music was joined by the band producing an incredible sound, a sound raw and wild. He watched, an erection pulsing at his thigh. Watched as her hair fell into her eyes, watched as her breasts undulated with each breath she exhaled into the trumpet. She finished the song and the crowd went wild, standing one and all in adulation clapping ferociously whistling, screaming, everyone except O'Neill who sat rooted to the bar stool. The sensation he felt was the same as the first time he was shot in Belfast, during the hunger strikes. Whoever the motherfucker was must have been a crack shot; he was hit from a range of four hundred yards with an SLR rifle. The same sensations visited him now, breathlessness, numbness, heat, and time slowing to a still. The instinct that kept him alive all these years, the instinct that had made him crawl, run, hide, the instinct he swore by, told him to go, screamed to him to down his beer in one and get the fuck away from her, But as she sat back beside him he felt now as if he was being electrocuted.

They ended up at a Casa De Particulars she knew in Miramar in a black street that looked like it harboured many secrets. Grace answered cautiously, and let them in. The room was full of little fans rat tatting, offering little solace from the wet heat of the humid night. O'Neill surveyed the contents of the room, there was a stone bust of Lenin on an old wooden radio, and three wooden chairs, a black and white photograph of a young pretty woman straddling a tank gun in uniform, with an old carbine that he thought was interesting. He thought to himself he would have liked to meet that gal at that time in the photograph.

"We must give Grace some money for the room?" Mauritza said. "How much?" O'Neill said.

"Fi'ty U.S dollars."

In the states you could stay in a motel with a Jacuzzi and all night porn for fifty dollars. But he looked at the old woman, her irises clouded by chalky cataracts, and then the archaic photograph of the revolutionary beauty on the wall and plucked fifty U.S dollars from his pockets. Mauritiza paid the old woman, speaking in Spanish and placed a kiss on the palm of her hand and then placed her palm on the old woman's forehead. The women spoke quickly and tenderly to each other, with the old woman getting off her wicker chair and entering a room, returning with a brilliant white, tiny sequinned dress that Mauritza gushed over, like it was something.

"Isn't it beautiful O'Neill?"

O'Neill liked the way she mentioned his name in the request; he had been here before, with women all over the world.

"It is created hizpecially for me by Grace"

O'Neill looked at the old woman, she was hardly a fashion icon. He bought her the little white dress.

"Maybe I'll see you in it sometime..."

"Maybe,"

They entered an old bedroom that had, at least fresh cotton sheets and one pillow. He then realised they were using the old woman's' bed, with more fans, and old lace curtains jaundiced by heat and age. He paid her in a hunk. She uncomfortably counted the money, avoiding his stare, and satisfied she placed it in her purse. She undressed with dignity and provocation allowing him to imagine. She turned revealing her full and beautiful body the skin glistening all over in a silky tan. He noticed a caesarean scar above her hip that shined silver on her dark skin. He wondered if her child would grow up as beautiful as her. She noticed him looking at it and she placed her hand over it shielding it like it was precious. She placed a hand on his chest. He didn't know why but he kissed her, she responded, they bumped foreheads and both smiled, the kiss surprised them both, him more so when she responded. He ran his tongue over her small but perfectly formed teeth. He enjoyed this, she bit him lightly on his tongue and intermittently gently sucked it. His hands hustled to her private place and she pulled him close, a long leg curled around his back, stroking his spine with the sole of her foot. Their lust was veering on pain now. She flicked him with skill onto the bed, grinding hard against him, she pushed his head with force down to where she wanted him. O'Neill went. The taste was strong and intimate but not at all unpleasant; this invoking hisses and slight moans from her, that encouraged him on, whilst her hand went to him strong with skill, until neither could take any more. She turned and lay on her stomach silently telling him what her favour was, and guided him in. O'Neill pounded her hard, and she expertly stalled him with the slightest of painless kicks to his testes with the soles of her feet.

She spoke in tongues of pleasure, a hybrid language of whispered Spanish and lust dictating the pace with her hips, increasing the pace until she sensed him close to the finish. Then she switched positions, her now on her back and blood striping his spine. He had been with so many whores before. He knew their ways, hammy acting, rehearsed deliveries to make a man climax quick, and fast, but somehow the way she

socketed her pelvis tight to his, the way she clutched him with her slow delicious hips told him that the words she uttered were tinted with the truth. That there could be the slightest possibility that she was enjoying this, for it seemed she had no intention in it ending soon. She thrust harder to him taking him deep, bracing herself on the wall, and absorbing him fast until both their bodies undulated as one, without control. After they had finished O'Neill took a piss in a toilet by candlelight. The stream of urine was needle thin and as accurate and made him aware of another sound, the different cumbersome plopping sounds of something else in water. He took the candle and directed the light in that direction to reveal an old tin bath, and something in it. He recoiled on sight of what was in the bath. A huge live sea turtle plopped in five inches of bath water with a shell the size of a bin lid. O'Neill stared in amazement. Recently he had watched a wildlife programme, stuck in a hotel room in Florida in the middle of a hurricane, there were apparently only around four hundred of these fucking things left and one was about to be made into Sunday stew! He blew out the candle and went back to the bedroom to discover Mauritza gone. He walked to the front door to see a taxi cab pull away in the black street. Mauritza went to the back seat window. He looked at her, as she winded down the window of the car. "Slainte"
The word came from the cab like a fleeing elegy..

"Fucking whore." O'Neill spat under his breath, watching the taxi's red taillights fade into the distance. O'Neill got dressed and left firing a look at the old woman who sat on her wicker chair sewing more sequins onto another dress. For some other sucker O'Neill thought. She at least looked guilty.

CHAPTER 5

In her little house in Vedado, Mauritza bathed in the cold water, using some bath soap she had taken from the Nacional. She dried off, and hung her red dress in the wardrobe and put on her low cut black dress, the dress he liked her to wear. Three old fans clacked air at her as she read the time on the old alarm clock 2.20. She took a seat and applied her new makeup thinking of the Irishman. She had never met an Irishman before. She liked the way he talked, his speech was fast, lilting and non-understandably funny, but more than that she could sense something in his face – some unspoken connection, some private wound that only those who had suffered could sense.

It had been a long time since she had been physically attracted to a man. This she thought was a reality a side effect of having sex with strangers for money. But the sex was good. Being a Doctor she could understand bodily functions and responses. This was not unusual, a physical response to sex was normal especially if a client was attractive and the Irishman was, but a kiss? No matter how much she tried to rationalise this she couldn't qualify it. So long since she had met a man to have a drink with, a boyfriend? She almost laughed out loud. She had left quickly embarrassed by her feelings. Any more time spent with the Irishman and she would have been expected to contact the photographer.

She placed her cheap jewellery and looked at the photographs of her as a young girl with her Father and Mother on a summer's day on the beach. All those years ago, her mind a clean slate, then filled with ambition and hope for the future.

She fetched the old cigar box where she stored trinkets and private artefacts, guiltily aware of her own truth. She gently fetched a baby's pink wristband in from the old box; she removed it with care and put the wristband to her nose. The fragrant smell of her baby had long gone. She read out loud the fading ink of the birth date and name, then kissed the little plastic wristband and placed it back in its special place, her only document of her child's' identity. It was a ritual she repeated every night.

She left later than she had expected, it had taken more time to compose herself, and she had noticed this more recently, like she had noticed grey hairs amongst her black mane. She walked through the badly lit streets, past the hisses from teenage corner boys drinking rum.

"Where you going at this time Mauritza?" She didn't answer. "She must be desperate."

One shouted loud enough for her to hear. She passed them with her head down. "Whoever it is, is one lucky guy." She was glad they couldn't see the tears in her eyes.

***

With the city in constant blackouts, and a failing electricity grid, O'Neill thought the old city a great place for vampires. At night Havana had very little light. The old men who played checkers on the street used their lighters to see the board. O'Neill entered a dark and moody bar in Prado where he had heard there were cigars for sale. The bar was occupied by a few rough looking whores who looked pregnant but weren't, wearing dirty all in one striped jumpsuits that must have been the latest women's fashion and old men supping on inch glasses of Havana club. All a man had to do was wait in Havana, wait and it would come. Sex, drugs, cigars, death.

"Some nice ladies for you senor?"

O'Neill looked at the hustler pestering him, wire oval glasses, small and slight in stature with a rat face and a pencil thin moustache that looked like it needed a lot of work to cultivate. He wore a little pork pie hat and a boating jacket. O'Neill stared at the little man with disdain, like a dog curling his lip.

"Where?" O'Neill spat with sarcasm.

O'Neill flicked his eyes to the rough looking women in the bar at the back the bar. "Not here, theez are the ugliest ladies of Havana".

The little Cuban whispered it as if it was a dirty joke, but still the women heard him. Some type of women these Cubans, O'Neill thought, as a bottle whizzed past the little Cuban's head. He ducked adroitly as if he magically detected it on internal radar that O'Neill knew most victims in life possess, and spat insults in his native tongue in the direction the bottle came from. O'Neill watched in amazement as the bottle bounced harmlessly off the bar and skipped onto a table into an upright position completely intact now, an omen of benevolence. A big whore in her fifties screamed obscenities at the little man from the back of the bar; backing him up quick as she mock charged O'Neill's money was on the woman.

"No more fucking women for me..." "How about Cigars

senor?"

O'Neill ordered another Cristal beer from the bar where an old barman with the largest hands O'Neill had ever seen and a face scrapped by time, tended the bar. The big-handed Cuban returned quickly with a Cristal beer in a can, glad to see dollars instead of the useless pesos. O'Neill stared at the beer tiny in the horny hands as big as Serrano hams, gratefully took it and then addressed the little Cuban.

"I'm going to say this once – normally this comes at the end of a conversation, but in light of recent events, I don't think I'm making it clear to you people? If you bring me a cedar box that's been stolen from the factories, and inside there are cigars with authenticated cigar bands that have been also stolen from the factories, I touch that cigar, I smell that cigar, and I smoke that cigar, and that cigar is not stolen from the same factory? That cigar is not what you say it is – I'll stop your fuckin' heart."

The little man stepped back. In mock surprise he took his glasses off and blinked his eyes. "Whoa I know who you are – you are Rocky Balboa," the Cuban said.

He was funny O'Neill would give him that.

"My friend I am not like those putas and cutthroats that hide on the street corners, I am the real deal, my cousin he work in Partagas factory – I have for you Monti-Christo, Romeo's, Cohibas".

"Gimme your id?" O'Neill demanded clicking his fingers.

The little Cuban hesitated, probably becoming aware that O'Neill wasn't an everyday tourist that could be hustled for a quick buck. O'Neill knew that all Cubans, especially in Havana had to have photographic id which included a fingerprint and address. The little Cuban pulled out his id with a bad photograph, which depicted the same individual without his hat and glasses. The man's name was Victor Hernandez Obispo. He was from Old Havana and he was, to O'Neill's shock, 44 years of age, occupation dentist. O'Neill handed the little man back his id memorising the address.

"There you go Victor". "No one calls me that..."

O'Neill chugged on his beer smiling.

"My name is "Tony Montana, like movie – Scarface."

O'Neill laughed, he knew who "Tony Montana" was; the little Cuban took off his little pork pie hat.

"At your service - Drinky for me?"

O'Neill decided the joke warranted a drink. He bought the little Cuban a beer. "Now Tony tell me about these Monti-Christos..."

Three hours later O'Neill, half jaked on rum and whiskey, found himself following thirty yards behind the little Cuban. This was normal in Havana a Cuban could get jailed just for speaking to a tourist. Soon they were in the Chinatown district beside a little street stall that sold pork rolls and churros. They stumbled into a young black man convulsing on his back at their feet and screaming in the street. The man babbled in mad tongues that reminded O'Neill of fundamentalist preachers he had seen on cheap American cable stations, the language indecipherable.

"Santeria religion" Tony Montana explained noticing O'Neill's interest. "Jesus," O'Neill said.

"No Jesus, is not here my fren, this is the other guy, he communes with the black saint Oggun, we must not disturb," Tony explained, blowing an sssh on his lips, O'Neill still staring at the shuddering man on the ground. They hurried on, O'Neill slightly disturbed at the young man's screaming, the beer had him lit and on guard. Alcohol did that to O'Neill, he had learnt this from a very young age the hard way. Drinking in shebeens in West Belfast, amongst men who were fighters, brawlers, and killers. He waited watching Tony Montana pay for the cigars from the little stall; across the street through the murky night he noticed another group of men with rickshaws. There were three of them and none wore shirts; fit men, which was apparent in their lithe physiques rigged with muscles. O'Neill could see by the way they talked and smoked, pointing at Tony Montana that they were agitated. Trouble was coming no doubt. He knew these men they were the same around most street corners all around the world.

"Churro my fren? Drinky gives me munchies"

Tony Montana handed O'Neill what resembled a doughnut on a stick, O'Neill shook his head slowly, watching closely the three men across the street with the rickshaws, guiding his concern to the little Cuban with his eyes.

"You know them?" O'Neill asked.

Tony Montana looked across the street and squinted and on his face came an expression that was all O'Neill needed to know about the situation.

"We must go my fren now."

O'Neill spat on the ground and glared at the little Cuban. "Thought that. You get the cigars?"

"Yes, yes we must go, problem."

The little Cuban turned and walked away at a canter on his heels, turning into an even darker street. O'Neill glared at the three rickshaw guys on the opposite side of the street, one actually limbering up like a sprinter before a race.

"Fucking rickshaws." He said to himself.

Across the street the men followed, leaving their rickshaws, quickening their pace, O'Neill took the opposite direction from where Tony Montana went, and the rickshaw guys. He followed a left and right that took him into an even more derelict street. Surveying the black streets for some sort of weapon, O'Neill evaluated the situation. He owed this little shit nothing, this was nothing to do with him he was a meddling fucking tourist to one and all, but he abhorred people being outnumbered, a person being beaten by people. It reminded him of being beaten by screws in the jail for failing to wear a prison uniform, it reminded him of a group of British Army squaddies beating him with rifles in a dank alley, him drunk and vulnerable, unable to defend himself properly, his reactions numbed by cheap booze, like he was now. It stirred his primal urge to defend the less strong, roused by the slow heat of the night and the black streets, the rhythmic rattle of drums from a salsa party somewhere in the old city, detonating in his ears like the prison screw's batons on plastic shields, but most of all it was the need to compete, and his belief that only true opponent to violence was increased violence, the violence that had haunted him most of his life. To his extreme left was a Spanish type villa that was in the process of being renovated. O'Neill cut across the dusty street to see if workmen had left any tools he could use. He broke into a light jog over crumpled corrugated iron and into the cool confines of the house, there was little to be salvaged from the site, a few long tail shovels and mounds of rubble.

The night's sanctity was broken up by high-pitched screams, that came from O'Neill's extreme left and O'Neill was sure who they belonged to. He ran from the empty house and alongside the dark streets to its source locking onto the louder shouts of extremis. He crossed the street and went down to where he had last seen Tony Montana. As he came around a corner he saw the men beating the little Cuban into a ball of blood on the dusty ground.

Three men, three men against one. O'Neill knew the only chance he had was to knock one or two out quickly, and then that would even the odds. O'Neill had a big right hand; that all the opponents he had faced were told to beware his right hook. A sports journalist in a local newspaper had once described it as "murderous". It had served and saved him many times in his life and he needed it now like no other.

The first Cuban he hit with it went straight to sleep. O'Neill caught him hard and from behind under his ear. The sound of the jaw breaking caroming like a rifle shot in the night. O'Neill could see the Cubans were off guard. One continued violently stamping on Tony Montana while the other rushed at O'Neill, a muscular black man wearing khaki shorts, who caught O'Neill with a useful right cross, jarring his head backwards. This awarded the Cubans an opportunity and the other that was beating on Tony Montana an alert, for he stopped beating on Tony Montana and rushed to help his friend. Immediately they went to grips one trying to gouge at O'Neill's eyes the other hold him still. Under pressure O'Neill loaded all he had in his right arm and then slammed the hook hard to the black man's rib cage, splintering ribs and breaking him in half like a piece of bread, leaving O'Neill to grapple with the last man.

The Cuban was strong. O'Neill could feel the wiry strength jingling through him from the Cuban as they both fell to the dirty ground, O'Neill head butted him continually to distract his hand to O'Neill's head and then pounded him hard in the kidneys and in secret places of the body that only dirty fighters knew where to hit. A man could hide his head, close it tight to his neck, make it an awkward target, by moving it, but no man could hide his body. A man that could work the body the way O'Neill could was to be watched, he was to be feared. The shot hurt the black guy and O'Neill rolled hard using his weight and momentum to gain the initiative until he was on top. He choked the Cuban until his eyes rolled into the white world of unconsciousness.

O'Neill got to his feet. His chest felt like a furnace and his eyes were sore from their dirty fingers. He wiped dirt and blood from his face. There were four men in various states around him including Tony Montana, O'Neill helped the badly beaten little Cuban to his feet.

"Motherfockers" Putas!" The little Cuban screamed.

The little Cuban stamped on one of his assailants and slammed a sheet of corrugated iron across another's head before he left. He led O'Neill in a half jog through a maze of streets until they reached the well-lit area, which the tourists seemed to have colonised. They entered a little fast food Rapido café where they ordered rum, and after a while, they drank bitter espresso coffees. O'Neill inspected the cigars in the bright light, he squeezed one and was surprised to see it retain its shape. He lifted another from the bottom of the cedar case to his nose and expertly inhaled the dark tarry aroma, the way a wine aficionado would a fine pinot, almost detecting the aroma of a woman on the fine leaves. O'Neill then finally lit one up, chugging deeply drawing in the rich pungent smoke, and after what seemed an eternity (to Tony Montana anyway) he exhaled in short sharp puffs.

"We have a deal Rocky Balboa?" Tony Montana enquired. "A deal it is Tony Montana!" O'Neill said.

They clinked espressos and O'Neill noticed the little Cuban's face was busted up bad, he had lost two teeth, which made his appearance even more comical, his glasses were spider webbed with glass fissures and a cartoon like lump surged from his forehead.

"In a little while, my fren' I will go to my apartment and I will take my 45. out and I will kill those motherfockers".

O'Neill let him talk, bravado bullshit that would never be consummated that told O'Neill all he needed to know about the little Cuban - he was a weak man in mind and body. O'Neill had known men who were weak in body but strong in mind, men from jail, from the organisations, who could absorb obscene amounts of punishment, and never make a threat but the minute their antagonists dropped their guard cut them to fucking pieces, strong men didn't tell you what they were going to do strong men did it.

"You fight good, you a bad boy."

O'Neill ignored the comment; watching as the little Cuban worked his fingers in the pulpy, pink mash of his gum.

"Fockin" dentures man."

"How many cigars can you get me?"

Tony Montana removed delicately from the interior of his torn coat another two boxes of what seemed equally good, large Romeo Y Julietas.

"Tony Montana take care of you my friend - Drinky for me?"

O'Neill collected the cigars studying them; again they were good quality the tanned leaves moist and well packed. He nodded approval and then placed them in a brown paper bag.

"Drinky for you."

O'Neill ordered another drink and looked at the little Cuban smiling at him with no teeth and gums charred with blood, amused by the spunky smile. Although he had been solitary in his existence for a period of time, he could recognise and begrudgingly admire those of spirit, those who could smile through the pain, weather the ignominy of defeat.

"Who were your friends?" O'Neill asked.

The little Cuban slugged on his new drink like it was his last.

"Hass'holes my friend, they think that all of Habana belongs to them and their boss, Tony Montana don't give a fock about them!"

O'Neill rocked back on his plastic chair, unable to stymie the burst of laughter. The smaller man seemed riled by the laughter aware that O'Neill did not take him seriously. "Oh I see, you think that I bullshit you. Irelandes?"

The Cuban checked left and right like a spooked child about to cross a busy road. The little man leaned across the stained plastic table in preparation for a whisper.

"There is a man my friend in Huba, a Devil my fren in this city? This is his realm, the cops they work for heem, he haz no fear of the Government, or The Horse – this is his Government."

The little man gestured to the open air a universal opening of his arms. "His is the Government of the night, the parliament of knives."

The little man could hold a story, he reminded O'Neill of Seanachies in jail, the organisation's storytellers, who kept the younger men's attentions rapt. Men who could paint vivid pictures with their articulate tongues, men who enthralled through the bars kept waning spirits up, and the blood bubbling. They were priceless.

"Who the fuck is The Horse?" O'Neill asked intrigued.

"Tourist – Castro is the Horse."

"What happened to his great cleansing of the gangsters?"

"For day there must be night, for good there must be bad, and The Horse like all of man, he like young pussy, fresh pussy, they say – not me, they say that he has 'The Horse' in his…"
The Cuban opened his torn coat and showed O'Neill his interior pocket.

"You fock with this man my friend – bye bye. He keel a lot of people with a click of his fingers, a man can be focked up very nice for a good beer in this city, this man this Diablo, personally he likes to take life my friend, in his Government of the night, with his parliament of knives."

It was a yarn that flourished with the small man's natural oratory, and strange appearance O'Neill concluded. And from a yarn sprang a story and from a story a myth finally resulting in a legend. These ghoulish reputations existed all over the macho worlds from men taking other men's lives. O'Neill knew this because he had one where he had come from.
"They say he keel over eighty men in knife fights."

O'Neill looked to his new beer cracking it open and blowing the froth away, some of it hit Tony Montana. Eighty men was a lot of dead hombres, eighty men with a fucking knife! Even if it was exaggerated, and there were thirty men there was a lot blood, a lot of gore. There was a term they used for a close quarter assassin in Ireland - "Up close and personal," that's what this man would be. O'Neill had a mental picture forming in his head of what this man must be like, it was just like when he boxed he would find out who his opponent was, then he would compile a dossier in his mind of what type of men they were. If it was true what Tony Montana was saying, this man was a winner and a champion, a man of stamina and ferocity. Growing in strength with every fight, every victory, he would devour his adversaries souls, amplified by the arcane knowledge of the dead's last words, and their killer's face would be the last faded image their eyes would see. O'Neill knew this because this was the special relationship killers had with their victims, O'Neill knew this because he was one and the same – a life taker. With each individual opponent an invaluable experience that would arm the man with more deadly knowledge, after eighty kills a man could be forgiven for thinking himself invincible. Tony continued, flushed by caffeine, and adrenaline, the alcohol dictating his tongue.

"In this city a man can have his throat cut for selling one cigar to a tourist, every whore on this Island he owns, every Pitbull dog his, even the banty fighting cocks are his." The little Cuban dunked all what was left of his beer down his mouth pouring it into the pulpy maw.

"But don't you worry with you a tough guy and with Tony Montana at your side the streets of Habana will be safe."

O'Neill looked at the little man and smiled. "I feel a lot better now."

They clinked beers like they knew one another. "One thing

Tony Montana?"

"What my fren?"

"I'm not your friend."

Chapter 6

Mauritza lay naked on The Caribe's bed, staring at the gnarled wooden ghouls carved into the headboard of the antique four poster bed, marvelling at the laser beams of new sunrays that streamed in through mampara doors, striping her supple body with strips of light, and the feeling of space. Space not afforded in the cramped world of Havana city and Cuba. She stared at The Caribe sleeping beside her watching the massive torso rise and fall. She studied the torso flecked in scars, white aged fossils encased in the black granite wall that was muscle. The scars ranged from a large scimitar one that ran from his throat to above his heart, to a thousand nicks that dominated the meaty, sinewy forearms. Above his heart was a tattoo of a serpent in green permanent ink, of a snake with fangs. Soon he would awaken, flush for sex again, big, physical, rough sex. But it wasn't the sex she hated him for; sex was the simplest part of life she thought. In fact in the bed was the only time she got revenge; she would respond to his slaps with profanity, vicious bites, raking nails, and spittle. She hated him for other things, her Father, the possession, but most of all her daughter. And because of the various political regimes those in Cuba would always be conflicted over being owned. Older people remembered before The Horse and Che, the corruption, the gangsters. Some clandestinely lamented the absence of dollars, others rejoiced in the old man's leadership. It was mostly older people who called it leadership, the younger generation regarded it mostly as a dictatorship, and were bored with the old man's four hour TV repeats. Mauritza herself hadn't really thought about it that deeply, as her own personal circumstances dominated her mind more than politics. Sometimes, when she awoke before him she would contemplate plunging one of his knives into his heart, but she feared him, feared his strength, the almighty power she had witnessed first hand, and most of all the doubt that a knife pushed by her could kill him. She brushed her hand over the great frame that lay beside her, to feel for human vital signs, sweat, heartbeat something that would reveal a chink. It was untrue to say that she held nothing but contempt for him. She had first met him as a slight girl with the figure of a boy when she was twelve years old, he twenty. She remembered the scale of his person first, his huge hand engulfing her hand on introduction, the gentle handshake, the dark face with the fine features ruled by the black eyes, that reminded her of some black raptor bird from the family of butchers. The muscular body decorated by fresh scars. The Santeria people said he had been in jail for killing a man with a machete when he was just eight years of age, and when incarcerated as a child he had had his boyhood robbed by many reprehensible men in the dank dungeon cells of the jails. That was until he made his pact with the dark Saint Ochun and who took him as one of his black apostles. People who believed in the santeria said that it was Oggun himself that inhabited the young boy's slight and slender frame, and made him grow big and strong into the physical specimen he had become. At the start of their relationship she enjoyed the protection of his presence, and how he would bestow her with gifts, but as she had got older she had sensed his influence become all consuming. She had wanted to discover other aspects of life, travel, maybe the possibility of other people, and that was when she noticed that his domination of her had become obsessive. Now it was anger that drove her. In other societies a man and a woman broke up, they got divorced, they moved on, in the archaic society he enforced and she inhabited that was forbidden. Forbidden because he was who he was, forbidden because he loved her. His love was no longer reciprocated, and no matter what he offered her, or forced her to do, that was what her heart testified to. She had tried to leave but he held the one thing that trapped her, the one thing, which made her contemplate the things she dared.

No she would need a sledgehammer and a sword to pierce that heart, if there was a heart and not just a black metal engine of sin. She saw him rouse, alerted by her minds' conspiracies, and she feigned sleep.

The Caribe awoke beside his woman, he licked her ear with his thick tongue, and nuzzled his head into her armpit, he liked the smell, the stale hum of old sweat, mingling with the fresh painting of new. It was the smell of orifice, it reminded him of pussy and he turned her onto her belly spooning himself into her buttocks. He drilled himself in using force, excited at the thought that he had caught her unawares, and it was over soon. It was his way in the morning, after a night with Mauritza, his memory still fresh with deeds committed from the night before.

"Fix me eggs." He demanded.

"Fix them yourself."

She didn't move and he clapped her on her backside hard enough for it to sting, she retaliated with a backwards kick, that she feared would antagonise him more. She was glad it did not.

"Maybe it's better only I eat - You getting a little chubby Mauritza."

This unnerved her more than anything, these piropos that hinted at intimacy, that brewed concern in her mind because of the ordinary nature of it - regular conversation between two irregular people.

"That's good then you won't want me anymore." He turned her head to him slowly.

"I will always want you Mauritza."

He rose out of the bed and left the room and Mauritza wished he would leave forever. The Caribe breakfasted on rump steaks and fried eggs, he drank bittersweet coffee, finishing it all off with a small cigar. He contemplated more sex with Mauritza but she had explained she was late for work. Her work was important she met many tourists; she generated a lot of money, besides, he thought he had to go to the ranch to watch the fighters. Mauritza watched him leave in the Fleetwood Cadillac, the black vehicular equivalent of a shark cruising depths. She wondered how he was so unopposed, in this oppressive place, and then thought maybe there was something in that story of him being an apostle of the black saints.

The Caribe arrived at his ranch eight miles outside Havana, where the fighters trained. It had once belonged to a Spanish aristocrat; the ranch was colonial and painted in a marine blue colour, which caught the sun in a way The Caribe liked. He loved the ranch, the baying of the pit bull dogs, the crowing of the fighting cocks, the ambrosial hum of animals, and the battering of bembe African drums that told him his warriors were training. The ranch was on the outskirts of the city distant enough not to arouse the interest of the Government, or neighbourhood watches, but close enough to ferry rich tourists to the blood sports. Youths trained Pit bull dogs on old rubber tires that dangled in their paddocks. The Caribe was an expert in such matters, he could tell by the definition of a dog's jaw muscles and the length of time they dangled in fearsome grips from the hanging tyres, which dogs had potential and would be champions. He headed through the paddocks and past young kids who teased coloured fighting cocks with dolls through the wire. The reputation of the ranch was spreading, men were coming every day. Bad boys from all the regions, business was good.

In a large corral central to the ranch seven groups of two men trained with machetes and daggers. The men moved with athleticism and grace swiping and thrusting with the knives at a fraction of their normal speed. The Caribe watched them carefully as Alfredo their trainer approached him limping on his bad leg and supping on one half of a hacked coconut. Alfredo was an old Cuban Army guy with one eye who trained the fighters. The old man spoke when he was spoken to.

"Who fights?"

Alfredo clucked on the sweet fluffy coconut flesh then spoke with his mouth full. "Beny".

"What one is he?" "El Negrito".

The Caribe spotted him immediately a snake-hipped skinny black youth who thrusted with vigour in the spars, quicker than his opponent, with hunger in his eyes.

"How many men Alfredo?"

"Four, his first in a tobacco field when he was sixteen."

"And his opponent?"

The old man wiped his mouth, noticing that The Caribe found him speaking with his mouth full, distasteful.

"The Farmer from Zapata."

The Caribe pointed at the man he thought was the one they spoke about, a tall Spanish looking man in his forties, with big shoulders who moved languorous and cagey.

"How many?"

"Six men, all with machete".

"Good Alfredo, good, how is my dragon?"

"Greedy, needs more than pigs and chickens."

"Good - tomorrow night he will have more eh?" Alfredo looked at The Caribe and feigned a smile.

"Si senor."

The Caribe left him, entering the villa, and the old man felt useless. Alfredo felt the bad diabetic sugar scorch his legs in the fiery tingling, realising that his blood sugar was rising, he limped to his shack to escape the morning sun, and stabilise it with a piece of mango. Inside his shack he lay down. There was little room; it was six by four with space only for a little stove and a spider that had created a wig of web on the naked light bulb that he rarely turned on to conserve electricity. Once he had been a leader of men in the army, now it annoyed him internally that he was led. Old age and the diabetes did that to a man he thought, robbed him of his balls his cajones, and the ability to get hard. And what was a man who could not get hard.

There had been a beautiful black woman Andrea who had worked in the country abattoir where he collected the cattle innards for the dogs. They had exchanged flirtations, her slimed in the extremities of meat, him with little electric yellow flowers of chicken feathers in his hair. She was not too young, forty maybe? An age where Alfredo thought local people would not be repulsed, the way they were when they saw the fat old tourists with the Cuban teenagers. They had gone on a date to a jazz club, and then back to her apartment. Half shot on rum, her sucking on his dead dick unable to be roused, like a turtle recoiling its head, her whispering filthy sex in his ear. He took her with his tongue, and she had come, and he was grateful that the opportunity was not a total disaster. But there would be no more dates, for he was old fashioned in that sense that a man wasn't a man unless he could get hard, and he would go so far to say that a man wasn't a man if he wanted to be led. But led he was. The ranch kept him occupied, the dogs, the chickens, the fighters, the only thing he was cautious of was the dragon. What possessed a man to acquire that? He had seen lots of things in his sixty-three years, in the army, as a fisherman in the sea. In Africa with the army whilst out hunting bush meat, they had killed a lion that charged them, trying to steal their antelope kill. Alfredo remembered the fiery amber coronas of the lion's eyes, as it lay dying. They had hit the lion in the lungs, and were covered the fine spray of blood as it perforated through the blood rich organs. In the Gulf Stream he had seen sharks, once a Great White that stole a huge blue Marlin they had caught, the shark eyes were black plastic orbs. But nothing had prepared him for the dragon. The eyes were antediluvian, they were eyes of the devil, the same eyes that pierced a man from the face of The Caribe.

***

O'Neill was awoken in his hotel room by a cock crowing. He stumbled from the old bed and out onto the balcony, where his entire wardrobe of ten black Guinness T shirts lay dried stiff by the sun. The sun beat hot and tropical. He looked across the magnificent grounds of the Nacional to the great cannons that governed the Malecon and the sea. Adjacent to his balcony around forty yards were the young couple O'Neill had watched marry the day earlier, drinking espresso coffees. They cradled each other in a single bed sheet, damp and embroidered with the gossamer stains of sex, admiring the same view. O'Neill watched the young lovers, wondering what they knew and he didn't.

He showered in the wonky shower receiving an electric shock for his trouble on touching the nozzle. The water spat semi warm in intermittent bursts over him. He walked out naked to see a pretty chambermaid, fixing his crumpled bed. She apologised and hid her eyes. More for her benefit than his he dressed quickly in shorts and in another Guinness T shirt vest. The girl had done a good job in cleaning his room.

"What's your name?"

"Olivia."

He surveyed the room; he could hardly recognise it from the mess before. "Good job."

"Thank you senor."

He rooted for a few bucks in pockets and handed the woman ten dollars, she refused. "I do not want, but thank you."

O'Neill looked at her twice, impressed. In a world of difficulty, in a place like Havana, it was refreshing to discover money wasn't important to everyone.

"I get paid enough."

"I thought your boss wasn't that generous?"

O'Neill pointed to the old TV blaring out more Castro repeats. "No my boss is a bigger boss, my boss is Jesus Christ."

"Oh that boss, I heard he's a hard man to work for? Especially in this place - With all this voodoo?"

"No not voodoo, voodoo - Haiti – Habana – Santeria".

He held his hands up a man admitting his ignorance, enjoying being educated. "You know he loves you?" She said.

O'Neill looked at the girl. "Who does?"

"Jesus Christ." She said. And not as an expletive. She said no more, cleaned the toilet and left wishing him goodbye, and it suddenly occurred to him, there and then that the woman had just given him the biggest compliment in his life. O'Neill had no religion, just superstition. Most of the bad hombres he had met in life had, boxers, assassins, omens happened for a reason and he wondered what this blessing would incur.

CHAPTER 7

The breakfast buffet consisted of ornate trays of fried eggs with skinny bacon and black beans. O'Neill selected a tortilla observing the other residents of the hotel, and took a seat on his own. The residents were rich, all of them dressed in Ralph Lauren, and Calvin Klein, wrists slack with jewellery and elegant watches. The room filled with eclectic language, Italian, French, Canadian. Mostly men - older men, in their fifties some with wives, a lot not. There for the young pussy or cock, to peel the scabs off their own inactive or bored sexual organs, and feed them to the exotic filth of Havana.

O'Neill ate a tortilla, bad as he had expected, and left to head to the cafe where he had arranged to meet Tony Montana the night before. As he headed down Vedado he noticed vultures drifting aimless on invisible currents over the city, floating like black embers in the big blue sky.

The cafe was a green fronted small building called "O'Reilly". O'Neill entered it's dark interior to discover a metal spiral staircase that shuddered as he walked up it. Upstairs O'Neill discovered Tony Montana terrorising a petrified parrot with a lit cigarette.

"Having fun?" O'Neill said.

"Irelandes you like uh? This is a Hi-rish cafe."

O'Neill looked around him apart from being green and having

the name, the cafe looked nothing like an Irish cafe, this apparent in the lack of graffiti and hairy bacon.

"This is named my – Irelandes".

O'Neill liked the way the little man caught himself on replacing "my Friend" with "Irelandes" It showed the ability to listen a trait O'Neill liked to see in people.

"This place the street, the cafe is named after 'Alejandro O'Reilly', a Spaniard whose Mother was from Irelandes."

"There you go now."

"See Tony Montana not just a pretty face."

O'Neill smiled at the little man's maimed face, garnished vivid violet and purple with big bruises.

"He got a plenty big fockin brain ready to take on the world."

They sat on a balcony overlooking the busy little street. Directly across the street O'Neill watched as an old woman on the opposite balcony washed white plastic bags and hung them out to dry. A pretty black girl came for their order.

"Coffee for me?"

O'Neill nodded a yes to the little man.

"My beautiful Senorita. Have you ever seen such beauty Irelandes? This is what makes me love Habana."

The girl frowned, used to this.

"I will have a very strong Espresso, and you Irelandes?" "I don't drink coffee - It makes me shit."

The girl left quickly.

"Irelandes if you want to impress the women of Habana you must not talk about shit. Believe me there is enough shit in Habana".

"I'd say you'd be an authority on that."

"You funny Irelandes, funny like a fockin heart attack."

"Now what was this you wanted to talk about?"

"What I have for you – iz good."

Below them the coffee machine hissed and spat like a wild cat, the aroma of fresh coffee wafted up the spiral staircase.

"Tonight, not far away - I have for you a dogfight!"

O'Neill looked at the little man, with his busted up face it seemed such a shame to let him down but...

"Bully for fucking you."

"Irelandes there is lots of money, connections to be made at a dogfight, cigars. The rich focking tourists pay in, they bet the dogs, drink a little rum, listen to the salsa, fock a pretty girl - dog fight is good, introduce you to a few people important people – this is who I tell you about? The Caribe the big boss, bad boy. The man that keel all the men. He has the face of a God; bigger than Savon the super heavyweight champion of the entire world, he is the son of oggun and he owns all the cigars in Habana."

The pretty girl returned up the staircase with the little coffee. O'Neill paid her and the Cuban sipped his espresso excited, his eager eyes alive. He watched the little old woman on the opposite balcony collect other dry plastic bags off the washing line as she hauled on a thick cigar, chugging out thick puffs of smoke. He was intrigued, morbidly fascinated, the way people would look at dead people or the interior of car crashes. What type of man could take all those people's lives with a blade? What type of man could hold this sway, in this toughest of places? This life taker.

"You must want to know Irelandes what the Devil looks like?"

"I must."

"These people very important people, if you like the dog fight, the very next night you may be lucky, you may be very lucky, if they like you they give you the invitation." O'Neill stared at him, extracting the information without a word.

"To go to knife fight, the executive game."

O'Neill could see that the little man was telling the truth, that it was a big deal, but somehow he didn't believe it. He didn't believe that in this time, feral and as wild as the world was, and none more untamed than Havana, that men fought with knives in duels to satiate the blood lust of tourists. It then occurred to him he didn't want to believe it.

O'Neill then looked across the balcony to the old woman as she folded her plastic bags, and it became clearer to him. People who were desperate would do anything, anything, to make their lives better. He knew that from Ireland after seeing friends and lovers murdered, from being beaten by cops, from jail, from being a killer. He had an affinity and empathy with these men, men who fought, an affinity borne from fighting in a ring, from competing in gladiatorial combat, an empathy from being the same as they were: desperate people in a desperate world.

"Organise it."

Tony Montana nodded his head. He saw the look on O'Neill's face a look that frightened him for a second, the look of a man that had no fear.

The huge pink bus was more lorry than bus. A lorry pulling a big humped smelly carriage with broken windows and hard seats. It collected them at a spot only known to Tony Montana, the outskirts of the city, beside a crumbling castle. The bus was jam packed with rich tourists. All men with girths like whales, their stomachs pregnant with alcohol and rich foods, emblems of wealth in this mostly skinny country. They reeked with the sweet stench of expensive colognes, cigar smoke and close sweat, their Cuban guides stood beside them subservient, and hustling amongst themselves for scraps, like dogs under a king's table.

O'Neill sat beside a large German in his fifties, who was

drinking miniatures of rum. Bubbles of sweat swarmed on his rotund face dripping constant onto O'Neill's trainers, O'Neill decided against saying anything, it wasn't the motherfucker's fault he was obese. O'Neill watched Tony Montana hustle the Cuban driver for a cigarette at the front of the bus.

After a little while they arrived at a ranch in the middle of the night. Huge rusted bins that burned refuse and cast a methane unholy haze over the ranch, illuminated the night. The tourists departed the bus to bawdy Afro - Cuban music that assaulted their senses, they filed into a line and paid a huge fat Cuban at the gates one of only three fat Cubans that O'Neill had ever seen.

"Fifty bucks".

O'Neill looked twice at the big Cuban; amazed he was paying for a ringside seat to hell. "Irelandes this is what you must pay."

Fifty U.S. and this was to just to enter the place. Inside the ranch he could smell the cooking of meat and the hefty odour of animals, and hear the frenzied barking off dogs so loud that it dominated the music. O'Neill observed pretty women scantily clad in Cabaret dresses, flirting with the fat men, serving seared chicken and pork from a large barbecue pit. O'Neill watched the men eat, appalled. O'Neill refused food and drink. He liked to be hungry, it sharpened senses and instinct, and instinct had kept him alive so far. He could feel the tension living in the air, an atmosphere of severe violence like a riot brewing, a storm cooking in the men making them a mob, spiked by the drums and drink. They took seats around an old bullring corral where people had congregated.

"You OK Irelandes – You like?" "This is a fucking freakshow." "Problem? Is good".

Tony Montana pointed to a young girl who fellated an old man twenty yards away, O'Neill spat on the ground.

"Great," he said, sarcastic.

"This is the Diablo's place Irelandes, the man I spoke to you about, The Caribe, it is a great privilege that we be here."

O'Neill looked at the little Cuban sucking on a piece of pork, and then to the bull ring as two skinny Cuban youths were towed into the centre from opposite ends by two Pit Bull dogs. O'Neill watched the dogs, one black, one white. The white dog was apoplectic with blood lust; foamy suds of saliva like the head of bad beer, had gathered at both corners off its bawling mouth. It was a magnificent animal bustling with condition comically marching nearly upright on its hind legs. On sight of its opponent it somersaulted on its leash unable to contain itself for the fight. The youths matched the dogs up and O'Neill couldn't help notice that the white dog's opponent, the black dog remained still, but focused. The black dog was a smaller animal with a white star in its chest, and fine muscled hindquarters. O'Neill concentrated on the black dog's eyes. They gleamed with desire, with heart and intelligence in comparison to the white dog's murderous insanity. The white dog was doing it's fighting on the lead. The black dog conserving its energy for the fight. The black dog was the winner O'Neill thought.

"That fockin white dog man, can you imagine taking heem" for a walk! He take you to eat a kid!" Tony Montana said.

"Have your lot on the black dog."

"Are you crazy? Look at the fockin" thing!"

The white dog in frenzy began to tear at the wooden corral fence; its teeth tearing up the tough wood like a chainsaw.

The men released the dogs. The dogs smashed into each other like vehicles in a head on crash biting furiously. The dogs fought for a few seconds standing on their hind legs pivoting and slashing inflicting big bites to each other's heads, the scuffle kicked up mud and dust to mask events momentarily, and when it settled the white dog had the black dog by the head thrashing the black dog hard with violent shakes.

A small old Cuban man with one eye and a limp, in his sixties took bets. O'Neill read his face a graph of hard living, a tight frame for his age and size with good shoulders and big hands. O'Neill then took a crumpled hundred dollar bill secreted in his trainers.

"One hundred dollars on the black dog."

The old man accepted his money adding it to a bulging fist. "You sure senor?"

O'Neill looked at the old man, the old man smiled wryly.

"You have been at dogfights before senor?"

O'Neill had in Ireland, a misspent youth in quarries with Bull Staffordshires and Wheaten terriers, in old barns and housing estate garages, he knew dogs, but more, he knew from fighting, in street brawls in shebeens, from having it sanitised in the ring, call it what you may it all was fighting, hurting pain.

"You loco? This is over." Tony Montana said.

The white dog with great exertion, superior strength and weight had dragged the smaller black dog to the centre of the corral. The white dog's chest caved in and out like bellows and foam engulfed its flanks and hindquarters.

"Welcome to death dog, the lock bite is too strong; it will inflict too much damage..." Tony Montana talked the whole way through like a sports commentator.

"It's not what dog can inflict the most." O'Neill said. The little Cuban blinked his little rat eyes twice.

"Oh it is not? Oh, I sorry it must be me that is loco."

"It is the one that can suffer the most." O'Neill said.

As if invoked by their conversation, the black dog suddenly came alive. The white dog had slackened its grip and the black dog had twisted inside one of the folds in its skin and seized the white dog by a front limb.

For twenty minutes the black dog chewed the limb until the white dog began to wail hideously through it's clenched jaws, and the white dog began to go red, until it fell to the dirt and the black dog switched bites, eventually killing the white dog with a throat bite. It then ragged the corpse. The tourists booed and jeered their contempt, most had clearly placed their bets on the white dog, but not O'Neill. He waited quietly until the one eyed Cuban returned and paid him what he was owed.

"You know dogs?" The old man asked O'Neill.

"Lucky guess." O'Neill said.

"You like the fights senor?"

"Not as much as I like cigars."

"Cigars uh?"

"Cigars in bulk, Romeos, Cohibas, Montes. That I like a lot."

"You got the greenbacks gringo?" The old man starting to play hardball.

"Like I say you get me bulk, and they are genuine, the price not too hard, and maybe old man me and you got a deal?" O'Neill said.

The old man leant back on his hip and decided that O'Neill was worth a shot.

"We have a very special fight here tomorrow night, very special – an executive game." "The executive game?" O'Neill repeated.

"For executive people, aficionados - two men with knives senor, to the death." O'Neill didn't answer, men with knives killing each other for tourists? Why didn't it appall him? Again drawn to the prospect, like a hyena to carrion. The thought made him want to spit. O'Neill coughed a wad of phlegm from his chest and spat it to the ground.

"Maybe I could show you some of our cigars tomorrow at it?"
"How much?" O'Neill asked.

"For you senor - It is one thousand U.S. dollars, for the invitation. And for that you get to see it real, two men skilled, fast, and then after we deal for the cigars."

"Two birds with the one stone sort of deal?" O'Neill said.

"We may not speak the language, but we speak the language eh?" Alfredo said. "Not interested at that price." O'Neill said showing the old man he could play too.

"Senor not everyone gets an invitation to the executive game, not everyone gets contact with quality cigars. There are over two hundred people here tonight, out of two hundred people, fifty three bet on the black dog, those fifty three people I offer the invitation too...You know why?"

"To get your money back." O'Neill said and the old man smiled. Tony Montana feeling neglected chirped in.

"They know about fights that is why?"

O'Neill and Alfredo ignored him. This was the interesting part.

O'Neill knew he was being played, but the bottom line was he was interested. "If I go then my friend here? My guide he can come too..."

The old man looked at the little Cuban and shook his head gravely. "Senor only tourist must come…"

Tony Montana stamped his foot like a petulant child. "I bring the focking tourists to you!"

The old man glared at Tony Montana, O'Neill interrupted the possible situation by defusing it.

"Then we have no deal, he is my rabbit's foot".

The old Cuban smiled slowly, the grin taking it's time.

"You come tomorrow, bring heem" As long as he don't pester anybody and he pays the tariff, and we'll let you have a look at these cigars OK? What hotel you stay?"

"The Nacional." O'Neill replied.

"Very good hotel senor we have a lot of people come here from there, someone will collect you at eight o'clock in the lobby."

The old man moved off, collecting and distributing the bets, O'Neill looked at the little Cuban who spat a piece of pork gristle from his mouth and spoke slow and deliberate.

"Irelandes we with the bad hombres now." Tony Montana said.

O'Neill looked at his accomplice and for the first time since they had met he knew he was right.

***

The Caribe looked at the mound of well-worn money that his men had assembled on the old coffee table in the veranda of the ranch. And then he had a cursory glance at Alfredo to make sure he had taken his shoes off whilst inside the interior of the house. He had.

"Good night Alfredo?" "Good night senor..."

"Tomorrow night will be much better." "Si senor."
Alfredo limped to the door. "Alfredo?"

"Si Senor."

"You fed the dog to the dragon yet?" "Not yet Senor."

"Good I would like to watch."

Alfredo left, he was sixty-three years of age and he obeyed the man young enough to be his son like a beaten dog. There were reasons. He hoped he would die soon, taking The Caribe with him.

Chapter 8

O'Neill sat in the Nacionals' bar of fame. "Bar of Fame", whoever named it had had a profound sense of irony. The bar was upholstered and trimmed in green leather, with a stone floor, and more photographs of old movie stars like Errol Flynn, Ava Gardner, and Judy Garland. A huge freezer which looked more like a vending machine than a freezer, that sported fashionable Corona, and Heineken beer bottles. In the corner of the bar there was also a flashing neon Wurlitzer. O'Neill found the anachronisms and paradoxes of Cuba fascinating. For all the vehement propaganda and espousing of communism, there seemed a latent and powerful attraction to the billboards of America, seen in the fifties cars, neon jukeboxes, right down to the street hustlers adopting movie character names. O'Neill drank creamy cocktails at the hotel's late bar. He played songs on the Wurlitzer fucked off at the pathetic selection, which seemed to consist mainly of the defunct Queen rock group and European soft metal. Through various compilations he discovered a Prince CD and played a song that had reminded him of his dead lover Meabh back home in Belfast, a relationship that had been interrupted, because of the conflict, because of murder. The song was "Little Red Corvette" he remembered the song because of a line – "Pocket full of horses, and some of them used." Meabh had explained to him that Trojans were a condom brand name in the U.S.A, with the image of a stallion on their front. He in due course would make jokes about this form of contraception "I'm away to get some Horses" he would say, intimate moments that he enjoyed and feared were fading too soon from his memory. Meabh was knowledgeable like that; she once won a pub quiz on her own, even though he was the other member of her team, him as useless as tits on a bull. Her with the university education and the rebel heart. He wondered how she had become involved in the organisation? Her from the nice family, and Protestant in laws, with the two cars and schoolteacher father. O'Neill knew it was inevitable that he would become involved, it was in his fighting nature, easy to channel aggression with the apparatus assembled against you. But a young, educated, middle class woman? What was that about? He sometimes wondered and he knew if she were alive she would have torn him to pieces, if there were a sexual element to her commitment? He knew the thought in itself was a betrayal of her memory, but he couldn't help think about it. Before him she had shared the bed of the officer commanding the organisation, and he knew the word she would have used in the hypothetical guessing game if she were alive, "Insecure". It wasn't as if the campaign came with the mighty revolutionary credentials that Cuba had. It was a grubby little guerrilla war fought from shadows, bushwhacking combatants slacking in their security routines. O'Neill watched a big toasted Mexican with a million pock marks, and a tough face cry like a baby at the bar drowned and drunk in sorrow. O'Neill wondered why a man like that cried, there was something terrible about a man crying he thought, something helpless, when men cried there was tragedy, death. He remembered the last time he cried, over Meabh – they had come for him, but only found her. A man like him, only under a different banner. Sledge hammering the door and emptying a pistol's worth into her. The memory still stung, as did the realities; him scraping the brain matter off the wall with a coin. The laughing forensic officers, and the senior cop quoting the bible at O'Neill. He wished the beautiful Doctor would enter the bar now and give him a distraction. It seemed a waste he should drink such nice cocktails all alone in the beautiful night with the framed photographs of Judy Garland looking at him and the saturnine memories. Blame it on the drink; all the Irish ever did. The CD began to jump at the vital moment of the song and O'Neill decided to go for a walk out onto the grounds of the hotel.

He followed a well-lit path down to the great cannons, which shot over the Malecon. The walls were surrounded by thick brush threaded with razor wire and judging by the smell -human shit. O'Neill took one of the many light plastic seats that littered the grounds and headed to the walls where the inevitable rumba and Salsa music grew louder. At the walls he sat down and slugged on a bottle of Corona, crickets fizzed in the air and lizards flickered across his path.

Unbelievably he heard sounds of sex that came from the sky. O'Neill looked above his head as a couple fucked on one of the huge cannons that jutted out from the hotel grounds over the malecon. He smiled to himself, mentally applauding their sense of adventure. He scanned the dark streets of Havana, and the Malecon. This was the place. He never wanted to leave, a place of sex, and excitement of dog fights of beautiful women and bad hombres, of music, and bad food, a place where a man could still test himself, where common sense never prevailed. This was the real Cuba, where a real revolution happened and eighty men on a boat felled a government, where a man's dick never stopped being hard, this was the place.

***

The Dragon had come from a small Island of Indonesia, smuggled in at the command of The Caribe. When it first arrived it was six feet long and underweight. The crew on the ship had fed the big lizard rats and twice the ship cats. But within months of feeding on the lush carrion generated by the ranch's nighttime activities, the lizard had flourished. It was now over ten feet long from the stone hard head to the whip lash tail, with teeth like broken glass and a bite that was laced with poisonous venom. Its claws were like meat hooks and with a quick lash of its tail it could snap a man's femur like a twig.

The Caribe kept the dragon in a pit at the back of the stables where it lay basking beside bleached bones on the crumpled hearts of palm fronds soiled by blood, flickering it's forked tongue.

"Isn't it magnificent Alfredo?"

Alfredo nodded his head weary from always agreeing.

"An evil ancient. From time began it's ancestors marauded with dinosaurs killing then as it kills now."

The last thing Alfredo needed was a natural history lesson. His brain buzzed from the beer the night before and his throat was cracked from shouting bets.

"Such power Alfredo, almost immortal."

Alfredo stared into the lizard's black eyes, turrets of destruction; dragon was the right name.

"You know what would be interesting Alfredo? A man - a man against the dragon..." Alfredo looked into The Caribe's black eyes glittering at the thought."

Alfredo had seen the dragon feed. To fight a man against the dragon was against nature, to fight a man against the dragon wouldn't be a fight it would be an abomination. Alfredo was astounded at what constituted as interesting in The Caribe's fevered imagination.

"Interesting, si senor." Alfredo lied. The Caribe moved quick, kicking Alfredo's bad leg and dragging him with one arm over the Dragon's paddock. The basking lizard moved quicker than lightning in a storm across the paddock expecting a feed, like a crocodile taking to water.

"Senor, Senor please!"

The Caribe swung the little man back from the paddock and away from the anxious Dragon which lashed it's tail so hard that it cut it streaking the paddock's white washed walls in fine lines of blood. Alfredo felt his aging heart tremor in his chest, like an engine with no oil, it spluttered, the bad blood sugar surge in his legs, as if hot kerosene had splashed over them. The Caribe patted him hard on the back, guttural and heartily.

"Alfredo you're getting old my friend, there once was a time when no man could surprise you."

"When I had two eyes senor..."

"Are you not grateful I left you one?"

"Very grateful senor."

The Caribe left the old man to enter the house with a cruel smile on his lips. The old man bent over his hands on his hips hoping for more breath and gathering his senses, and in his mind he cursed him, cursed him.

***

The tropical sun sucked sweat from O'Neill's body like a child squeezing fruit. He walked along unawares into the market. The market stalls consisted mainly of mediocre art, trinkets and wooden musical instruments, and the ubiquitous image of Che that adorned and dominated everything, from cups to Conchs. As popular as Coca cola. O'Neill, sad for a second at the irony, thought more about Che in that fucking Bolivian jungle with a bunch of keystone cops, trying to knock them into shape, asthma tugging on his chest maybe contemplating his luck running out when an oil painting caught his eye. It wasn't a great painting, even to an uneducated eye like O'Neill's it was pretty bad. The painting was three quarter length, aqua marine in theme and in colour. It depicted a woman, a dark, classic Latino woman, beautiful, and voluptuous standing on a dock topless, her left hand pushed her lustrous ebony hair from her face obscuring one of her eyes, her mouth ripe and as red as a chilli, partially opened in a half pout. With her other hand she dragged dark blue panties over a silky large hip revealing a tantalising glimpse of pubis. On the dock overlooking the sea rested a ripe tomato and a bitten coconut.

"She is pretty company?"

"How much?" O'Neill enquired.

The artist was a young man, in his twenties, wearing a Thai dyed shirt, love beads and a bright expression that told O'Neill he was a haggler.

"She embodies the archetype male machismo fantasy, the raven haired hourglass figured senorita we all desire..."

"I'm saying this one more time then I'm walking. How much?"

"Companero this is a market? I am an artiste once featured on the "Buena Vista club". O'Neill removed his shades displaying his hard eyes, to the man.

This seemed to have the desired effect. "One hundred U.S.dollars."

"I'll give you eighty now".

"Ninety and you have a deal".

"Seventy or I walk"

"Eighty it is then companero".

O'Neill removed the crumpled money from his pocket slapping it into the painter's palm and lifted the painting with one hand.

"Thank you Senor may she provide you the solace in your long lonely nights that she provided me..."

O'Neill flipped him a finger and walked on, past a man with

bookshelves that stored Malcolm X, Che, and Ernest Hemmingway autobiographies. He walked into magnificent courtyard marred only by begging street waifs and an ugly turkey vulture plucking on a dead rat, reminding him he was hungry, and was there anything on this Island that wasn't hungry.

O'Neill sat down out of the sun in an outdoor cafe under a sun umbrella beside a little plastic table and chair in the middle of the courtyard and ordered a mojito staring at his newly acquired painting. A crowd had gathered to his extreme right where a young Cuban man with his entire face pierced charged tourists a dollar to take a photograph.

O'Neill stared abhorred at the man's face; every visible millimetre of skin was pierced, with silver rings and steel bars. Fresh wounds suppurated pus and the man opened his mouth baring the interior of his mouth like a schoolboy with a festered brace on a dentist's chair. O'Neill watched in disbelief as tourists filed into line, handing the man solitary dollars. O'Neill smoked a cigarette wondering was there any degradation Cubans wouldn't stoop to for money. He took two bites from a bad ham and cheese sandwich and pushed the rest away to the street waifs who gobbled it unconcerned about flavour.

O'Neill lit a cigarette and looked at his painting when something occurred to him – Where would he put the painting considering he had no home, O'Neill lived on the wing, in motel rooms, the back seat of rented cars and any woman who would have him for a night. If he went back to Ireland there was always a bar or a flat he could borrow calling in old favours for dirty deeds committed, but he had no residence, no belongings.

Typical, he thought of his life, solitary as a Tiger. He had never thought about his life in depth, but it did occur to him that in some sense he was lonely. Lonely from the fractured conversations he had with strangers at airports, motels, doing deals with scumbags, fucking whores.

But that's what his life was; it hadn't suddenly happened, this was the way he always had been, created by the necessity of survival. It was the behaviour of an assassin, because that's what O'Neill had once been. Now he didn't know what he was, some rogue transient, chasing fast money. An old woman on a bicycle with flowers approached him, she looked tired, O'Neill stared at the flowers wilting and fading fast in the heat. He pushed her a dollar left over for the waiter, man didn't deserve it after the quality of the sandwich.

"Flowers senor?" She asked.

He shook his head slow.

"I read palm senor?"

"Your alright old woman."

"Senor I insist, it is a gift like the gift you give me?"

She waved the dollar at him, and before he could speak, she took his hand in a tough hooked grip with her little wizened hands.

She read his palm, "Warrior senor?"

O'Neill frowned and sucked on his cigarette, it wasn't that hard to tell, his hands were graveyards of floating bone and cartilage, his nose reset badly at the bridge.

"I used to box."

"That I know from your hands."

He smiled and pushed the front of his nose down with his index finger. She smiled back, with but two teeth. The old woman's fingers felt cool and soothing on his broken hands free of sweat and calm on his veins.

"And a lot more senor, and a lot more..."

O'Neill looked into the old woman's face as it grew sad on this revelation.

"There is a woman senor, a beautiful woman."

O'Neill looked at the old woman then at the huge painting of the Latino woman dominant between them.

"You don't say?"

"A very beautiful woman, she is in great danger."

"This sounds silly, old woman but isn't this where you say 'And so are you?'"

The old woman smiled furtively releasing his hand gently. O'Neill stared at his hand as it belonged to someone else.

"And so are you?"

O'Neill smiled and stubbed out his cigarette on the plastic table, melting the surface the way a bullet would skin. He gathered up his painting and strode away. The old woman called to him halfway across the square.

She rode her bicycle effortlessly with one foot pushing a pedal passing him repeating with the words that hung in the air.

"And so are you"

O'Neill watched the old woman glide down the cobbled streets on her bike with her dead flowers. He spoke to himself, as if he were someone else.

"Another fucking omen".

***

Mauritza nearly fucked the man's brains out. He was handsome, verging on pretty, that had shaved pubic hair, he smelt of too much deodorant and perfume, a young Chilean playboy. She had met him at the tacky local disco "The Commordoro". The sex had been angry and violent; he had instigated it by slapping her hard on the ass and trying to watch himself in the mirror. He wanted to fuck himself Mauritza had thought. When he pulled her hair hard she retaliated with a bite that drew blood and nearly took his tongue. The sex then descended into a brawl, only for Grace to break it up by hitting him over the head with her old revolver - Fucking tourists.

She dressed quickly, doctoring a bruise left on her cheek with the little makeup she had left, she looked once more at the young man, a he came to on the bed. Fucking machismo. The Latin world had a lot to answer for. She balled up her fist and planted her feet, as the Chilean playboy's eyes started to open and a plaintive moan came from his lips. She threw a right cross, that scored direct right on the button of his chin the way her father had taught her as a child, and he went straight back to sleep again. Grace burst out laughing at the gorgeous lady with the jack hammer right cross.

"Not so tough now Grace."

"Chileans never had balls", Grace said.

Mauritza kissed Grace on both cheeks, paid her her cut and left. Warmed by the fact that the next time the Chilean playboy got rough with a woman he would remember Mauritza, how she nearly took his tongue and knocked him the fuck out. She smiled at his scored back striping the sheets with blood. Men were there to be fucked up and fucked over.

She sensed anxiety within herself, rage at such bad fucking luck with her life. But something had occurred here with the Chilean that made her realise she was no victim, and nor would she ever be.

Chapter 9

Tony Montana looked at his crying babies, twins, just his luck he thought. In a world where it was difficult enough to feed one baby his wife give birth to another two. Another two on top of the three he already had. They lived in a rat hole apartment block in Chinatown where life was a never-ending sequence of arguments and fights.

Overcrowding, over food, over the one toilet that catered to all the apartments on the block. The summer before there had been two suicides and a domestic stabbing, which was fatal. Tony Montana had tried to intervene in that one, he had known both parties, but a woman scorned was a woman scorned and to fuck another neighbour was no bright thing either. Besides he was a family man, a man who loved his wife and his kids, he had no desire to disturb that. But his kids were hungry, and he had to do something.

He fed them a little powdered milk and contemplated killing the pig they owned that lived on their cramped balcony. In another time, in another place, he'd probably have more kids but not here. He was afraid to fuck his wife now for fear of her getting pregnant, and knowing his luck she would probably have triplets the next time. His wife Berta was a pretty mulatto with cinnamon skin and large open eyes that could never betray truth. She approached him as the children slept fatigue webbing her pretty eyes in bloodshot.

"Victor we need meat?"

"You want to me to kill the pig?"

"It is Mercedes' pet."

Mercedes was their oldest daughter, a tomboy waif of a girl who doted on the pig.

"Tell her it jumped off the roof."

"Victor she would never believe that, you know that pig, more goat than pig it is..."

Victor loved his wife, she was an educated woman who once was a schoolteacher, a woman who could speak with authority on most subjects. He felt aggrieved that an educated woman like that had to live in such shit and squalor with him a two-bit hustler in a pork pie hat.

"What do you want to me to do Berta?"

"Make it better."

There was one thing he could do, he thought, that would give him instant cash. But it would be dangerous. More dangerous than hustling the tourists with the Government and the Castro brothers who ruled the day (although The Horse hadn't been seen in months, Tony suspected they had him on ice somewhere in deep freeze to be wheeled out on a special occasion like a pizza from a freezer) The Caribe ruled the night and all it's minions. The cigars, the hookers, the coca rocks. He waited until the sun hung low in the sky and Berta went to sleep, then put on his little Pork pie hat and removed the big silver Colt 45 from their broken down refrigerator. An ex U.S. marine working on a Canadian boat had given him it for taking him to some nice whores in Chinatown who had sucked the ex Marine's cock until it was a drop. The man did proclaim that his cock had never had so much fun and therefore honoured Tony Montana with the big gun. He waited until Berta took her siesta jammed the big gun into the back of his trousers, kissed his babies on the soft part of their heads and left hugging Berta accidentally waking her. He got on his old motorbike and raced along the Malecon to a small port where he knew the fishermen would be returning from their lobster pots. A man could sell fresh lobsters to the hotels, for more money than cocaine to tourists. Cuba and it's empty shelves, and devastating poverty and no one allowed to earn except The Caribe, and man and beast bent to his iron will and summary justice. Tony Montana knew the consequences of defiance, but as long as the losses were minor, and the treachery slight a man could evade serious attention, and the obsidian gaze of The Caribe.

He parked his bike close to the dock facing the road, and watched as a beaten up fishing boat, swarmed by gulls, off loaded it's catch. There were two men, one as big as a silverback gorilla with no neck, the other middle aged with a cigar and missing an arm.

They worked quietly dropping their catch into a large wooden box on the dock. Tony Montana pulled his pork pie hat over his face and approached, pulling out the big Colt holding it in his two hands like he had seen Andy Garcia doing in "Jennifer Eight", which had run for the past six years at the local cinema

"Senor, the lobsters? Hand them over – please."

The two men stared at the big silver gun in disbelief, not at the request but at the audacity, that a man would dare rob them. They paid The Caribe eight dollars a week for the dock, and six dollars for every lobster caught, which they sold onto the local hotels for ten dollars who in turn charged tourists forty. This was the food chain in Cuba and most knew their places. It was only when idiots like this interrupted the system that problems and difficulties arose.

"Motherfockers! The lobsters or I blow your fockin' brains out!"

Tony Montana jabbed the big handgun in the one - armed man's face.

"How many?" The one armed man asked.

"Them all!"

He liked bawling at the men, he liked the ephemeral sway the weapon gave him. He who had always been bawled out by others from infancy to adulthood. The perennial loser enjoying the temporary reign of power. The big black man picked the lobsters out from the box; nipping pincers and twitching antennas, purple thoraxes mottled with sea lice, and approached Tony Montana. Tony Montana extracted an onion sack from his pocket and dropped it close to the big black man; the man placed them inside the sack, which magically began to move on the dock with the motion of the lobsters, and handed them back to Tony Montana.

"Thank you senor, you have been extremely gracious."

The big man looked closely into Tony Montana's face.

"You know who owns them?"

Tony Montana returned a glance full of arrogance.

"Yeah Me! You know who I am? I'm the fockin' Taxi Driver man."

And with that he left, tearing off on his motorbike down the Malecon. He bought pork, beef, chicken necks, cow's milk, light bulbs and shampoo from a corrupt hotel chamber maid who worked in the Ingelterra, and a large bottle of fine rum that he and Berta would share some night with the kid's asleep. The rest he would invest on bets at the ranch later.

Berta looked happy as she fixed him food, he loved how her eyes would reflect her happiness, and he thought how close a man could get to happiness if life wasn't that difficult; sex and sunshine, shampoo and shower, music, sleeping babies and a wife with pretty eyes and a nice ass.

***

Dusk turned Havana to gold, burning O'Neill's eyes with rays of flames. O'Neill stood on his balcony tugging on a fine Cohiba. He checked his watch it was time to do more business with the cigars. If it were significant bulk this deal would be his last, and finish his time in Cuba nicely. O'Neill headed downstairs to watch men slay themselves for other men. The old gold lame elevator descended slowly, like a tomb entering the ground.

He walked into the majestic foyer of the Nacional to find Tony Montana bickering with a young concierge, who wore a uniform three times to big for him, and was threatening to phone cops if Tony Montana didn't get out.

"Irelandes tell this hasshole who I am?"

"It's OK - he's with me."

The concierge nodded obediently glaring at Tony Montana as he followed O'Neill out of the foyer and to the front of the hotel. They sat on the cool steps, watching the government taxis and their owners beep horns eager to attain a rich fare.

"You know Irelandes, tonight I feel lucky man so lucky I feel it everywhere, tonight could be my night my man, get me some money, get me Government taxi - that's what I want."

He jabbed a finger in the direction of the taxis, mostly Lada vehicles.

"What? A taxi or a Lada?"

"Taxi means tips, get a catalogue of the pretty pussy. Some real nice stock. Take the hombres on tours, where the Coca hides out, drive round all day, air conditioning on whistle at the chikkas on the malecon, Berta, my babies, everybody be happy, that's it man, I tell you."

O'Neill enjoyed the little man's aspiration and dreams. They were attainable; they were current, not some myth that involved necromancing the dead or a beautiful Cuban obsession. O'Neill pointed over towards the fleet of

Government taxis, eager for their trade.

"You know what type of cars they are?"

"I know."

"Ladas."

"Good car amigo?"

"Back home they used to say, "Ladas are Lada shit"."

O'Neill looked at the Cuban's face, the joke hadn't punched in.

"Lot - of - shit."

"Oh I see, Hirish humour - Is good, real fockin" funny, here for that you win a cigarette."

O'Neill looked at the cheap white cigarette the little man handed to him, he accepted half in shock.

"I have a very good day at the office, fruits of the sea my man, fruits of the sea, some day Tony Montana show you how."

A bigger horn beeped, and they both turned to see a large red Sedan pull up, driven by a black teenager who had to sit on a box to reach the steering wheel.

"Here it is Irelandes, now the fun begins."

O'Neill stepped to his full height and rotated his neck the way he used to before he fought. He allowed Tony Montana to enter the car first and got into the ancient car, red as hell and probably older. Time to watch men die he thought...

CHAPTER 10

Beny was born a bastard, and continued living his life very much in that vein. Beny blamed it on everything; on having to grow up sharing a room with sixteen other people, the stench of shit polluting his atmosphere so much that he thought he would always reek off it no matter how much he washed. He could smell shit in his dreams, when he ate, when he trained, the stench haunted him. Before he had become a knife fighter, he had stood at the graveyard in the old city and exposed his cock to tourists for whatever donation they gave. He had a large cock ten inches fully erect, and obese Canadian women and old queens especially enjoyed it. The graveyard was fine in the afternoon, but lethal at night. Under the cover of darkness the graveyard would fill with Goths and other desperados. Beny was particularly spooked by the Goth's after two of them had asked him to fuck them both but Beny wasn't a fag due to his abhorrence of shit, and told them so, and one of them had hit him with a bicycle chain giving him a scimitar scar, and a dented head. Another time three crazy santeria Priests under the subterfuge as fags had tried to hack it off as a gift for one of their black saints. That was the final straw for Beny in the graveyard. One Canadian lady Jenny, from Vancouver, would visit him regularly every year, and in return for the services of his big cock. She would feed and clothe him most summers. Once she smuggled in a pair of Nike Air Max for him that had practically started a riot in his apartment block. For three weeks local gangs pursued him like a hunted animal for those shoes. They caught him one day at the malecon and beat him until he was unconscious, and when he awoke it wasn't just the Nike Air Max that were missing but his shirt, socks and trousers. All Beny had left at the malecon was precious little dignity and his big cock, there for all to see, only without any donations. He had still continued to see Jenny but found it a chore fucking the elderly with a big cock not only were there lubrication problems, but the fact was it was dangerous with their brittle bones. And last he had heard Jenny had cancer, so that avenue of opportunity had closed.

The knife was his only escape from the smell of shit. He practised his moves lunging, moving shrugging his body closing his vital organs from imaginary attacks. For every knife fight he received a hundred U.S. dollars, paid to him by Alfredo. He now had four hundred dollars. Soon he would be able to pay off some smuggler, fuck rafts, too many sharks and storms. He had heard too many stories about people dying on rafts like his uncle Faustino, who left in 1980 and was never heard off again. He would get the fuck out, his Mother had told him that he had relatives who ran an exotic pet store in Miami, where he would receive a hundred dollars a day for selling Chinchillas, and coloured fish.

A hundred dollars a day without having to kill a man or even worse get killed. Beny prayed for that day as he tended the little black altar to his saint, fixing perfume and lighting a little candle. The black saint Beny worshipped was Oggun, who seemed to reap the most dividends with those of a coarse nature. Desperate men often turned to religion, and Beny was no different. His adoption of santeria was down to catching any sort of an edge over an opponent, for some fighters were intimidated by the religion's practice. In the tiny room at the ranch he rented he paid tribute to the black saint with an iron pot and plates of avocado, cassava, pepper and some wild honey he had rooted from a hive whilst out running, training for the fight.

He bowed twice before the pot and hoped for the strength to win another hundred dollars.

He had prepared well, so much so that he had fasted all day drinking nothing but a little sugared water. He liked to be hungry when he fought, he knew his opponent, knew what he fought with - a machete. The man was tall and rangy, but older than Beny, a man with kids, and a lot more to worry about than Beny. Beny assumed he had too much aggression for the man, though it would be foolish to think that it would be easy, killing a man with a knife was dirty, bloody, and close. There were easier ways to make a hundred dollars, and all were in America.

Alfredo tapped the wicker door to his room with his walking stick, alerting Beny that it was time. He practiced his kill strike one last time before leaving the room thinking about a hundred dollars and what chinchilla shit smelt like, cold sweat misting like dew on his back.

There were around fifty tourists at the ranch. They were seated on an old baseball stand that had been crudely assembled around a dirty, empty swimming pool, which acted as a makeshift pit and miniature gladiatorial arena. O'Neill immediately noticed the crimson tidemark of blood and dirt.

The crowd was what he expected rich, fat and obscene, smoking cigars and drinking rum and beer, gold ringed their fingers and capped their teeth. Omniscient was the man that Tony Montana had spoke off with great fear. Tony Montana identified the man in whispers, his hand covering his mouth. Like a tribal war chief O'Neill thought, directing runners and minions who obeyed his every motion. The man wore a white linen suit that accentuated his colour and physique. The man was muscle bound with great muscles and thick veins that switched with the slightest of movement. A structure like that was all about one thing – explosive energy; he was built for sprinting and not for the marathon.

The big man stood on the baseball bleekers, watching over all.

A while later The Caribe was joined by the woman Mauritza. O'Neill surprised by the connection, felt pangs of rage swell up from his organs, and felt angry at himself that he could harbour such feelings for a whore. He spat to the ground as he watched the big man place her hands on his big shoulders which she proceeded to massage.

O'Neill concentrated on her face; she was without doubt one of the most beautiful women he had ever seen. Wisps of her ebony hair fell into her face, and with gentle puffs she blew it back onto her head. She wore a low cut linen boob tube that revealed most of her breasts buffed with a lotion of sweat by the evening humidity and that swayed with motion, threatening escape from the inadequate top. There hadn't been too many memorable women in O'Neill's life, Meabh and now her had been the exception to the rule, yet there was something else to their tryst that still confused him, some unmistakable notion that there was something going on that wasn't supposed to be, some unspoken thing that left what had happened complicated. He wasn't naive, he wasn't gullible, he'd been with a lot of hookers, knew their ways, knew what it was - mostly cold pussy. For that was all what it was, and whatever it was it hadn't been the same with this woman, it had stirred feelings that he didn't believe he had.

The impenetrable immoral firewall that guarded his heart, which he had assumed unbreachable had been breached. Breached by a woman who supplemented her income, by chugging on cock and spreading her legs, a sucker for a whore he thought.

Chapter 11

She scanned the crowd and caught O'Neill looking at her; to O'Neill's shock she raised her hand in recognition, a half wave that made O'Neill check behind him in the stand to see if she was waving to someone else.

Mauritiza did not know why she raised her hand to the Irishman but it was plain that it was a stupid thing to do, failing to consider both their futures. The Caribe turned slowly on his seat, glaring at her with his dead eyes.

"You wave to the crowd, you have a friend here? Who is it? Your boyfriend?" The Caribe queried.

"No, the sun it was in my eyes".

"The Sun?" The Caribe's words were inflected with a hint of anger.

"The sun, and then there was a dragonfly in my hair". Mauritza trying to assuage the big man, knowing how seismically his anger became rage.

"The sun in your eyes and the dragonfly in your hair, at the same time? You remember whom you represent; you raise your hand to acknowledge another? You remember who you are with the next time a dragonfly lands in your hair, or the sun shines in your eyes. You remember in Havana I am the sun, I am the dragonfly."

It was enough, enough for now, he turned reading the crowd for a man that dared incur his wrath.

"Keep your hands on my shoulders, nowhere else, you hear?"

"I hear." Mauritza replied kneading the lactic acid from his trapezium muscles, eager to release his tension.

Tony Montana waved his hand in front of O'Neill's face the way a thief would a blind person.

"You know where hell is Irelandes?"

"What?"

"Keep looking at that chikka and you'll find out."

"I know her."

"You know her! You can fock all the ladies in Habana for money, you probably even focked her my friend – that is acceptable a business transaction, that will bring in money, but the one thing you must not do, Irelandes', is to know that woman. I am afraid to think out loud it is too terrible a thought, I speak no more, we have a fight to watch."

Two fighters entered the swimming pool at opposite ends. They were stripped to the waist wearing nothing but underclothes and dirty shorts. On closer study O'Neill thought he knew immediately who would win, and which man's new blood would refresh the tidemark. The eyes - the skinny black youth had a fixed glare, alert, focused. The older rangy man's were fixed to the ground, in his eyes were the previous hauntings of a man who had seen hard times. His desire in life was to survive, whereas the youth wanted to win and this was what O'Neill thought designated him a champion.

"The older guy is good Irelandes, I talk to a amigo, they say he keel" many men with a machete, a machete is good, better than a knife, taller man too, longer reach..."

O'Neill looked at the Cuban and shook his head.

"They have a saying back home, it's not the size of the dog, it's the size of the fight in the dog..."

"Always with the sayings Irelandes."

Tony Montana sucked on his cigarette and thought about what had been said with deliberation, as if the saying were profound. The little Cuban waited a while before responding.

"You know they also have a saying here."

"Yeah?"

"They say always bet on the black guy..."

Even though O'Neill tried not to he laughed out loud.

"You know wee man you can be alright sometimes."

Tony Montana turned and stared at O'Neill as if outraged.

"Time to bet Irelandes."

And with that he whistled to the little man with the walking stick and the one eye.

***

Felipe was Beny's opponent in the knife fight. Images and thoughts raced through his mind before the fight started, thoughts about his wife and kids. This was not unusual, it was a life-threatening situation, and a man would think about the things important to him facing death. But he had come through it six times before, and now he hoped this would be lucky number seven. He thought about his kids, and the wife that had left him. What type of person was she he thought, to leave him and their four children she had borne to him, for another. And to force him into the situation he now faced now. He had applied himself to the task of being a father and a partner with dignity. In their little farm on the Zapata peninsula. He had worked hard with citrus fruits, on the marshy and fecund land.

There were few days their table was not full, and the laughter of children resonated their little house. She left him, left him for the sex, coca rock the mind numbing grass and cheap booze in the city. Once she had returned, beaten and bleeding, on her breasts were small incisions made by a knife. Through her slow drugged words and her voice cracked from screaming, Felipe was able to decipher that her pimp had near killed her. Felipe propelled by the love of his wife hunted down her assailant and hacked him to death, only to discover on his return home that his wife had left him again.

Felipe had once fought for his kids, fought to give them the things in life he felt they missed out on, not having a Mother, but now he fought for the pain. At first he had tried to replace her with other women, but none had been able to rouse his feelings like her.

And now as he approached fifty he had conceded that there would not be another to replace the one woman who had owned his heart. Felipe was a simple man, a farmer with great hands, that planted, tended and fixed. In the great scheme of things he thought he could never love again, and this, he thought was a good way to enter knife fights this was his fuel.

The fight proceeded with the sound of drums being battered by rough and ready hangers on with cigars and scars. The two fighters circled each other finding each other's range, their feet shifting lightly on the pool floor, sometimes stubbing on the bolus mounds of blood soaked sand. O'Neill watched carefully noticing how the taller older Spanish looking man had balance in his toes. The smaller muscular black youth moved with less grace but his feet firmly planted. O'Neill noticed he had great muscle groups in his thighs. Man needed legs in a fight, as much as he needed anything else.

Beny attacked, quick lunging twice, trying to cut the opponent's hand which held the machete. Felipe countered with a swift swipe, missing by the slightest of distances taking off the black youth's hand at the wrist. Both moves displayed speed and installed caution in the two men, Beny veered left running at speed in a circle out of range trying to dictate the pace. Felipe watched him run focused, he held the machete above his head ready to strike, like the way he had seen herons in the Zapata shallows strike fish. The crowd was quiet, attentive, occasionally a hushed conversation from one of the rough hangers on was audible, but that was it, that and the relentless drums.

An opportunity presented itself as Felipe slightly tripped on the congealed gore of the swimming pool. Beny struck fast and hard driving the knife into Felipe's left bicep arm. A man in the crowd shouted out involuntarily as if it was his person that had been struck. Felipe winced as the strike drove home, aware of serious damage. Felipe felt pain, real pain, the hot sting and numbing wet. He dared not look down at his arm, for he knew the strike had succeeded, the important thing for him now was to stay focused and return fire.

The bicep muscle disengaged from the sleeve of skin like a baby being born. Seconds after the cut being inflicted another tourist in the crowd vomited and O'Neill glared at him, if it was blood he wanted this is what he would receive. O'Neill felt like frog marching the nauseous man to the pit, and rubbing his face in the visceral effluvium. His weakness pitiful in view of two men battling for their lives. The blood loss sapped Felipe's strength as he stood centre, fending the circling Beny off with his machete, tracing his younger opponent's movement with the blade. Beny jinked in and out of range; the more work Felipe had to do the more blood he would lose. Matter of time now, Beny thought to himself as Felipe stumbled backwards his blood clotting the sand on the already stained floor, his left arm floppy limp and dead, the red raw distended bicep muscle jiggled in the motion.

Beny followed like a bird of prey hovering, ever so slightly out of range but close enough to strike. For Felipe breath was coming slow in respiratory difficulty, his energy reserves all but tapped out, like he had a boulder on his back as well as a bad boy in his face with a knife. Beny leapt to strike, aiming his strike low, targeting the groin or kidneys only to receive a heavy hack from Felipe that bit a lump of flesh from his shoulder like a blitzed watermelon. Beny retreated at speed, the top of his shoulder stinging like someone had set fire to it. O'Neill winced, placing himself in the desperation of the situation. The thoughts and images flashed faster than before through Felipe's mind. But now he thought mostly about his kids, about the six hundred dollars he had left with his sister in Miramar. One hundred and fifty dollars each wasn't a bad last will and testament in Cuba. They were all nearly reared up, considering his situation he hadn't done a bad job.

He wished his father had left him as much, plus they had the farm, the fecund marshy land, and the citrus fruits, if one wanted to be a farmer. He thought of his farm and the taste of fecund mangos, the coral colours of hummingbirds and the smell of burned coffee beans; pleasant memories as his life force left him in great rivers of blood gushing from his arm and the flies were already beginning to plague him. The blood rushed down his arm streaming down his legs through his toes, leaving bloodied footprints like an ancestor on the concrete floor. The loss of blood making him go cold in the hot night and he could feel his heartbeat pop in his ears. The crowd around him seemed as distant as stars in the night sky, their faces anonymous and amorphous in the quivering light provided by the huge steel bins, aflame. Felipe tried to concentrate on his opponent who moved slower and closer in ever decreasing circles.

Like a shark - O'Neill thought, getting closer and closer to finish.

Beny could feel it, the adrenaline racing through him making his big cock hard, making him anxious, that the strike should present itself soon. The older man's eyes drooped like an old man groggy from rum sitting on the Malecon.

The night air shimmered in front of him and Felipe thought about how magical it seemed, and he wondered if his wife ever thought about him (if she hadn't died someplace) and would she be sad on hearing that he was dead, sorrow filled in his heart accompanied by a Toledo steel blade driven true and hard into it

Alfredo paid out what bets he owed to the tourists, their features haunted by the reality of what they had seen. Alfredo liked this, liked the fact that some would have sleepless nights; it lessened the God forsaken burden he had to carry in this trade of life for money.

He approached the Irishman. The old man wanting to see if the blood sport had any impact on him.

"Amigo" what you think of the knife fight? You win again?"

"I think desperate men do desperate things," O'Neill replied.

O'Neill collected his winnings and nodded at the old man.

"You ever fight, box?"

"I'd say more a brawler."

"It's all fighting, that's what life is one big fight, from you are born, life and then death, and two of those you know about, the third the great mystery. What weight you fight - light heavy?"

"Middle," O'Neill said.

"The hardest weight amigo."

"So they say."

"You ready to check out my cigars?"

O'Neill counted his money as if he had not heard what the old man had said.

"Yeah let's check the hoagies." O'Neill said.

"Just you, leave your guide dog." Alfredo nodded towards Tony Montana.

"That I can do." O'Neill obliged and followed the old man round the back of the baseball stand.

"Cruel, the executive game, eh?" Alfredo said.

"Blood puts manners on all men." O'Neill said.

"I like that Irelandes. Many men have seen what you see, many tourists come to the cock fights, the dog fights, then the man fight, a lot of men they, feel different after. Some men they not sleep at night, not able to shave themselves in the mirror, the men that can, I can tell, I may only have one eye but I see, they are from another place, another way that can only be reached by fighting, by killing, companero I think you are such a man..."

"I don't know what way to take that?" O'Neill said.

"Take it the good way, and here we are, cigars."

Alfredo reached an old blue Studebaker car, and popped open the boot to reveal ten boxes of fine Montecristos. O'Neill conducted his taste and touch tests, both with favourable results. They agreed on eight hundred bucks a box. O'Neill paid him, and both parties were happy with the deal. Alfredo offered to help him carry the cigar boxes back to their car, O'Neill declined.

Tony Montana waited on O'Neill at the big red Chevy suspicious that the driver wasn't there. He took the winnings from the fight, a hunk of dollars as thick as a brick, and jammed it down his balls. He cooked the sums in his head, glad that he did not know the exact amount, this on top of the money he had made from the lobsters gave him a warm feeling inside, that dropped his guard a little. It was a feeling of progress of fulfilling his duties as a man and happiness at a little luck. That's all a man wanted in life, a little luck.

He smoked another cigarette and farted and thought about kissing each one of his babies and his wife as they slept when an explosion of white light engulfed his world of temporary joy.

O'Neill returned just in time, his arms full of cigars to see two men drag the unconscious form of Tony Montana across the dusty courtyard. Undoubtedly the little man had fucked up again, it was in his nature. O'Neill had learnt that from the prior experience with the rickshaw men. People like him always fucked up because they had no sway; they were foxes in a world full of wolves. He knew this would escalate, he could see the moves before the play, and the odds were not in his favour.

"Hey what the fuck?" O'Neill shouted to the men. When were the odds ever in his favour?

The men stopped, dropping Tony Montana supine to the ground, a puff of dust rose. The two men were middle-aged, one with one arm, the other man big and black with a pickaxe handle.

"No problemo amigo." The one armed man said.

The man pointed at the prostrate body of Tony Montana.

"Big fucking problem – that's a friend of mine." O'Neill raised his voice.

"Amigo not your problemo." The one armed man repeated the word louder, matching O'Neill's voice for volume.

O'Neill was getting anxious, he was outnumbered again in this place that made him feel more vulnerable than any Havana side street. They were isolated, and the tourists gone, O'Neill unfamiliar with the terrain.

"Like I said my friend, he is with me." O'Neill had introduced the word "friend" hoping to take a little edge from the situation, it didn't.

The man with one arm looked at his cohort with the pickaxe handle and nodded, the man stepped forward to meet O'Neill. The time for talking had passed. O'Neill advanced but they were halted by a deep voice from behind. The voice was rich and sonorous, one that O'Neill knew belonged to authority. He turned to the huge frame of the man he had seen at the night of the dogfights, and with Mauritza. The man that Tony Montana had described to him as The Caribe.

Eyes like Sonny Liston. That's what O'Neill thought, the very same eyes, as if they were taken from that big bad dead fighter who had wrecking balls for fists, and plopped into The Caribe's noble head. Eyes without humanity, but seen all.

"What is the problem here my friend?" The voice enquired and demanded in the one sentence, O'Neill aware of the seniority by the one-armed man and his companion taking a back seat to the situation and again cautious about the use of the word "friend".

"This man is with me." O'Neill reiterated his point.

"You must be mistaken, for in Habana I think you will find all are with me."

Telling O'Neill the way it was, without bluster, or ego these were the facts.

The man moved with power towards him. O'Neill noticed his stride sure and confident. He passed O'Neill, he thought simply to emphasise that he was taller and heavier. The big Cuban lifted Tony Montana's face with his hand, like a hunter inspecting something in a trap.

"Where are you from?"

O'Neill waited before responding, a gap of round twenty seconds.

"Ireland."

"What iz it they say? - 'The fighting Hirish?' Well my fren, my man here he likes lobsters, and the tourists like the lobsters, and I like most tourists – the ones that don't give me any shit".

O'Neill animated his own face by raising his eyebrows.

"That's the problem with lobsters, everybody got boners for them."

The Caribe half smiled, an unnatural smile on a face that held no laughter lines. It was good to meet men with character – a luxury only afforded to tourists for all the locals he already bested. He recognised that the Irishman had character, unafraid, a physical presence too, with big shoulders and heavy hands.

"You had a good night. The executive game, your cigars?" The Caribe pointed at the ten boxes of Montecristos in O'Neill's arms.

"In US that's a pretty good day at the races no?" The Caribe added. The man was right, with what he had already and just acquired O'Neill would create a clear profit that could almost render him rich, all he had to do was walk away. O'Neill sat the cigars down on the ground freeing his hands almost knowing he was about to slip into a quicksand of regret.

"I guess I'm just a sucker for tender lobsters." O'Neill said.

The Caribe stared at him intently, his generosity fading.

"But the lobsters that you like and that he likes are different lobsters altogether." The Caribe stepped closer to O'Neill. This made the large black man and accomplice of the one-armed man retreat further back.

"Yeah how's that?" O'Neill asked.

"Well for hizample the lobsters you like you eat in a restaurant yeah?" The Caribe spoke to him slowly as if he were mentally handicapped. O'Neill aware of the subtlety in the insult.

"And the lobsters that he likes, he steals off my fishermen who sell them to the restaurant yeah?"

The arrogance now apparent on the bigger Cuban man's tongue, it came from someone at his peak.

"Go back to your hotel, with your cigars, forget about Cuban problems, take the profit tourist. Tomorrow see the sights, go on the tours, wear the Argentinean's T shirt, but you forget the night, and this night for the night belongs to me."

O'Neill looked at the fortune in cigars at his feet. He knew the man was giving him an exit, the choice was explicit; turn a blind eye and everything would be okay. O'Neill weighed up the one armed man and the large black guy, they were not the problem now he could hit them fast and hard enough they would think they were surrounded but this other man installed a healthy respect. The Caribe was quiet now, silhouetted in the night by the little light that was available from the bins casting the muscled Cuban as a hellish image.

"My friends will take you to your hotel, free of charge." The Caribe gestured to the two assailants, who now were placated by his orders.

Time to bite his tongue, he was a tourist he had everything that he had come for or had he? The Cubans wanted no heat from fucking with tourists, even The Caribe. In the current economic downturn tourists where what had kept the whole country alive, with the whoring and heathen blood sports. The Caribe knew bad publicity with a tourist would provoke a potential war with the Government.

O'Neill gathered the cigars back into his arms. He had to cut his losses sometime. He had already done his deed of a lifetime saving the little Cuban before, and he just hoped they wouldn't kill the little man. O'Neill stood back and the two cronies returned to their prostrate victim. O'Neill fixed a look in the Caribe's direction and nodded his head, the slightest affirmation that he was taking the offer. The Caribe treated him to the same slight nod, acknowledging the gesture.

As he walked past Tony Montana lying sparked out in the dirt, O'Neill said "Sorry Tony" under his breath to his guide. The larger black man proceeded to drag Tony Montana in the opposite direction when from the ground there seemed to be an explosion as if someone had stepped on a mine. A strobe light of gunfire flashed, partially shedding light on the lethal situation. The big man with the pick axe handle staggered back holding his abdomen, eventually folding to the dusty ground as Tony Montana on his back discharged shots from a huge flashing silver pistol, blowing the big black man along the ground. O'Neill stepped back half deaf and numbed by the gunfire, as the little Cuban on his knees discharged rounds smacking the other Cuban with the one arm direct in the face, blowing an exit wound out the back of his head the size of a pool ball into the night.

Tony Montana pushed himself to his feet still letting bullets fly. The pistol felt hot in his hand, and kicked like a wild animal caught in gin trap, his two assailants were down and the life was leaving them. Tony Montana pivoted to shoot The Caribe, more out of fear than deliberation but there was nothing but empty space and dark night, and the Irishman. The motherfucker could move, O'Neill had known this, the muscle-bound frame dictated it. The big man was gone. Tony Montana stood gun in hand, breathing slack and fast and nearly as laboured as those on the ground as he turned to the Irishman. They looked at the two men on the ground as indescript as rags, the black man's stomach inflated and deflated fast. Tony Montana looked at O'Neill outraged; the Irishman was holding his ears.

"What in the name of good fuck?"

"You focked me man, you leave me to those fockin' animals!"

"You dug your own hole. You stealing fucking lobsters?"

Tony Montana nodded his head looking to the ground like a child caught pilfering sweets, O'Neill knew by his shell shocked face that he had never killed a man, or for that matter, men before. O'Neill knew adrenaline was keeping the little Cuban afloat, before reality set in. And it was about to.

Shouts; automatic gunfire snaffled at their feet. Then screams, dogs barking, people with torches, danger. O'Neill began to think fast, first and foremost of his cigars then of The Caribe, the imminence of the new threat. The man's awareness, his common sense, his instinct. The minute the firearm was produced the situation was out of control, an unfair advantage that alerted his instinct and sparked him to flee, dissolving into the night. The Caribe had cunning he'd be plotting his next move. "We must go Irelandes – now."

But O'Neill was gone, just like The Caribe. They raced back towards the ranch O'Neill seizing an old sack from a fence and piling the cigars into it, Tony Montana in O'Neill's slipstream. O'Neill had decided to head for the place they, would be least expected to run to - the large ranch villa. They passed the Pit Bull kennels where the dogs raged, chewing the steel wire of their paddocks with excitement. As he raced through the kennels, O'Neill let Tony Montana catch up and ushered Tony behind him, as he released the Pit Bulls one by one, using the steel wire doors as a barrier, guarding their legs from their ferocious bites, before the dogs found one another in mortal combat, like betrothed lover's clinching in unbreakable kisses.

Other Pit Bulls barrelled into the night, fanged bullets seeking targets. O'Neill heard the august screams of their pursuers as they met the dogs, and the bursts of automatic gunfire as the dogs were dealt with. The sound of their pursuers was now closer in the air, men shouting and screaming. O'Neill felt like an animal that had been hit by a car, energised to flight, unsure of the damage. They ran blind tearing through a wooden fence into a battery of chicken coops. O'Neill smashed through the flimsy chicken wire of the first coop, sending fighting cocks and bright coloured feathers everywhere, Tony Montana ploughed behind him. At the back there was another obstacle in the form of tall corrugated iron that was used as segregation, and judging by the sounds O'Neill imagined as more pit bulls.

O'Neill charged the corrugated iron fence, ramming it with his shoulder bending it, sufficiently for him and then the Cuban to clamber over it. They dropped into another dog paddock full of pit bulls, which swarmed to attack them. The little Cuban shot wildly at the pack until he realised the dogs had their mouths bound by wire. O'Neill kicked down a gate where they sprinted blindly through more dog paddocks, sending other dogs mad and free. They emerged close to the ranch house, the sounds of men behind them screaming in Spanish getting closer. A kennel boy walked inquisitive from a stable with water buckets and into a fierce hook from O'Neill that put him into an untroubled unconscious, putting any more curiosity out of his head. They sprinted over broken glass, and more crumpled corrugated iron, until they reached a courtyard facing the ranch where they took refuge in the defunct fountain, amongst the maggots of stubbed out fags and well-chewed cigars. They crouched low and peeked from behind the fountain wall, O'Neil brushing an arc of sweat from his shaven head that marked the night air. They watched a man with an Armalite rifle and a torch jog in their direction. Another smell assaulted O'Neill's senses - dog shit. O Neill surmised that he had walked in it when he realised that Tony Montana was covered in it.

"What the fuck did you do roll in it?"

"I fell".

Gunfire jerked them back to more pressing matters.

"How many rounds you have left?" O'Neill demanded.

"Not enough, two or three."

"Fuck, gimme the gun!"

Tony looked helpless, no doubt traumatised by the reality of his reactions.

"I need the fucking gun?"

O'Neill repeated the request without emotion in his voice. He contemplated taking it but reneged on the basis that he should expect the worst. Experience had taught him that when a situation arose it was him left to deal with it, a fucking storm chaser, in circumstances that always seemed to spiral out of control.

The little man handed him the gun, O'Neill cocked it and crouched even lower into the shadows, putting his hand over it to stop the silver glinting in the night. The figure of the man grew closer, shining the torch in obvious places. As the man came to within a few feet O'Neill got to his feet from behind the corrugated iron and gave the figure with the Armalite a hole in the back of his head that he would never remember.

O'Neill got giddy with adrenaline as the man went down, slumped unnaturally against the courtyard wall. He never even saw his face, O'Neill thought and he was grateful for that. He took the armalite and sprinted towards the ranch house, followed by Tony Montana.

As they ran O'Neill handed over the colt 45 to the little Cuban like a sprinter with a baton in the relay race, amazed he didn't drop it. O'Neill fiddled with the safety catch on the rifle and ran around the ranch, seeking entry via the rear, as machine gun fire pricked at their feet. At the back of the ranch they were met by another man with a pistol, tall and middle-aged man. O'Neill cut him to the ground with two shots. O'Neill veered away from the rear of the ranch to the sanctuary of a group of parked vehicles parked fifty yards away at the extreme left of the ranch. He knew their only hope to survive this clusterfuck was to get away from it. It was the right choice, as more men poured out from the ranch. They hid behind a mud brown Chevy. O'Neill put the rifle to his shoulder, it felt coldly familiar, this was the single most important weapon in the history of Ireland's recent conflict. He remembered as a boy ferrying them away from operations in wet nappies, their muzzles still hot from use. He remembered the men that used them, older men, men that feared nothing; jail, torture, death. What cigarettes they smoked - Park Drive cigarettes, their trigger fingers dipped gold by the strong tobacco. They were the men that blooded him, they were the men that moulded him into what he was, and had been. O'Neill let rip; the rifle was a fearsome weapon, from any range.

"Get a car." O'Neill barked the order to Tony Montana.

He covered the little Cuban as he scurried behind him face in the dirt, opening and closing car doors, checking the ancient cars. To O'Neill's extreme left, he heard men coming fast, and now the hunting dogs. He kept the rifle trained on the area at the side of the ranch and back doors where he suspected their main threats would come.

Two pit bulls, no longer allies. Sprinting at speed yelping excitedly noses to the ground, one with a hacking bark that sounded out their position. O'Neill dropped both dogs with two single shots, the high velocity pops of the bullets sending one of the dogs six feet into the air, the spent casings skipping from the rifle, one down his shirt scorching his nipple, the other clinking to the ground.

One wounded dog attacked the other now dead, pit bull, baffling O'Neill. The dog put off its trajectory by the bullet and misappropriating the blame associated with the newfound pain, it's back leg trailing useless, shaking its former comrade's limp torso in its fierce jaws. Furious at it's static companion, some dogs these pit bulls O'Neill thought.

Men came, four or five bare chested, covering each other in military formation, carrying carbines and automatic machine guns. They began to take up positions, running low alerted by the gunfire and yelps of the dogs. O'Neill squeezed off single shots, to conserve ammo. Other automatic guns returned fire, tearing out the windscreens of cars, chunks of glass splintering from the windscreens, leaping into the night like scattered diamonds, Gunfire spiked car metal, cracking batteries and rupturing engines, bleeding vital automobile oil, discolouring the ground at O'Neill's feet, and filling his nostrils with the potent reek. O'Neill retreated and got underneath a car where the chrome grill was blistered and warped from fire. From this level he could see the feet of his attackers, most of them wearing sandals.

He took aim and let one burst of automatic fire go; a result as he heard men scream in agony, invoking heavier fire. He retreated more cars back, aware from other gunfire that men had taken up positions within the ranch, and that at least one had a shotgun as a sleet of shot showered the mud brown Chevy where he had been, sounding like gravel tossed at a window. The roar of an engine was barely audible over all the noise, as Tony Montana pulled up four metres away on a motorbike complete with a sidecar. Bizarrely it reminded O'Neill of old war films, where Nazis always seemed to drive them. O'Neill sprinted from behind the car the rifle now like a cannonball in his hand as he tried to jump into the sidecar missing as Tony Montana started too fast, leaving O'Neill spitting dirt, in seconds he was up again and this time he made it.

O'Neill twisted into an uncomfortable lop sided position into the sidecar holding the armalite trying to force the second and last taped magazine of bullets into the rifle.

Through a fog of dust, a bullet smacked into the backlight, as they raced through stables and onto a dirt road which nearly capsized the bike on a crater like pot holed road, racing into the night.

"Can't you do anything right? I said car."

"Cars in huba" don't have petrol amigo."

The road ahead was a long sleeve of gloom where the only landmark was the sparse lights of Havana city, eight miles in the distance that illuminated the coffin black of the night like the Kleig lights of a distant stage. O'Neill watched behind in the distance from his uncomfortable position as the lights of vehicles blinked in pursuit. The speedometer on the bike flicked over seventy. Too fast for this road, where every pothole and bump registered on O'Neill's balls.

"Fucking lobsters." Was all O'Neill could say.

"Fockin lobsters." Tony repeated.

"We making it Tony?"

"Trust Tony Montana Irelandes trust me..."

O'Neill watched as the lights in the distance got closer, evil eyes that dilated in the hot night. They took a corner too fast losing balance, O'Neill felt the bike lurch violently to one side, the engine snarling like something speared. O'Neill now as if in slow motion and horror as the Cuban, wrestled vainly with the bike's handlebars and braced himself as the side car ploughed into a granulated iron guard rail separating from the bike.

The collision kicked up a bloom of dirt blanketing O'Neill's viewpoint, but increasing his fear of the unknown as he flew through the air at speed, landing in a skidding ball, in stinging all round agony as the rough surface of the dirt road peeled the skin off his buttocks and legs like aged paint, cigars strewn everywhere like the animal droppings of some unknown beast of burden and transporting him with considerable momentum into a large boulder, and the black sleep of concussion.

Lobsters, and Pit Bulls and Pit Bulls and lobsters. Pit Bulls eating lobsters scoffing them whole, crunching their pincers and thoraxes with mighty bites. Two lobsters hanging off an insouciant Pit Bull's ears like surreal earrings. These were the vivid images that haunted O'Neill through his concussed sleep; it was better than the reality he was to face.

***

The Caribe surveyed the scene, five men dead, four men wounded, eight dogs dead, one a champion that had won many fights. The two men had inflicted a heavy toll on his camp; even his fucking kennel boy had a broken jaw. The thief would pay, pay for his insolence, pay for his disrespect. But, by all his men's accounts the tourist was the man who had done the damage. The Caribe ruled with an iron fist, this was an insult that could not be ignored. The Irishman would have to be made an example of - tourist or not.

Alfredo helped load the dead, men and dogs onto the old truck, there was excitement and fear at the camp where he heard the knife fighters talk amongst themselves about how the blonde Irishman with the armalite had taken on the whole camp. Alfredo knew the Irishman had balls, he had seen that in how he had conducted himself on the two occasions that they had met. He also knew The Caribe and his epic pride, the pride that forbade him defeat, the pride that demanded constant respect from one and all. After the wild chaos of the night, he knew that the Irishman's previous status as a tourist would be lost to The Caribe's terrible wrath, that there would be hell to pay, and he would die a horrible death. Two helpers accompanied him from knife fighting camp, as they tossed the corpses of the men onto the methane bonfires in the great rusted bins. He recognised one, a light coloured man called Reuben who had served under him in the army in Angola, and he stopped the knife fighters.

"I know this man."

They looked at him with the dull eyes of the servile unable to think for themselves.

"I will bury him."

They sat the dead corpse to one side, where it's legs lay crooked and abnormal. They continued tossing other dead men into the huge bins, roaring with flapping flames, holding their noses as the corpses caught flame.

The Caribe's men found O'Neill and Tony Montana ten minutes later. They loaded them roughly, still unconscious into the back of a green Ford truck where they roused them with lit cigarettes, only to beat them unconscious again. O'Neill felt as if it was happening to someone else; he seemed that distant from himself, a sensation of such pain that it felt as if he wasn't there, but at least he had some relief from the frenzied lobster and Pit Bull dreams, the pain confirming reality.

From the condition of the tourist the men decided their efforts weren't being fully rewarded, so they concentrated on the more coherent Cuban, whose screams echoed through the night as they transported them back to the ranch. O'Neill felt the lights go out again in his head and the pit bulls and lobsters came back.

And awoke to them, only this time it was his own screams, like a lungfish, the remnant of a parched riverbed. He gasped for life, tugging his head that was glued to the dirty ground in old blood. He found himself in a dog paddock, beside the chalk of mummified dog shit, and a badly torn piebald Pit Bull with a head on it like an anvil, licking O'Neill's torn face, oblivious to its own festering wounds. The dog's skin hung in tattered strips from it's throat, none of it's ears remained and it's left front leg was grotesquely swollen, with the consistency of broken glass thick with sepsis fluid.

The dog had at first terrified him with its intentions. He tried to move away but nothing seemed to work. For one slight moment he was frozen with the fear that he was paralysed, but he found that if he concentrated through the throbbing ache, his legs worked fine. O'Neill stared into it's little piggy eyes which were filled with dumbness, but seemingly no malice. The dog took to one of O'Neill's prominent wounds, a large gash in his forehead, and lapped at it with its sandpaper tongue. At first O'Neill thought this abhorrent, but the sensation won him over and he allowed the big dog to tend it. The paddock was no bigger than ten by twelve, with paw marks in the concrete that bizarrely reminded O'Neill of a pet food product trademark. The paddock was surrounded with corrugated iron with a wooden sheet that acted as a bed where Tony Montana lay before him unconscious, beaten to a pulp, the place saturated with blood and pit bull traces like some avant-garde art work.

O'Neill was grateful for the dog's soothing tongue, and even more that the dog was friendly. He gently patted it on the head with an uncomfortable and fearful tap. An insect buzzed above the dog's big skull, and the dog snapped at it engulfing it in it's well armed mouth, swallowing comically. A silver filament of saliva leaked from its mouth shivering from a black nippled mandible, that repulsed O'Neill so much that he flicked it away with his butchered fingers. O'Neill watched the little Cuban, who intermittently would convulse, then cough and then remain still. O'Neill knew by his companion's appearance, the dog's dumb stares and how his own body felt that there probably wasn't much difference in all their conditions except that, ironically O'Neill was the best off.

But that was nothing to be proud of, considering their situation and the environment. The paddock reeked - from dogs, blood, shit, something much worse, imminent that he thought emanated from them all, Death?

O'Neill checked the little Cuban's pulse. It throbbed weak and distant. Both the Cuban's legs were broke and it looked like he had lost an ear. Occasionally he would retch and splutter as he inhaled blood, his lungs making grotesque gurgling sounds. On the Cuban's arms and face were the festering purple blisters of cigarette burns. The fall from the bike combined with their personal torture, had rendered both men in dire straits. O'Neill knew that if they didn't receive medical attention they would die, and even with medical attention the odds were against his companion. O'Neill luckily enough had no broken limbs, but suspected from the severe pain in his torso that four or five of his ribs were broke, and his internal organs felt as if someone had taken a blow torch to them. Sight was available only in his left eye, as the other was closed. His tongue was as thick as a bridle in his mouth and he had lost teeth, it annoyed him that, he had always had good teeth even though he smoked, had boxed, taken big hits from the hardest hitters and never lost a tooth and here he was, not the first time in his life against the ropes, but the first time he wanted to throw in the towel, the first time he wished some unseen corner man would come to his aid, and take this agony away. His face felt like ice cream left in the sun, both his hands were broken, tendons and ligaments leaked from his knuckles in bloody ligature the skin on his legs felt as if flayed by a whip.

Every breath he took felt as if one of his broken ribs was piercing his heart, blood pounded so hard in his head he felt it was going to explode.

"Some water amigo?"

O'Neill turned in agony to see a half shorn plastic carton full of murky water, being pushed towards him from under the locked kennel gate. With a great deal of effort an image formed to reveal Alfredo. O'Neill slurped on the water through his mushy mouth, he then used some of it on Tony Montana, who stirred a little, then passed it to the Pit Bull who dropped a grateful tongue in it.

"Your friend not too good?"

"Which one?" O'Neill replied.

The old man smiled.

"A very, very good dog, he win all hiz fights."

O'Neill looked at the pit bull, that's what a winner looked like. It didn't look like he was going to win the next one. The dog could barely drink, its big head was slung to the side, and the left leg was even pulpier with the broken glass sepsis than before.

"He have heart, but he iz - How you say getting a leetle long in the tooth, like me senor."

The old man counted on his hands and under his breath.

"He haz been matched with sixteen dogs, undefeated. But now he take longer to heal, he don't eat as much, don't bite as hard."

O'Neill knew there was a point to this but what?

"Just like me."

O'Neill looked at the old man, both of them equal now in the peripheral field of groggy one-eyed vision.

"What is going to happen to us?"

The old man shrugged his shoulders, and shook his head.

"For every action there is consequences, I know this."

The old man pointed to the canesecent orbit of his dead eye.

"This is your consequence, these things sometime we have no control over, your fren hiz life iz the consequence. You know what you need, Irelandes now? Another fren from huba; I have another gift for you Irelandes…"

O'Neill watched the old man as he limped forward surreptitiously and pushed a knife through the wire. The knife had a dull black plastic handle, and a slender, razor sharp blade. It looked to O'Neill like a steak knife, the type of knife a butcher would use to fillet thick meat. O'Neill crawled and collected the knife from the kennel floor; he looked at the old man.

"Bad things need a sharp knife." The old man said.

O'Neill scoured the old man's face for betrayal; he was cute enough to know that favours in these hard places didn't come for free.

The dog finished lapping at the water and O'Neil took the carton and sipped some more, contemplating the wisdom of his words.

For a long while, he studied the knife wondering its purpose. A gun would have been better. If he had wanted him to escape, it would have been a gun, besides he was in too bad a physical condition to run, or drive. No there was a specific reason why the man had given him the knife, an event.

The old man was no Houdini, but with the homage of the knife there was a connection to be cultivated. He lay working out the old man's play. There was a plan, but it wasn't O'Neill's it was the old man's, O'Neill didn't know his role yet, but as long as it involved breathing and getting the fuck out of this place he was willing to go along with it. There simply wasn't any other option. He did not deny it worried him, worried him on top of a thousand other current worries, because he was in no condition for any event, bar urgent medical intervention but he hunkered down using the old dog as a comfort blanket grateful for warm blood, contact and a source of heat in a union of the broken, secreting the knife wondering what path his flimsy destiny offered.

CHAPTER 12

Mauritza knew by his way that he was angry; something had clambered under his skin and worked its way into his system. When they fucked he would usually whisper vulgarities with tender obscenity. It would have been a lie to say that she did not enjoy their couplings, in the same way she had a healthy appetite for sex with her clients.

Mauritza enjoyed sex, she could come most times, without having a skilled lover, and she liked the post coital release of endorphins. She was as red blooded a Cuban woman as he was a man. But she could tell he was not his usual self. Five times he would normally come; she had been having sex with him since she was fourteen years old. Three times at night, once occasionally if he had a little rum, and without fail two times in the morning, his shuddering like a horse confirmation of his climax. As she lay on the bed she could recall only once during the night, and she could tell by his inability to sleep, and lack of usual sexual vigour that something vexed him. He liked to smell. Her armpits, the dew of her lust on his hands, after he was inside her. The night before he did none.

She did not ask the reasons why, for such reasons were personal, and to be personal and private with him sent out the wrong signs. She wanted to exit this relationship which had been dictated by his demanding terms, not sustain it.

She laid on his bed in the vast bedroom, beside a tall open window with a huge grille watching him clean his knives. The sound of knives grinding over the stone made her nervous. It seemed more like a jail cell than a bedroom. The room was filled with expensive ornaments, a jade figurine depicting men fighting with knives, a limestone statue, almost life-size, of a python with a goat in a constrictive embrace that had been stolen to order by one of his underlings from the Zoological de Piedra, a zoo in the country where all the animals instead of being alive, were created from limestone; a tall, gnarled oak cabinet with nothing in it, and a mirror in a gold frame that displayed the Caribe's reflection as he cleaned his large array of knives from the cigar box with a shaving belt, and the more modern steel ones on a granite stone. He glanced at her sipping on rum. Her dark coloured sex prominent against the brilliant white Egyptian cotton sheets.

"Cover up woman."

"What, you're complaining?"

"No chirp back tonight Doctor, just fuck, then quiet."

She obeyed when he called her "Doctor." She knew this state, this was the state that dictated death, and this was when he would kill men.

CHAPTER 13

Tony Montana regained consciousness late into the night on the fourth day of their incarceration. He had been awoken by his fevered nightmares. A heat glittered all over his aching body like magic dust, he groaned involuntarily and O'Neill pushed over the little water he had saved. It took the little man a while to regain his powers of speech.

"You look like shit Irelandes." Tony said

"You wanna" be in here looking out," O'Neill replied, warmed by the fact that Tony even in his condition had, till now, retained his wit. The little man read the Irishman for anger at him, for creating this set of circumstances that put them in this jeopardy. He had a guilty look on his Cuban face as he busked for laughs and O'Neill would have obliged only both knew that laughter with their broken ribs would hurt. The little Cuban sipped the murky water, wincing, realising that they were joined by a third companion in the form of the busted up pit bull that lay panting heavily beside O'Neill.

"What the fock iz that?"

The little Cuban would have tried to move away if he could.

"Don't worry Tony he's on our side."

"The losing side, he looks like shit too."

"Seems to be the only stipulation," O'Neill said.

This time they did laugh, guarding their sore torsos with their broken hands.

"What can I say, I very sorry Irelandes? This trouble is all my fault…"

O'Neill looked at the little man. He didn't have to say that. If atonement was accepting responsibility for actions then the little Cuban had learned a very valuable lesson. But O'Neill's judgement was that it was too late for both of them to learn about each other's instincts; the little Cuban's propensity for clusterfuck, and his inability to be a criminal, and O'Neill's own propensity for violence, and inability to avoid confrontation. They were one and the same, two perpetual losers.

"The only sorry you should feel Tony is for crashing the motorbike." O'Neill thought he could do with a morale boost.

"For involving you in all this, it is not fair, you being a tourist, a visitor".

That could apply almost to everything in this fucked up world… You a good guy Irelandes, you fockin U2, Bono eh?"

"Fuck Bono." O'Neill joked.

They laughed again, O'Neill noticing the smaller man's speech becoming more slurred, one side of his face freezing up.

"All through my life, people beat me. I not tough like you Irelandes, I had enough of being beat on, and of being served shit with every sunrise, that's why I shot those Motherfockers…"

"I know," O'Neill said and he did. He knew because he too had been served the same shit at sunrise only in a different country, under a less tropical sun.

The little Cuban had no option to respond to the situation. It was exactly what O'Neill, and any other man worth his sand, would have done. O'Neill thought himself unfortunate that he had now become embroiled in an issue which, if studied, didn't really concern him. But in fairness his nature always led him that way, so he couldn't feel that surprised or annoyed by it. Yes, no doubt the Cubans were going to kill Tony Montana, that had been evident from his negotiations with them and The Caribe's intervention. People like Tony Montana didn't really matter in the big picture, or the criminal machinations that kept the world spinning. He was a cautionary footnote to those who dared steal lobsters off The Caribe.

"Sorry Irelandes".

"That's twice, no need for a third time, within my experience it's better to concentrate on what is going to happen instead of what happened, and on that subject when it will happen." O'Neill scolded him.

The little Cuban looked at him and O'Neill saw all that he needed to know, he wasn't going to make it. Not only because of his physical condition, but because his will to survive wasn't strong enough, it would be easier to fade than to recover and most people chose to fade.

"What is your name Irelandes?"

"You know my name."

"Your first name, the one your mother would call you?"

O'Neill looked at the little man with cynicism, his mother like his father died when he was young. Care homes fed and housed him and the conflict reared him. He had had these moments before, they were no good except at the end of bad films.

"That bad uh?" O'Neill noticed the left hand side of Tony's face now almost permanently disfigured in a distorted grin, and the dropped eyelid more prominent.

"For me yes, maybe not for you," Tony Montana said. The words coming slower and misshapen from the voice thickening in his throat "Tourist."

"Tourist." O'Neill echoed.

They shared another smile, no longer laughter, and the bloodied, murky water.

My first name is "Setanta."

"Setanta" what a type of fockin" name is that?"

"I was named after an Irish warrior." O'Neill explained.

"Setanta," if I ever have another son I might call him that."

They paused, both knew he wouldn't. The little Cuban foraged in his clothing, hooking his one good hand around for some hidey-hole on his person, he retrieved a soft crumpled cigarette packet. He opened it to reveal one last bent cigarette, as precious as a jewel. The little Cuban straightened it out with precision and with difficulty angled it into his frozen mouth. O'Neill smiled through his own broken mouth. The little Cuban then from his balls removed an expensive silver zippo lighter, no doubt pilfered from some unsuspecting tourist.

"Tourists."

He tutted and ignited the cigarette and after four or five heavy chugs passed it to O'Neill, blood on the butt. O'Neill sucked on it letting the smoke drape his lungs, the nicotine hit flush to his head. Two friends sharing a cigarette, killing what precious little time they had left, blanking the reality that something horrific was about to happen to both of them, through the sanctuary of tobacco.

"They have a joke here. A father and son are walking along the diamond white sandy beach at Varadero."

O'Neill found it difficult to interpret the words now. "Father" sounded like "fadder", and the Cuban's speech was enunciated in slow motion. O'Neill attributed it to some brain trauma, probably his brain swelling, but he gave the man his stage.

"They have lived there all their lives, they are separated from the tourists by razor wire on the beach they call home, father looks at his son with pride and says son what do you want to be when you grow up? Son looks at his father who has ambitions for hiz only son -Maybe a doctor, politician, a teacher. The son looks at the tourists with the cocktails, and food through the razor wire, he sees the pretty chikkas, the tourist's big bellies sipping the cocktails, son says "I want to be a tourist".

O'Neill smiled acknowledging the irony.

"The small things in life, we not know, how important Irelandes they are until -".

"It's too late."

O'Neill finished the conversation for him and handed the little Cuban back the cigarette, and the man nodded gratefully.

"My fren'."

"Setanta to you Tony – and consider yourself privileged as I only allow my friends to call me that."

The little Cuban laughed, and then coughed spitting black blood.

"Setanta, I want you to do something for me? For my family?"

From another secret place on his person the man handed O'Neill a chunk of bloodstained money. And from another, a little pen, and he wrote down an address on a blood streaked dollar bill.

"Apartment two hundred and sixty two Ipa 22, my wife's name is Berta."

O'Neill absorbed the information then looked at the money as the little Cuban offered it to him.

"Please give my wife this."

"You know it's not over yet, you know things can happen, the will to live, is a funny thing Tony. I've been in jail, busted out. Been in scrapes that didn't look like it was going my way, but made it go my way."

The little Cuban started to shake involuntarily like an old man with Parkinson's disease.

"This is not going my way Irelandes…!"

"What will I tell her?"

Tony Montana looked to the sky; his half dropped eye getting lower it was the look of resignation, of failure.

"Tell her I tried."

O'Neill looked at the little man, there was bravery in his fear and acceptance. They talked intermittently through the night amidst sequences of unconsciousness, until the fighting cocks crowed. O'Neill let the little man talk and babble through his coma like bouts.

O'Neill knew little about head injuries but imagined, due to the Cuban's incoherence, violent shaking, and delirious shouts that the brain had finally swollen. A little after sunset, the little Cuban seemed to rally and had an episode of lucidity speaking about his life, love and now his imminent demise, and like a priest receiving the last confession on the death bed, O'Neill obliged him. He had remembered a former comrade back in Ireland telling him about his younger sister dying of a cancer in a hospice. He had thought the story poignant, the sister being much younger than the other hospice members, taking great solace when a senior nurse explained to her that everyone she knew would die, thus alleviating some of her distress. O'Neill relayed the story to the Cuban who also seemed to derive some succour from it.

Four men finally came, armed with machetes and a shotgun, lead by Alfredo. They put both men on a wooden trolley used to drag heavy objects from the stables, and pulled them into the courtyard and out beside the derelict swimming pool where they had witnessed the men with knives fight. Sunlight seared their eyes and O'Neill could hear the little Cuban mumbling nonsense slightly in front. The cold steel of the knife felt good at the back of his leg which he had locked to the joint to give the impression that it was injured, at least some other Motherfucker would suffer too he thought. The Caribe stood wearing linen trousers and a black leather waistcoat, flanked by his knife fighters, all in all around fifty men, lean men, all different hues with scars and tattoos, who smoked and talked excitedly.

O'Neill could tell by the way they clustered around him that he had their fear. Respect came from fear. Knowing whom the man had defeated, watching his victories, aware of his power. Tony Montana coughed up another wad of blood and spat to the ground. By this stage his world was a kaleidoscope of shapes and sounds. He called to O'Neill, eager for a friend in this savage carnival of strangers, and oppressors, and extended his hand blindly to O'Neill. O'Neill managed to hi five the small palm, before he was ripped to the edge of the swimming pool. Where The Caribe delivered the requiem.

"It is unfortunate that we are here today, but let us send a message out to those who dare declare themselves our enemy. This man and his cohort took the lives of five of our comrades; five good men lost their lives to this scum. To our fallen comrades, we salute you, to our enemies we smite you."

The Caribe directed two heavies with a nod who dragged the slight frame of Tony Montana off the wooden trolley and to the swimming pool. O'Neill leaned from his own trolley and strained to see into the pool only to recoil in horror at the sight of a huge lizard. He recognised the lizard. It was the length of a crocodile with huge claws, an animal called a Komodo dragon. The little Cuban began to scream hysterically in an ill chosen moment of lucidity at the same sight. His antagonists dragged him to the edge of the swimming pool, Tony Montana spewing forth obscenities at the big man; the accomplices tossed him in a sickening heap into the derelict pool. The little man screamed in agony on landing as fractured bones were fractured again.

O'Neill could not bear to watch, but he read the expressions of the hardened fighters' faces as some turned away, as the dragon tore the man to pieces still alive. It was incredible O'Neill thought in this century, that a man could commit what he had just seen committed to another, a fucking Bond Villain wouldn't have committed the crime he had just witnessed. Havana was a primitive place. He had discovered this from his own personal experience, from the attitudes and machismo, the open sewers, the al fresco sex, electricity blackouts, and the draconian measures applied by the Government. He had known this from the open practise of the Black arts, and Castro's laborious repeated speeches and archaic manifestos, but most of all it was confirmed to him by what had just occurred. They had just tossed a man to a dragon. The man, a newly acquired friend, father, husband. O'Neill fixed a glare at the Caribe as the little man's screams subsided until the only sounds apparent were the sounds of flesh being sucked and torn. Then the same two arbitrators who had tossed the little Cuban came to lift him, and with difficulty they hurled him into the pit.

He landed hard in the pen but luckily he rolled transferring the impact without any bones getting broken, and more importantly, without dropping the knife on contact with the ground. O'Neill retched at the stench of shit and dead meat. The Lizard was at the opposite end of the pool, worrying the disemboweled corpse of what had once been O'Neill's friend.

The odds were not in his favour, an invalid with a knife. The big tail thrashed, slapping the blood licked concrete like a bull whip, leaving cochineal streaks on contact, that brindled the entire area of the makeshift feeding ground, and real life dragon's den.

The Dragon turned, facing him. It's face a bloody mask. Like a dinosaur he thought. It reminded O'Neill of those stupid creature features that he used to watch avidly as a child on Saturday afternoons that often seemed to feature the much-maligned actor Doug McClure, where Iguanas would be filmed on miniature sets. It made a sound, a terrible, unholy, terrifying sound that O'Neill thought came from a hundred million years ago.

The dragon moved, awkward and saurian, like a body builder trying to run, the big biceps in it's taloned arms flexing, O'Neill got to his unsteady feet, the dragon stopped on his movement, O'Neill took the knife from behind his back. He was unaware of shouts from above as the people at the ringside seats noticed the blade, the same way that in a ring there was no one there but you and your opponent.

As the dragon cautiously advanced O'Neill moved and the dragon froze, tasting the air with its forked tongue. That was how they smelled O'Neill thought. He had an idea he advanced and the dragon retreated, making the terrible sound. Now it was pissed.

"Fuck! Fuck! Fuck!"

That's all that came into his head, terror, fear. He had to use it, use it like fuel, direct it into his arms, his shoulders, and change it from its crude source into energy, using the prospect of survival as the slick alchemist. He thought hard, trying to raid information in his head that would help. The dragon was a predator. Predators expected prey to flee - that was it, he wouldn't flee. He hadn't much choice, looking at the torn messy corpse of Tony Montana in the corner and the approaching back wall of the swimming pool, there was fucking nowhere to flee.

And it was huge; bigger than a fucking crocodile. In the creature features the way to kill the things was the head, drive that fucking knife up to the hilt into its pea sized prehistoric brain! Like Doug Fucking McClure!

This thing was fucking nuclear. Everything about it was designed to destroy other living creatures, from the powerful muscled tail that acted as a fifth limb to the venom in its mouth. O'Neill inched forward, the dragon stopped, he outstretched his arms making himself bigger, the dragon turned making the unholy sound again. O'Neill moved forward slowly until he realised he had backed it into a corner, suddenly it exploded towards him attacking. The great tail lashed hard sweeping O'Neill's' legs with such immense power that he thought he had tapped into an undiscovered and terrifying kinetic energy. The dragon then rushed biting. O'Neill pivoted in desperation and, with every ounce of his waning strength drove the blade upwards through the animal's leathery chin, piercing through the roof of the fetid mouth and into it's dull brain. O'Neill withdrew the knife quickly and directed hard thrusts to the head region, as repulsed as he was violent, killing the animal as the great tail subsided on the concrete. Hot blood spat onto his body as the velocity of the tail's slaps decreased to little pats.

O'Neill pushed the twitching beast away and stared above him blinded by the morning sun where he could see the black silhouettes surrounding the mini amphitheatre silent with the dumbed mouths of the fighters and The Caribe.

He screamed at them exultant, and defiant with his profanities and victory.

"Motherfuckers!

Was all he had to say.

That was until they put him back onto the wooden trolley and tied his hands and feet with barbed wire. O'Neill oblivious to the new pain, adrenalised and apoplectic with rage.

"You fucker, you Cuban cunt, you bastard, Motherfucker, tough guy fucker! Fight me fucker, fight me!"

He was mad from the sun, the infections and the battle when they hauled the victorious Irishman out from the pool.

"You should be quiet if you know what is good for you." Alfredo whispered to him.

"Fuck you old man, fuck you and that clown that runs you all." O'Neill said.

Alfredo looked at the Irishman with secret admiration, at the seeping blood on the wooden trolley, the barbed wire handcuffs, the face swollen three times it's natural size threatening the big boss. The Irishman had courage. Not many men had the ability or sense to turn defence into attack like the Irishman had done the night before; not many men could kill four men with a machine gun and escape from the camp, and kill the dragon. Alfredo had big plans for this one. That was the reason he had given him the knife. He could be the man who could do the things he should have done, the man who could release the people. A man like this you did not want as an adversary, a man like this you wanted as an ally.

The Caribe approached. He noticed a tattoo on the inside of the Irishman's right arm of Che.

151

"Tourists, they all want the image of the Argentinean. That is not the real Cuba, this is the real Cuba." He kneeled and balanced over O'Neill's face, tilting his head to focus, then he unsheathed a significant blade from the small of his back and drew it slowly horizontally across the cursing Irishman's face, which if he ever survived another dawn, would inevitably be scarred.

"That was for my dragon tourist."

The Irishman spat claret saliva onto him.

"You've no balls you know that?" O'Neill raged.

The Caribe did not reply but wiped the blood away with the back of his thick hands, transferring it almost delicately to a stain on O'Neill's ripped shirt. With that The Caribe stamped on O'Neill's head with his cowboy boot, and Cuban tipped heel clouding out O'Neill's world with a black veil of unconsciousness he was now getting used to.

"And that was for me." The Caribe said.

Mauritza watched from the balcony of the ranch, as the men filed away from the swimming pool. She watched as The Caribe cut and stamped on the Irishman, turning her head, feeling his pain, and watched as they hauled him away lifeless on the trolley to the mercy of the midday sun and it's myrmidon leaving him to bleed in the stifling heat.

Mauritza closed the blinds and rushed to the cellar where she knew The Caribe kept first aid items to tend to his favorite dogs, and, to a lesser degree his more useful fighters.

Mauritza worked fast, taking hydrogen peroxide, vials of antibiotics and dressings from the Green first aid kit. She replaced the precious milky antibiotics, with some government sun cream from her hand bag, careful to syringe the exact amount back into the vials replacing the first aid kit, unsure of what side the box had been facing when in her haste she had opened it. She decided the first aid sign had been facing her, then decided against and put the green box in backwards, then hid her precious cargo underneath the bed.

After the men had placed the unconscious Irishman directly beside the main dog kennels supine on his back and bleeding under the fiery nimbus of the sun, they stood awaiting their next command. None was forthcoming; instead The Caribe stood glaring balefully at them saying nothing letting his heat seeking eyes scorch into their very souls.

There was no need for words, the torn cadaver of Tony Montana in the swimming pool and the mangled Irishman at their feet laid testament to those who defied, of those who dared, of those who challenged, of those who failed to obey. The Caribe walked close to Alfredo.

"Feed him to the dogs in the evening, but let him char for a while, let him tenderise in the heat Alfredo."

"Yes senor. In the evening."

The Caribe got closer to Alfredo, hunting information with his eyes, intimidating with his physique. He towered over the older man.

"I have one question for you Alfredo."

"Yes Senor?"

"You are the trainer of my dogs, the trainer of my fighters, my bookie?"

"I am."

"You my maker of unpleasant decisions, my fixer, my conduit to the fighters, the question I ask you is this? How did this piece of shit have a knife?"

"He must have had one, when he was captured." Alfredo replied, annoyed at himself for the quick answer, as if it was rehearsed.

"That is a remarkable coincidence, because I recall the very same knife inhabiting my kitchens at one stage or other, and you know me my old friend, I never forget a blade. It makes me the man that I am. We have an infiltrator in our midst, who for some reason is not happy. This we must address, for we all know that the penalty for treason and betrayal is death, and now that I have no dragon, I fear I will have to go back to the tools of my trade."

The Caribe opened the interior of his black leather waistcoat, revealing the super enhanced eight pack of abdominal muscles and a tool belt of ferocious blades. The Caribe turned to another accomplice.

"Beny make sure the other fighters know this, that a reward of a pretty girl or boy for the night will be the order for those that expose this traitor."

"Yes sir." Beny said, nodding his head in affirmation like a dog begging for meat.

The Caribe nodded his head slowly and walked past the men in the direction of the ranch. The violence of the morning had aroused him, even though his dragon was dead. He wanted sex now, sex with Mauritiza.

***

Alfredo knew that like a tilted hourglass, time was running out as he sat in his shack, avoiding the afternoon sun drinking rum and watching the spider that lived above his naked light bulb cocooning a fly. He had thought many times about the morality of his existence, and he could tell lies to everyone except himself. It was wrong. It was barbaric, a sanguinary vaudeville where the players really died. Alfredo knew from the cave drawings that man had always killed man with tools, and that the blade was as much a part of man as man was himself. From the honed down animal bones of history to the contemporary combat knives he had used in the Army. The knife was the past of mankind, and its destruction. It was rudimentary, and sophisticated. He had first learned the art of the blade in the army; there it was justified as close combat, but how far he had fallen from the grace of being loyal to

Cuba to what he did now. Was it even an occupation he thought? He refereed blood baths, arbitrated between the desperate, and satiated the blood lust of the rich. A thousand years before he would have probably thrown Christians to the lions. He did not how it had come to this; the proximity to the ones he loved was one legitimate reason, and easy money in a hard world. But each day in his little cracked mirror he found it harder and harder to face himself. His daughter had tried to explain to him, those feelings of self-loathing, and that other such feelings of what he felt were the bona fide effects of his blood sugar. But that world of science and doctors held little allure for Alfredo, with the hands of time ticking. His body now was mostly muzzy with sleep and his mind was filled with the complex mysteries of what happened to a man when his body was interred in the tomb of Cuba's ruddy earth that he had picked out in the country beside his beloved wife, with the reality that he contributed and participated in the training and encouragement of the men of Cuba to gut each other like fish for a measly few bucks and a full gut. That was his real problem, as he sat in his shack drinking sickly sweet rum, feeling the sugar rise in his legs like mercury in heat.

CHAPTER 14

The black corona of the flaming sun induced feverish hallucinations in O'Neill's brain that made the concussed dreams of before seem kids fairytales. The palate of his mouth was like sand, and he sometimes thought he was subconsciously trying to swallow his own tongue, to end his own life. Che Guevara in space! That was what was in his brain, and he knew why. He had remembered a story he had read many years before in jail, that a Cuban astronaut on a mission with Russians had left a statue of Che in orbit. The image had always stayed with him, oscillating through the black void a little Che, armed with nothing but his little beret with its' silver star, his bandit moustache and steely determination, inspiring oppressed aliens in different galaxies. The image replayed in his head over and over, until he too thought he was spinning through a black galaxy. And in reality he was, a black galaxy of colossal heat, where the once gold halo of the sun was a blistering black, where the natural sounds and sensations were drowned out by his thundering heartbeat and peeling skin. He dried to drive his face into a crack of wood on the trolley to evade the heat but it was to no avail. O'Neill did not want to scream, so he did the next best thing and sung a rebel song that inspired solidarity in the nearby Pit Bulls, who wailed in with an unholy choir. The fighters in the barrio watched the mad Irishman singing in the hundred-degree heat. There were examples and there were cruelty, and even though they were in the pain game, somehow what they considered a brutal existence paled into insignificance compared to what this gringo was going through. At the start there had been a considerable amount of ill will towards the gringo, considering that he had been directly responsible for the deaths of some of their peers. But as happens with men accomplished with taking other men's lives, as with soldiers, a begrudging respect was beginning to gather for him. They had all feared the dragon, and with killing it he had earned their respect.

O'Neill awoke in the evening, in a better place, back in the dog kennel with fluid singing in his mouth, filtering down his throat. His smudged vista revealed Mauritiza, applying soothing Aloe Vera on the damaged inflicted by the sun's flames and wetting his mouth.

O'Neill thought she looked nervous, glancing behind her, front and back like prey at a waterhole. Still beautiful, her hair snagged and wild, the different coloured eyes, her full mouth half open displaying her small even white teeth. Sex, is what he detected, from the rough bruises garnishing her neck, and the indentations of big fingerprints on her deltoid muscles. He was amazed that considering his condition this was what was on his mind.

But that was life, sex and death. He blamed it on her breasts. He knew it was a stereotype; he knew that was such a cliché, but he was being truthful with himself.

Mauritza's nipples pricked through the slight linen top, the butterscotch aureole studded with dark nipple. She was aware he was looking at her as she dabbed a damp cloth, steeped in antiseptic on open knife wounds, and other wounds.

"Well doctor, what's the diagnosis?" O'Neill asked.

His voice sounded like it belonged to an old man or a stranger; the words were heavy with strain.

"Mostly superficial, you could live, if you were not here." She answered matter of factly, planting.

"Can you get me out?"

Mauritiza continued on as if he had said nothing.

"Can you?" He repeated, the words eager.

"I have ears, he would find you." Mauritza answered.

O'Neill had few options. He was travelling on a fake passport, he was living on a dead man's credit card, and involved in contraband activity in a world he knew very little about, and what he did know he was sure no one else wanted to. A third world country, with crippling poverty, run by a dictator by day and this underworld king at night, where defiance was rewarded with people being thrown to dragons, and the entertainment was two men with blades. In this arena of corruption, where The Caribe owned the very fish in the sea, who on earth would risk their life for a stranger, and some meddling tourist at that. O'Neill was a realist; he knew it was madness to even consider cops, or media. He knew about cops and media in the Western world, the supposed civilized world, and they were all rotten to the core. Considering Cuba's economic plight he imagined this crew would be twice as bad, given the sway The Caribe had, it would be totally futile. O'Neill foraged for something in the bristling darkness that was his ebbing future.

"Mauritza I am a tourist – people will come for me?"

"Don't you understand? It doesn't matter what you were, now you are his enemy, in a world where he has none." She spoke with clarity, each word reaching the destination clearly making sense.

"You are here, so you must forget about the authorities. He is the authority, to people here is he more important than Castro..."

"You have to help me Mauritza!" he implored.

She shot him a glance, and pressed and bandaged his broken hands.

"That's what I am doing O'Neill, helping you." She heard masculine voices outside the dog kennels and an abrupt bang on the corrugated door. She gathered up the soiled dressing and proceeded to the corrugated iron gate, it cracked open and O'Neill noticed the old man Alfredo hurry her out.

"Now you convalesce O'Neill". Mauritza said and she was gone.

"Convalesce," he repeated mimicking her Spanish tongue. He loved how she spoke, what she knew.

The old man Alfredo brought him a thick broth, of black peas and some rice later. He could hear the ungodly cacophony of dogs howling and barking in disharmony, hell's symphony. O'Neill was unable to eat the food, with the sound and discomfort.

"Feeding time at the zoo." Alfredo said.

"Hope they're not getting what I'm getting." O'Neill countered, noticing Alfredo go quiet and serious.

"The fighting dog must be fed meat, otherwise he has no strength, beef preferably, but in lean times, any meat will do," Alfredo looked at the cracked Irishman, and the Irishman back at him.

"Any meat?" O'Neill said.

"Let you into a little secret Irelandes? If I get you out of here, you must do something for me," Alfredo said.

O'Neill started to piece it together the knife, the warnings, bringing the Doctor to tend his wounds, the old man was making his play and whatever he was selling, O'Neill was for buying.

"I have a friend in the country, by the beach, he could help you convalesce…"

The minute he said it, O'Neill knew that Alfredo was Mauritza's father. It wasn't the repeat of the word, but the exact same expression on the old man's face that told O'Neill they were inexplicably linked; the way O'Neill thought twins could read each other's thoughts.

"You must get strong again. Let the wounds heal then you must return and kill The Caribe". Alfredo spoke in deadly earnest, his one good eye not blinking once.

"That simple uh?" O'Neill countered.

"That is my terms."

"Well if you could get me some men, a few assault weapons, then we might have something to talk about old man."

"You must kill him, kill him with a knife there is no other way."

"Old man there are a million ways to kill people, guns and bombs – bombs are better."

O'Neill reasoned in an unreasoned conversation.

"It must be with a knife." The old man was adamant, set in stone.

"Look get me to the hotel, I have money..." O'Neill said.

"No you have nothing. They have already been to the hotel, he had one of his thieves take your money from the security box, your cigars are gone and another man, your same size, with the same colour of hair checked out under your name." The old man delivered the bombshell cold, insouciant.

"What about my fucking money? My fucking cigars." His fucking painting!

"Gone. There is nothing any more, nothing except your life. As far as one and all are concerned you are nothing but a ghost".

O'Neill paused and searched for lies in his antiquated face, this was the truth.

"I want a gun." O'Neill demanded.

"Listen to me we have very little time, and I will not tell you again, a gun is no use the only way you will survive this, is if you challenge him with the blade. That way he cannot have you killed and fed to the dogs like he wants me to do tonight." Alfredo removed a .38 special revolver from his jacket and cocked the hammer. O'Neill stared at the weapon, the old man was pissing down his back and telling him it was raining.

"That way is the Cuban way. That way has been man's way since time began, a duel. The fighters they think you have cajones, for killing the dragon, for standing up to the big boss, they will hold no respect for him if he has you killed any other way. It will not be easy, he is the master of the blade, a man doesn't achieve his position from being anything other." Alfredo spoke with the same clarity Mauritza did.

"And a bomb just wouldn't do it for you?"

Alfredo looked at him amazed that even in this condition, and situation that he could discover humour. O'Neill thought it an Irish thing.

"Gringo it's your funeral, he is too well protected, he has many people. But with a knife, if he will not fight, the knife fighters will kill him. He is the greatest knife fighter in all of Cuba, his power is in the blade, is in his ego, in his dick, take this and he is nothing."

163

"Listen, all I know is guns and fists, that's all. I know fuck all about knives..."

"The man in the country, he will show you."

"The only thing I need shown is the way out of here."

"This is your only way."

"I don't know about this."

"You know O'Neill, if you don't go tonight they will throw you to the dogs."

"They means you old man?"

"I am old, if it falls between me and you O'Neill then "they" means I, but if it means the liberty and redemption of the only two people in my life that I love, if it means that the legacy of my ancestors lives on, if it means that my daughter's jailed heart is released from her jailer's key? If it means that one young Cuban isn't forced to kill another with a blade to fill a man's pockets with bloodied dollars, then Irelandes I am "I", I am me. Better to die an opponent than a begging dog." Alfredo said.

And O'Neill believed him.

The old man moved him at gunpoint to another secluded part of the ranch. A derelict aviary, with the confetti of dove droppings scattered like molten lava in the eaves, and bird feathers that drifted somnambulist through the air. No doves, the old man explained that the knife fighters had eaten them all, their bodies screaming for protein after the hard training sessions. He had told O'Neill the reason for his moving was in preparation for his imminent flight. O'Neill did not know what to make out of his situation, which seemed to be in permanent thrombosis. Late in the night, he was awoken by Maurtiza, and injected with a hefty concoction of anti inflammatories and another dose of antibiotics that she thought would keep him medicated for the long journey he was about to embark on.

"Alfredo is your Father?" he enquired.

"That is correct." She said.

O'Neill had thought the dynamic had changed between them now. There had been something soiled by their transaction for sex, that jeopardised the possibility of something larger.

"He is taking a big risk, I appreciate that." O'Neill said.

"We are taking a big risk, but you the biggest if you fulfil the obligation you agreed to?"

Good old Mauritza back with the obligations, and transactions. A life for a life, to kill a king, to free the damsel.

"All a man can do is try." He did not believe it was within his being to fulfil the obligation that was asked. He did not think it a deliberate betrayal of the obligation, but just the well-honed self-preservation that had kept him breathing for the duration of his life. O'Neill had no choice but to accept what was offered him by Alfredo, but now this close to

Mauritza he detected that not only was this his way out, but that he was hers.

She looked at him, eager for him to be mobile. She loosened a tourniquet around his hand and O'Neill flexed it and felt the circulation get better, she inspected the wound on his face.

"You will scar." she said.

"It can join with the rest, besides a scar is a memory." he said.

Maurtiza liked the way he wasn't vain, not vain like the Latino men, who talked through their cock, not vain like The Caribe with the personal shaves, the massages, and Italian Colognes. There was a roughness and a readiness to him that she liked that was distinctly unlatino, the fresh smell of sweat and the blonde furry stubble that covered his face.

"We all have scars, some we do not want to remember" Mauritza said.

Her great eyes looked to her bronzed abdomen, almost sheer through her linen and she brushed the silvery scimitar scar engraved in it, her private caesarean scar and melancholy memory. The eyes quickly darted back to tending to his face and the job at hand.

"Scars heal."

The minute he said it he thought she should have said it instead of him, but it was the last word on the subject.

She finished tending him with saline water and he came up well. Most of his injuries were superficial.

He watched her as she packed her little kit in the aviary thinking about how he would miss her cool soothing hands on his cheek, on his busted hands, when he heard her let out a yip of surprise. At her feet in a mound of thick sticks he noticed the stiff form of the piebald Pit Bull that had earlier been his cellmate and first nurse to his wounds. The old dog must have crawled into the aviary seeking somewhere quiet to yield to death. She noticed him staring solemnly at the dead dog rigid with rigor mortis, a blood stained tongue lolled out of the gin trap mouth, and with tenderness O'Neill closed it.

"Friend of yours?" she said

"You could say that." O'Neill replied.

"Well take a good look. That is the alternative." Mauritza said.

She was as hard as any he had met. She got to her feet and proceeded to unlock the aviary door.

"How do you know I won't just get the fuck out of this shithole? And leave you here to rot with this fucker? You think about that Mauritza?"

She turned without answering, and glared at him.

"How far would you get in that condition?"

She was right, he knew he had to be taken, helped, and tended. The best he could do would be to lie and rest. As she left, he was unwilling to allow her the last word, wanting her to be appreciative of his worth, of the quest they had set out for him.

"Why do you trust me?" he asked.

"I don't."

And with that she left, leaving him in the straw with the dead dog and amazingly the glowing embers of an erection.

***

Alfredo made coffee for both of them in his little hut. It was late into the night, and he had removed the collection of sepia photographs from the music box under his camp bed.

Mauritza sat on the edge of the bed enthralled, at the photographs of her and her Mother Ingrid. A happy smiling wife with her daughter on the malecon in the late seventies. The photographs had been singed by tobacco smoke and old age, but still retained a fresh quality that appealed to both father and daughter.

"She was so beautiful," Mauritza said.

"She had to be, to catch a big marlin like me." Alfredo joked, and Mauritza smiled.

He poured the hot liquid from a rusting saucepan into two tin camper cups and allowed them to cool and stew. As they waited Mauritiza tended the empty cavity that once held his eye with saline and ointment.

"You must go to the hospital in the city Papa, in case of glaucoma."

"SSSShhh, that is a hospital where a man goes in the front and goes out the back in a pine box." Alfredo replied.

She put his patch back on and kissed him on his lined forehead.

"Grump lines." she said.

"She says that too." Alfredo replied unsure if it was the right thing to say, and in the moment of quiet that followed he thought it wasn't. The moment became a minute. Until Alfredo decided the coffee was ready, fixed her coffee and handed the cup to her handle first so that it would not scald her hand.

"When did you last see her?" Mauritza asked.

"Three days ago, in the ranch"

"And?"

"She is beautiful, like you my love."

"What did she talk about?" Mauritza asked.

"Oh you know just kid things, puppies, flowers, horses, chocolate."

"Chocolate?" Maurtiza sounded concerned.

"Chocolate is bad for children, cavities, her teeth."

The old man looked at the concerned Mother. She blushed realising that this was a minor peccadillo in the greater scheme of things.

"Tell me more Father, does she ask about me?"

"His influence is strong, she is an intuitive child the way you were when you were the same age, and I think she feels it is -..."

The old man rooted through his old head for the right word, a word that would have to do two things; one assuage his daughter's concern and secondly articulate his Granddaughter's care.

"Impolite." The minute he said it he knew it wasn't adequate, that it didn't go far enough. It was all he had, and it was the truth.

She paused sending her melancholic eyes elsewhere in his room to veil her grief, then to his face, angry with rage. There was no need for words. He was the same as her, they felt the same, sharing the same lineage, the same genetic connection...

"The tourist, you think he is strong enough for the journey?"

"He is strong, his wounds are dressed, and he is on a course of the strongest antibiotics, that is all we can do, my only concern..." Mauritza hesitated before voicing it, knowing how much her Father had invested in this, knowing what risk he was willing to take.

"Speak Mauritza, what is your worry?" Alfredo demanded.

"Why would he come back, to this, this impossible task?" Mauritza spoke.

Mauritiza looked away ashamed at crushing her Father's hope. Her Father had still the romantic blood of a socialist flowing through his old veins.

"Because he has Che on his arm, that is why." Alfredo answered.

Mauritza looked at her Father, his one good eye defiant dancing, in his old head, and kissed him. She smiled proud of her old man, proud of how could he still have belief in the universal lie that was Cuba, through the miasma. But this was no reason. They were relying on a debt of gratitude, within her experience the people in this life who repaid debts were few and far between.

"We have nothing to lose Mauritza, except our lives?"

Mauritza took her time in replying, knowing her response would have to contain a witty riposte, in order to match his.

"What lives?" she said.

She clunked her tin coffee cup off his and she could see the old man's good eye soften in its defiance, the happiness filling it with a gentle glitter, like a bright star in the blackest sky.

"What is the plan Papa?" Mauritza asked.

The old man motioned her to come nearer, surreptitiously checking through a slit in his shanty tin hut that served as a window that no one was outside.

"There is no one here but a spider Papa?"

"All that hunt conspire, remember that my love, and all that kill are his agents! I saved a corpse from the gunfight last night, a friend of mine, Rueben from the army. There is no face."

Mauritza put her hand to her mouth disgusted.

"Mauritza now is not the time for a weak stomach. I will dress the corpse with the tourist's clothes, and leave it in with the dogs tonight. Tomorrow The Caribe will check to ensure that I have obeyed his wishes. I have starved the dogs there will be little left - we must take him to Jose at edge of the mangrove marsh, where there are arrangements for his travel."

"What happens if he wants me tonight?" Mauritza asked.

"Tonight he trains with his knives, if he enquires tell him you have a client in the city, a hotshot – his eyes will fill with dollar signs." Alfredo had it all worked out.

"Then what?" Mauritza said.

"Then we wait, and hope, hope that the tourist returns with the knowledge of the blade, hope he returns with the heart, hope he fulfils the promise he made." Alfredo said.

They looked at each other with eyes that welled with love and fear.

"If I was a braver man..."

"There is no braver," Mauritza said.

"If I was a stronger man..."

"There is none stronger Papa."

"I should've killed him a long time ago!"

"You tried Papa."

"And failed! I am sorry my love..."

The old man bent in half holding his salt and pepper tufts of hair in his hands, hiding his sobs low to the ground. She went to him, lifting his disgraced face.

"I love you Papa."

The old man looked at his beautiful daughter, at the marks of sex on her neck and the big green and black fingerprint indentations on her arms. He also thought he could smell the hint of his oppressor's sickly sweet cologne rank off her clothes in his little room, he looked at her with his one good eye and a swarm of pain in the cavity of his other.

"And I you Mauritza, and I you..."

O'Neill lay in the aviary devoid of birds on ragged straw. It reminded him of jail and the pulverising loneliness of thought. If he had been in better condition, he would have tried to engage in some sort of physical exercise, to avoid thinking, but he was not. His entire body throbbed with pain that was neither excruciating nor sharp, pain that was just there at all times. O'Neill thought about Mauritza, and thought about what he recognised within her – hate. In his life he had seen and committed a lot of things, but he had never considered the people whose lives he had taken as people he hated with the exception of one. They were the consequences of a fucked up situation. And with each day and year passing the people that he brutally murdered, became fleeting images and as distant as a stranger's experiences, that only stalked his consciousness in the purgatory of dreams.

The man he had hated had taken one he had loved. And working from this experience he thought that this was the reason for Mauritza's contempt. The man he had killed, that without a flag of allegiance he would have killed anyway, whose demise brought great satisfaction in the ending of life, and of being there when the bullets tore into his body.

The sole witness as the blood crept from his body, slow and thick. He remembered the day, the intimacy of the murder. And there was intimacy in murder.

Belfast nineteen ninety-three. O'Neill had waited three days in the back of a van waiting on the man's return to his house. An AK 47 wrapped around his arm watching the back of the domicile on a summer day. The man finally turned up, O'Neill could remember the day vivid and down to every last detail, which set the murder out as very different from others, he had committed. O'Neill relived the moment the sun on his back, that must have created a fearful silhouette, his masked face his victim's final eclipse. The blood pulsing over the man's fierce tattoos, vivid portraits of gnarled ghouls, lightening bolts, and the flag he served, everything of that day and none of the other unfortunate victims, even down to the man's last word...

"Please."

He had wondered if Meabh had said the same? He wondered what terror had coursed through her as he looked at the man prostrate before him. Her hands raised in a defensive gesture pleading soft words of mercy, hoping her gender would offer her a lifeline, falling on the assassin's deaf ears. Before the man was spent, O'Neill had peeled the mask up off his face to reveal his identity, to scorch his antagonist's retinas with who his executioner was. The man had been a notorious assassin who revelled in killing, now fatefully aware of his nemesis.

Meabh was a beautiful woman, a smart woman Meabh, she was named after an Irish queen, and she had been a lecturer at a local university as well as a rioter. They had joked about their names, how they should have met in a different mystical world, her Queen and him warrior. He never knew how the enemy discovered he was staying at her house. Informers? Cops probably. But the day of her death equally live in his memory now, cold and wintry, such a foreign thought in Cuba's present wet humidity with his current, weeping wounds.

O'Neill returned in the early morning, from a night of no good, to a caved in door, and her porcelain face punctured by bullets, brain tissue welded to the ceiling; there were signs of torture on the body. The assassin had waited all night on him returning and when he had not the assassin slaked his blood lust on the poor girl. He was unable to touch or look at her corpse for shame. He saw parts of what he was in Mauritza, it lurked within her different coloured eyes, secreted in the dark confines of her soul, beyond reason, beyond time. He wondered what the real reason was. The man she hated, was an evil man, O'Neill could tell that from the way he had the little Cuban killed, in the way he conducted his business, but the man traded in skin and blood this was the reality of his world. Evil men were only regarded as evil by those they oppressed, by their enemies.

Evil men were oblivious to the concept of what evil was because they were immersed in the their truth, and this man's truth was blood and blades. In such places the O'Neill understood the consequences better than most for they were no more barbaric than a lot of things that went on in other places, places he had come from.

But something that emanated from the huge Cuban was beyond barbaric, beyond human, something in that balsa wood face, in the intricate scars that embroidered his body (none on his face), in his muscles, that troubled O'Neill. It was an atmosphere that pervaded beyond the natural, and he thought only the woman knew...

CHAPTER 15

Mauritza and the old man came for him in the late evening. They loaded him with difficulty into the back of an old Buick, throwing rags over him and told him to lie still for as long as the wheels turned. The sun was down and still it seemed hotter than ever especially under old rags. The ride was bumpy and short, and then they arrived at a crossroads beside the rusting cadavers of old train cars on a track. They helped him out of the old Buick, towards an even shabbier looking pick up truck with no lights. A skinny man in his fifties with slits for eyes seemed to be the designated driver. Jose was his name. The man had two charred fangs for teeth and wore a straw hat; he seemed a man from the country, with his rustic red tanned arms, with his hands crooked as hooks, with the fingers in the wrong places and dirt in the sills of his nails.

Mauritza and Alfredo helped him out of the Buick bracing himself on both their shoulders as he limped to the other vehicle. At the start O'Neill was surprised that the old man was her father. For some unexplained reason he imagined an older more aristocratic connection, but seeing both of them together it was clear. They communicated quietly to each other mostly glances and nods. The private language of those connected through blood and guts. With a great deal of effort, he finally made it into the back of the truck which to his great relief boasted an old striped bed mattress, rosetted with stains, which expelled a fog of dust on receiving his weight.

"This is Jose he will take you to the place where the old man will take care of you." Alfredo informed him.

O'Neill disliked this, strangers in charge of his future, as if someone else had already mapped out his destiny. He looked at Mauritza; she was so serious, nothing like the vamp trumpet player who had every man in Cafe Guerto wiping his mouth. Alfredo interrupted his staring at her by beating the filthy mattress, which bloomed even more dust and other unidentifiable shit.

"First class just for you senor. My old friend is called Pretan Tristo, I have told him all about you." Alfredo said.

O'Neill uncomfortable with the emphasis people seemed to be placing on him. He now felt like a fifty to one horse with a nation of poor people's life savings on him. He disliked the limelight, the responsibility of being somebody's last chance. This had been one serious fuck up of an enterprise what had initially begun as a quick buck was now deteriorating into the most serious fucking thing in his life. Why him? He thought, what made the old man and Mauritza believe he was worth trusting, worth nailing their hopes to? O'Neill knew from jail the importance of not asking what if? He knew that it pre empted what his fellow countrymen called "hard whack", tough jail time. But he believed in bad luck, and that's where he currently was, in the bad luck hotel. He'd lost every penny, and all the cigars. That crawled under his skin the most, when he recollected the risks involved and the less than salubrious places he had gone to get them, the dark places, the men he had killed, Tony Montana, and for what? The only thing he had left was his life and he was a cunt hair from losing that too. Every inept film he had ever seen had the absurd notion that there was one person, one talented individual who would save the day. It wasn't O'Neill, he was a lot of things - assassin, liar, cheat, smuggler, street fighter, and proficient in all but none of these were the qualities that were needed for what they asked. They needed a person with heart, not balls (there was a difference) a person with soul and if he was truly honest with himself it could be strongly disputed that he had either.

She handed him two rum bottles full of water and the first aid kit she had risked losing her life for by stealing from The Caribe.

"Good luck O'Neill". Mauritza said.

O'Neill traced her face for sincerity; it was there, it just had to be flushed out like some hunted, wounded beast in deep cover. And for the second time in his life the gut instinct that had never let him down was unsure. Alfredo banged the side of the pick up and the country bumpkin punched it, racing off fanning a large arc of dust in their trail. O'Neill fixed his eyes on the woman, fixed them on her as if there was nothing else in the world, before the tsunami cloud swallowed her. And there and then it occurred to him that there wasn't.

Chapter 16

Pretan Tristo no longer had any idea of how old he was. All he knew was that he originally came from Manila in the Philippines. He was the last remaining member of a great criminal family that had terrorised the Manila region for over two centuries. He himself had been a man of conflict, of violence. He had lived in Trinidad in the same simple jungle hut for the last thirty-eight years. Occasionally to attain a few pesos for rum and women he would train young fighters in the way of the blade. Pretan had killed one hundred and nine men in his lifetime. He had killed men with sticks, machetes, clubs, swords, six with a gun, but the majority with a knife. Pretan had studied the knife since he was nine years of age, it was compulsory where he came from. It was like national service for Cubans. When he was aged eleven he killed the first man in his young life, an old shopkeeper who had tried to decapitate him with a machete. Pretan laughed when he heard the Cubans cry about hard times under Castro, for this was paradise compared to where he came from. He liked the Cubans, he liked the Cubans better than he liked his own, and he had liked the Cuban women most of all. His family demanded that he hone his skill with the blade and he travelled from Sibiu to Mindanao, three days in a kayak.

Where the Grandmaster Kindaza trained him for another twelve years in many black arts, but specialising in the art of the blade.

Pretan had great memories of Kindaza's palatial residence. A gabion pit of snakes, the aviary of falcons and eagles, a courtyard of monitor lizards, great regal gardens full of orchids. In times of distress he would close his eyes and conjure up those halcyon days of youth, in the vast gardens, the memories so vivid sometimes he thought he could smell the sweet fragrance of the orchids.

He had a face older than the sun and marked by it. His eyes had retreated deep into his face, which had the same texture as a crocodile. He knew things some men would disbelieve. Pretan knew about the alchemy of snake venom, how the cause was the cure. Of how one must embrace the fear in order to conquer it. Pretan knew this not from books, or technology, not from Doctors or scientists. Pretan knew this from living, from fighting, from being snake bit. But now not knowing his age, but knowing it significant enough to have surpassed all his peers he could hear the hushed whispers of death on the wind, in the way his old body creaked, and in his perishing flesh. Content in the little wreck of a hut in Trinidad beside the sea, where he liked to fish for sea bass and trap duck.

Pretan was troubled with a bad dream. He was in a coal mine in a duel, there was no light, just the hymn of the blade searching for the heart through the air. His opponent moved more quickly than he did, he crouched low, somewhere in the black murk a snake hissed. For the first time in his ancient life the old man could not decide on the strike, he had been scared like no other time in his life. The unseen opponent was better, in a blind panic the old man lashed out with his best kill strike, the strike that had taken 96 men's lives with his personal dagger, the Ilongo dagger, the dagger that had been within his family for two centuries. He missed and the unseen force had slashed his hand, taking it and the dagger away - "De-fanging the snake," old Kindaza had called it. When an opponent is disarmed from the knife, the opponent has no defence, and with no knife, against a man with another there is no escape. All that the old man could do was to await the better adversary's strike, and hope it would be true. It had come too, the blade singing its hymn louder than the hissing snake. His buried eyes could see the fine blade slash through the dark, and Pretan knew that without a blade, without a fang he was a dead man. He had awoke before the impact his palm mat wet from new sweat and his old heart thudding hot and too fast in his chest. With great difficulty the hoary, old Philippine made it across to where he had some water stored, he poured the tepid water over his old head. And for some reason or other something told the old man that what he had just experienced was more than a dream, something from a distant world had just made contact, something from a dark place had alerted him to be aware.

Under his palm bed he removed the Illongo dagger stored in its tiger skin pouch. The old man removed the great steel dagger serrated both sides. The dagger that had tasted blood and killed men for two centuries, the great blade that held no discrimination for no man, that had slain peasant and prince. Pretan practiced with the great dagger, his old arms moving with grace making the blade sing it's terrible hymn, preparing for the unseen opponent that would dare visit him in his dreams, that dared disturb him in the twilight of his life. There was no lying down in Pretan, the invisible opponent that haunted him from the lair of dreams would reveal himself soon, and Pretan would be ready.

O'Neill felt like he was on a racehorse galloping over broken rocks and glass. He had never been as uncomfortable in his life, except when he was on the dirty protest in jail, smearing his own shit on cell walls. It seemed a lifetime ago, bullied into it by the organisation's policy, until he could stand no more and asked to be removed from the protest, asked to be removed from them. They could save Ireland themselves; his days as a freedom fighter were over. The longer he had resided in Cuba the more he felt connected to it. Not just the corruptions of the old city, but the beauty of the country regions too. As he sped through the countryside on the back of the pick up. He noticed great flocks of pink flamingos congregate, smothering the opaque lagoons in a pink smaze. His wounds wept, and sounds of discomfort came compulsory from his mouth as Jose raced the old pickup along the country roads as if pursued, and they were. O'Neill decided to lie horizontal blaming his discomfort and grunts on sitting upright. Flat on his back he watched in wonderment as above his head great royal palm trees wigged with fronds flashed by.

As he changed position on the long journey he passed fields of citrus and sugar cane with mountains shimmering in the distance, where men cajole oxen with sticks, driving them on lutulent plough, and the only other traffic on the road were farm labourers on horses. The country was beautiful, simple and archaic. The people seemed happy, untouched, unpolluted by what was going on in Havana by its moral corrosion. There were smiles on the young men's faces as they toiled in the fields. They passed three young girls trying to hitch hike, one that flashed her breasts to Jose who nearly careered off the road into a tobacco plantation. O'Neill found romantic notions flying into his head, he imagined Che and Fidel holed up in the adjacent mountain ranges, armed with nothing but carbine and cigars, relying on these simple peasant people for their lives, good people without malice, performing little acts of compassion, like pulling their rotting teeth out in exchange for chicken eggs, people who only sought what was fair, what was theirs. The reality was shattered when he noticed a plane's vapour trail stroke through the coral pink dusk sky, another squad of tourists looking to get laid, or hunt for cheap tobacco, same as he did.

Soon it would all be over, when old Castro died. O'Neill glanced back at the Oxen in the fields as they tilled the earth, turning the ground into a muddy surf in their wake, and imagined what a Burger King or McDonalds would look like in the vast field.

They reached their destination late on, rocking up a rough dirt path that wound into mangroves, where an old ramshackle hut stood scuffed and charred with dirt and faded paint. Chickens pecked at the skiddy soil outside. O'Neill got out of the back with difficulty. Holding his ribcage, he exchanged looks with Jose not knowing whether to thank or curse him. Jose said nothing, but drove off leaving O'Neill standing staring at the hut holding his ribcage wondering what manner of man would live in such conditions.

O'Neill approached the hut cautiously and pushed open a door made from palm fronds and entered the murky interior.

A Chinaman in a sarong! That was all there was. He reminded O'Neill of a baboon with his low brow that appeared to have no forehead. There one room in the hut, a kerosene stove, with dried fish that hung on a pole, their skins shiny like steel arrow heads that diffused with the little light that blinked through the hut, a rocking chair, empty bottles of rum, some shark jaws nailed to the delicate walls like jagged bleached bows. The old man seemed oblivious to O'Neill's presence.

"Hello?" O'Neill said, and there was still no response.

"Ola'?" O'Neill tried again.

The old man who looked like a baboon, had other interests. His tiny eyes which skulked deep in a relic of a face, concentrating on some other complicated business in his hands.

He had strange hands, big hands but with an uncharacteristic length to the fingers that could have belonged to a piano player, and giant thumbs. The hands betrayed his age, strong and sinewy, with a stratum of healthy veins. O'Neill watched what he was doing with interest. The old man tied fishhooks expertly to a pole, the great long fingers moving adroitly with the intricate knowledge of a craft. The old man satisfied with the end result, placed the pole with fishhooks in the corner of the room and stared at O'Neill a little while, O'Neill felt like a book being read.

"Pretan me?"

It took him a while to understand the old man was referring to himself. It wasn't until the old man pointed to himself with one of the huge orang utang thumbs, that the penny dropped.

"My name is O'Neill?"

The old man nodded his head.

"Irelandes gringo".

"Hungry me?" Pretan said smacking his lips and rubbing his belly.

"What?" O'Neill asked.

"Hungry me?" Pretan repeated.

O'Neill rubbed his own head baffled. Was it a question or the old man's current state? He stopped rubbing his head when he irritated a nearly healed scab.

"What?"

"Thirsty me?" Pretan said.

O'Neill concentrated mostly on facial expressions and the questions that punctuated the man's speech. He worked it out, "Me" meant you, it would take him a while but O'Neill was beginning to understand. He moved slowly, shuffling across the small space towards O'Neill, taking his hand, probing for the pulse at the wrist in a big rock-breaking grip. Up close O'Neill studied the old man's pachyderm face, an ancient parchment of transcribed lines that he thought could each tell a story The old man checked O'Neill's pulse closing the tiny eyes, counting quietly to himself in some unknown language then nodded his head as if things were OK.

"Shit OK?" Pretan enquired blowing a raspberry with his tongue.

O'Neill looked at the old man, the man was definitely insane.

"Piss OK?" Pretan said and then simulated both bodily functions with an imaginary defecation and urination.

O'Neill nodded his head.

"Hungry me?" Pretan rubbed his belly again and this time it became clear – me meant you. O'Neill nailed the mental note to this mind.

O'Neill shrugged his shoulders, it had been so long since he had thought about something as natural and normal as food but anything for a quiet life. The old man shuffled to the old kerosene stove and broke pieces of the silver skinned fish off and handed it to him breaking the fish into pearly flakes. O'Neill tasted a little, it was delicately flavoured, and tasted better than he had thought it would. It recalled to his mind an old Irish saying back home, something about hunger being a good sauce. The old man nodded his head seeking out O'Neill's approval; O'Neill returned the look, rubbing his stomach, confirming.

"Mmmmmmm, good". O'Neill said.

O'Neill watched Pretan slowly make his way to another corner of the hut. He liked the way the old man moved, shuffling his feet, the heels never leaving the ground, like a child unschooled in the simplicity of walking.

The old man lifted an old palm mat at the corner of the room and beat it with his heavy hands, knocking seven types of shit from it's interwoven fabric that clouded the atmosphere and littered the floor with debris, he then patted it down flat.

"Sleepy me?" Pretan said.

It normally took O'Neill time to warm to new people and especially strangers, but there was something magical and inherently decent about the old man and his basic gifts of food and shelter that he instantly liked. O'Neill limped to the palm mat, the old man extending one of his big hands if he needed it, O'Neill didn't and he bedded down on the palm mat.

"Sleepy me." Pretan repeated the old voice soothing to O'Neill's ears.

And O'Neill slept, like an old man, like a baby, like a cat, like a man who needed it.

***

The Caribe stood alone on the veranda, sipping rum and coffee, contemplating his life. The rum to wring the morning chill from his bones, the coffee to wake him up and make him shit. With his plethora of business interests there were so many things on his mind. A man had to be on top of his game to take care of all his dealings. From the illicit hefty commerce of the drug planes flying in from Colombia dropping their white gold on the disused military airbases in the Zapata peninsula, to the slighter trade of cigars with the street vendors in the old city and lobsters with the fishermen in the malecon. It all had to be taken care of, maybe not every day but every other day because it all turned a profit and if a man slacked then the food chain was disrupted and problems arose.

Sometimes he wished for a simpler existence, where he didn't have to have his all seeing eyes always open, where he didn't personally have to deal with all of Havana's problems.

Recently a hotel manager had made a complaint through an intermediary that one of his whores had taken a tourist's wallet, and that government officials would be getting involved. It was a pain in the ass but The Caribe knew that if not treated pains in the ass could become rectal ulcers. The wallet was returned, and the woman scarred with acid.

There was an uneasy truce with the government that was only preserved by The Caribe not stepping on their toes with the tourists, and as long as The Caribe kept his considerable house of crime in order, they left him alone. Indeed he provided an attractive if unofficial service to them with the bait of his pretty whores, all of whom he insisted in being regularly treated by his Doctors (Mauritza included) for STDs, and sampled by himself before being put on the street. Even his cigars were the genuine articles. As regards the cocaine, which was not his sole preserve he was one of three.

Two army generals, provided the muscle to deal with the Colombian drug cartels while The Caribe who provided logistical support and distribution.

The Caribe watched his fighters assemble in the courtyard, and begin practising their knife drills, he was especially proud of this operation. The Caribe loved it more than anything; he regarded the knife fight as the jewel in his unofficial crown. It was the executive game that reaped the most dividends. It appealed only to the very rich, who bet heavily, and required only two men brave enough to fight and in a country like Cuba, there would always be men brave enough to fight. The operation was simple and foolproof, they recruited the richest tourists, they kept the fight on site, away from the shit hive that was Havana, and unlike the other business interests, it had been devised and cultivated by The Caribe alone. It was his other baby.

He finished the rest of his rum and coffee, and noticed a nerve twitch wildly under his arm, no doubt spiked by the caffeine and alcohol. He observed the flicking nerve and flexed the hammock of bicep muscle to stop it. The Caribe knew that his physical condition was hereditary. It was inherited from an ancestry of champions, of warriors.

Men who refused to eat pigs in case their eyes became small, nor turtle, for the turtle was thought stupid amongst the indigenous people. The blood that ran thick in his big veins belonged to the blood of ancestors who feasted on the flesh of their enemies. He imagined them with pride, the same shape and size as himself, facing the Spanish and their awesome hardware of musket, cannon, horse, and war dog.

Brave men, armed with blades carved from horn and bone, shell and wood, and stone hatchets of diorite and serpentine. They offered no emblems of gold, or banners of quetzal plumes, no necklaces like the other native tribes; their only gifts were the carnage of the blade, war, and ferocity. Sometimes he thought himself born in the wrong century, he dreamt of ancient times, where he could taste the metallic rust of the blood of his enemy on his tongue, and when these experiences occurred The Caribe regarded them not as dreams but as his ancestors communing with him. There was only one way to oppose those who sought to conquer and that he thought was with more force. History intrigued him, and he had learned that whilst the Spanish disemboweled and reigned genocide on the indigenous people of Cuba, The Caribs retaliated by devouring their Spanish combatants. The Caribe could visualise the ferocious battles; the great Spanish war dogs, massive beasts clad in iron armour, the froth foamy on their tongue, unleashed crazed by the imminence of blood and hot sun, The Caribs standing their ground and slayed them by hand, until they were blown to smithereens by cannons.

His sires were men of strength and power, and pride, whose final persecution by the Spanish resulted in their mass suicide, rather than be conquered. The Caribe admired them because they were him; and no other had ever conquered him. He was undefeated with knife and hand, in the heat of battle, in contest, he knew it was these ancient things that drove him on, that supplied him the strength, the power, the will to win.

He stretched like a big cat, and lit a giant cigar basking in the new heat, with the rum running to his head, watching over the ranch, the morning sun beginning to blitz the countryside and warm him. The little girl joined him. "Papa, Papa can I have a puppy?"

The voice came from below him, The Caribe looked down at the beautiful little girl, dressed in a little white cotton dress. Natalia, was but six years old. He eclipsed her in his shadow. He lifted her with one hand careful to blow the cigar smoke away from her and brought her to his face, he looked into the young girl's eyes at her beautiful brows that arced and climbed when she wanted things. Like her Mother he thought; her features held Mauritza's stamp, its delicate bone structure and glossy dark mane of hair, but his darker skin tone.

"We will see little one." The Caribe said.

"But you have so many on the ranch, just a little one?"

"Puppies grow into dogs Natalia, I would fear one could turn and bite you."

"And I would bite it back Papa." The Caribe laughed like an echo in a well, she was the only one he would reveal his true humour to.

"Dogs are for work little one."

"I know Papa, I know what they do."

"You know you must not become attached."

"Can I pl-ease have one?" Natalia said.

"And what happens when it grows up, will you feed it, lift its shit?"

"I will, every day if you pl-ease let me have one".

"And when it is ready what will you do when it has to fight to live?"

"Do they have to fight Papa?"

"Everything in this world has to fight."

The little girl analysed the answer. The Caribe thought it important to portray life truthfully to her, it would enable her to deal with harsh realities.

"And what happens if it is killed in the fight?"

"My dog will be a winner!"

The Caribe gently smiled at her persistence.

"I'll train it to be the best fighting dog on this ranch!"

The Caribe looked at his little daughter, thinking whom she resembled the most now.

"Pick one."

"I will, I will!"

He sat her down and watched her race away and down the stairs to the house. He lit another cigar as big as a corncob and chugged on it, enjoying her fading screams of delight. She reminded him of his own brief tenure as a child for he too had possessed the same determination .She exited the kitchen door below him and tore across the courtyard towards the dog paddocks. The Caribe spent a small smile, privately enjoying the exuberance of her youth. There were few people in his world The Caribe cared for but she was one. There was the other but that was not reciprocated, and sometimes it hurt him, and other times it angered him.

He did not know why he forbade her release, he did not really understand if this was pride or another darker motive, all he knew was that if she loved another it would destroy him, like a wooden stake a vampire. She would weaken him with her absence. He like most Cubans held superstitions. She was his totem pole, lucky emblem and voodoo doll all rolled into one and the human weakness of his desire made him mortal, if she was to leave The Caribe thought all he had worked for, all whose lives that he had taken would have been in vain, and all would be lost. He took a little comfort from the fact that his daughter loved him, loved him without prejudice or a moral judgement. He was her Father that was all there was to it, and he enjoyed the role and even more the child's kindness, Natalia loved him not like her Mother. He knew Mauritza hated him, there were many reasons, the treatment of her father, his appetites, his demands but most of all he thought it was the fact that he had kept her away from her daughter, to him it was one of those realities of life, an insurance policy that guaranteed her presence, and if she never loved him then that would have to suffice, for she would love no other and life was better that way for him anyway.

He had always kept pets, - dogs, chickens, and exotic ones too, snakes, the dragon, once he even had a baboon, and it had killed many dogs. Until it bit him, and he killed it, a ferocious animal, unbeatable in the pit, but ultimately it was untameable, with the wildness never leaving its heart. In a way he acknowledged this trait, in the way he kept the men that fought with knives.

In a strange way he looked upon the little girl the same manner, sometimes he felt uncomfortable when she called him "Papa". Soon she would blossom into a beautiful girl, he could see that, he could see the features evolving, in her fine face, in her caramel skin. Then he would make sure she would not call him "Papa," for if she were a replica of Mauritza and possessed love for him, and then he secretly feared misplacing the moral boundaries and roles. And who could stop him having what he wanted in his kingdom of pain. The thoughts were uncomfortable in his head, and he sought to evict them, choosing to think of other pressing matters like the cigars in the old city and the lobsters at the malecon. But the thoughts remained; what use would all of it be if there were no one to share it with? And the one he desired did not? He concluded the train of thought by deciding he could do what he wanted, that was the reward for his efforts, that was the reward for competing, that was his reward for killing all those who dared to bite his cruel hand.

Far away he could hear church bells ringing dull in the distance, and he could taste the salt from the sea on a zephyr breeze. He chugged a little more on the cigar and thought he should dwell no more of these matters, and wondered if many men possessed such dark thoughts. There was no answer to his question. He noticed the black shadows of turkey vultures with their ragged feathered wings hanging, like kites in the evening sky, and it reminded him he had a consultation with his Babalawoo his Santeria guide.

The Caribe met the man in the back room of the ranch. The man that looked much younger than his years, some thought this was because he was in league with the dark saints, the reward for black pacts. They found it strange, the old face with ebony black glossy hair that still held the curls of youth. It had added to the mystery of his occupation.

Bogelio was The Caribe's Babalawoo, a high priest of the ancient Santieria religion. He was the youngest of nineteen children, his parents also high priests. He had practised the old faith for as long as he could remember, comfortable with it's trances, and the zombie rituals as a priest with prayer. Bogelio had always been regarded in his district as one who held special commune with the spirits and the Santeria gifts of foresight and the ability to exorcize demons from an extremely young age. As a child he remembered extinguishing evil spirits from the inflamed hosts and citizens of Las Yaguas barrios who had paid him in sugar, and cigars. In Las Yaguas barrio, his gifts were as revered as those of a baseball or boxing hero, before Castro's men razed it to the ground citing it a hive of crime. He had seen many things in the eighty-four years of his life, and he could see many more, as death grew nearer, with his divine powers. Bogelio spilt a little rum on the hard wooden floor, in tribute to the black saints mixing it along with spittle. The Caribe handed the man some coffee and fifty U.S. dollars and watched as Bogelio held a full coconut and a seashell, as if weighing both, sapping from the conduits. After a while he spoke The Caribe listened intently. He did not fully believe in all of the santeria, but regarded the old man's information as profound and foresight into the future, and for The Caribe this was invaluable counsel.

"There are threats." Bogelio said

"There are always threats."

"From a woman and a child. The child is yours?"

The Caribe nodded his head slowly, wary of the man reading his thoughts.

"There is conflict, conflict over your love for the woman, and – and the child."

Bogelio hesitated to reveal the last piece of information, uncomfortable with the revelation, and what he had seen. He moved swiftly on feeling the threat of danger sensing The Caribe's discomfort also.

"There is an old man, old but dangerous. He possesses great knowledge, knowledge that cannot be read about or learned, the knowledge from experience. A master."

The Caribe told the black priest all he knew with a shrug of his shoulders.

"A man who hunts sharks?" Bogelio enquired of The Caribe.

"I know no old man that has great knowledge and hunts sharks. Now santo" what is all this bullshit about?" The Caribe asked, frustration spiking his words.

"You ask for me to consult the saints, my friend, I cannot help if the information is unpleasant, or is not what you wish to hear. I tell you the truth. If you seek falsehoods they are not resident here." Bogelio thought his response fair, he had really wanted to tell The Caribe go to the charlatan fortune-tellers at the malecon, but he knew not to.

"Tell me what other hocus pocus you have?" The Caribe said.

Bogelio concentrated holding the shell conch close to his ear, communing through the centuries and the souls of ancestors, his heartbeat slowing to three beats a minute, falling into a deep trance. After exactly seven minutes the old man came to.

"What news from the dark plane?" The Caribe asked in a mocking tone.

"There is another, from another place, a place of rain – of green fields and old conflicts, a warrior." Bogelio said.

The Caribe knew immediately of whom the black priest spoke about.

"The man is dangerous. Unskilled now, but with proper training he will be a threat."

"Unskilled in what?" The Caribe demanded.

"In the blade." Bogelio responded.

The Caribe thought carefully about the old man's words.

"He could be no threat, to me." The Caribe said.

"But he will be," Bogelio answered sensing something he had never had with The Caribe, something that Bogelio had immense discomfort with, it was the sense of fear.

"He will have no time to, in the bellies of dogs." And with that The Caribe ended their consultation.

CHAPTER 17

Alfredo checked the swollen corpse; the skin tone was the right colour, and the face unrecognisable from where the bullet had exited through the face. He went to the paddock full of the voracious pups that yelped and belled on sight as he dragged the corpse into the kennels on a wooden trolley. He had some guilt, but such things needed to be done. He had known the man from the army days. Reuben was his name, he had served under Alfredo in Angola in the seventies with the Cuban army. It saddened Alfredo that things had ended up the way they had for them both. They had both served their country well, and proudly. There had been a real purpose to their lives then, with duties and solidarity. And now he was to feed Reuben to the dogs. Rueben had become a farmer on leaving the army but there had been scant return from the barren land and he had returned to Havana to be recruited by The Caribe to tend dogs, and fight with knives, seduced by occasional free pussy, Yankee dollars, and rum. A man could be seduced for very little in Cuba even though the penalties were severe. An old saying he had heard came to him "A day in the life of the Tiger is worth a year in the life of a sheep". Alfredo thought with nostalgia of this. Once Alfredo had been a political man, with no interest in money. He had done many things to avoid the way he lived now. He had collected trash, shined shoes, and sung ballads to tourists, but as he got older he feared that one day he would end up in the malecon ninety years old with diarrhoea and rooting through garbage for food, like many of his contemporaries.

Alfredo disapproved of the relationship from the very start. She had met the much older, mature, powerfully built man at the beach. The man from nowhere his wife had called him. At first Alfredo thought it was a rites of passage most teenage girls went through, a schoolgirl crush on a bad boy. Alfredo was warned by his wife that sanctions imposed would only encourage more rebellion, so it was with his cautious grace that he tolerated the relationship. Mauritza his beautiful daughter, magnificent in mind also. The huge hulking presence of The Caribe following her to school, the school teachers fearful of the muscled older man accompanying her, intimidating any who even dared communicate with her. Alfredo remembered he was younger then, not as useless as he was now, without the diabetes or the solitary eye. Not in his prime as he was in the army, but still a formidable adversary. The Caribe, younger, fresh from jail where he had earned his bones and his muscles. Alfredo politely telling the younger man that he didn't like the unhealthy interest he had in his daughter, The Caribe cold cocking him, looking through him as if wasn't there, as if his words didn't exist. The steel of the dead eyes, the ignorance. Weeks passed and The Caribe's vigil accelerated. At night Alfredo would hear him flick stones at her window, in the morning he would leave fresh honey and almonds.

Alfredo sometimes wondering what her position was in all this, dismissing it as a younger girls' infatuation until he had caught them in bed together, Mauritza ashamed, blood on the bed confirming her chastity, The Caribe brazen wearing his prick in an erection and the ultimate insult. The more Alfredo thought of that he wondered if the conflict that night had been choreographed by The Caribe. Mauritza never admitted that it was without consent, but there was something in his little girl's eyes that night that alerted Alfredo to the fact that something was wounded and corrupted. Alfredo had defended her honour, he pulled the knife. It was to prove the wrong choice, the younger man had taken his eye, and he was about to take his life when Mauritza begged for leniency, inadvertently surrendering herself to a Faustian agreement she could never get out off.

His life had seemed to descend into darkness since then. His wife had died then The Caribe took Mauritza's baby, his grandchild, denied them the right to see her, using the child to lever desires and ransoms. Alfredo had seen a lot of bad things, his memories were still full of colour. He could remember as a young boy serving American gangsters drinks in the Nacional, evil men full of the Devil, who spoke of terrible deeds and atrocities, that treated all before them as shit, sleeping in luxury beds while the locals slept in the street before Che and Fidel put them to their heels.

In Angola too he encountered the horrors of war, and the brutal consistency of violence. But never in his life had he met an individual of such insouciant cruelty as The Caribe. To him cruelty was an occupation as natural as a man building a wall or a carpenter tending wood. Alfredo sometimes thought the man's title had been self appointed, but in a million conversations with the old people of Havana, none knew who he was, like his wife had said, but he was known everywhere, his legend spawned from jail myths and knife fights. They said it was in jail that he had learned the blood crafts, from the secrets of assassins and when he was released he implemented them. Conducted late at night, in the black streets of the old city, in the shanty barrios, he faced all and none survived him.

Alfredo had seen him kill many men, men that were good with blades, bad hombres. Assassins, men who worshipped the black saints, leopard men from African secret societies like the Abakua, criminals, all had fallen before The Caribes' many blades. He had never seen such speed and power combined, he had never seen a man move as fast as The Caribe with the mongoose strikes. With none to oppose him, he soon seized power of Havana's criminal underworld. And now with his reign Alfredo thought The Caribe had achieved perfect symmetry with those gangsters of yesteryear, but now there was no Che, and Fidel too senile and oblivious. None of The Caribe's fights lasted longer than a few minutes. The man was merciless, ferocious. In the last few years, with more tourists coming to Cuba, Alfredo had watched as the dark man transformed his terrible talent for business into the brutal knife fights, where he lead men to their deaths for entertainment.

It sickened Alfredo but there was nothing that he could do, he feared for his daughter, his only grandchild. His pathetic life was one of damage limitation, often he dreamed of ways to kill the man, but some unseen force prevented him.

In a way, he thought it was cowardice, but in another way it was the fear of failure and what consequences his remaining blood would have to suffer. Alfredo remembered his old father telling him years before after he got into a brawl with another boy who bettered him in a fist fight, that he would have to strike when his blood was still hot, because time would cool it, this was how he felt now, time had sapped his strength, he was too old, too weak, like the old fighting dogs who could no longer bite as hard, their fangs broken.

That's why the Irishman was important, he could be the one, and he had the balls, the strength, there for all to see. The only real doubt Alfredo had was his commitment; the man seemed committed to nothing but himself, and survival, just like The Caribe… But they had spat on it and spittle sealed many a deal.

The dogs scared him, they fed faster than pigs, and he had seen them strip a horse in twenty minutes, a donkey in ten. He dropped the corpse into the kennel and watched as the dogs worried and ragged the corpse.

"Sorry Reuben, if it's any consolation old friend it's for a good cause." Alfredo thought it a pithy requiem, but the least he could do.

He turned and limped out, hearing the dogs squabble. There were a lot of worries on his mind, first and foremost the fact that he had underestimated The Caribe's eye for intimate detail in recognising the knife as belonging to the ranch's kitchens. The second, and more important worry was he feared that The Caribe suspected it was him who had smuggled the knife in.

"Alfredo , Alfredo, Papa has said I can have a puppy?"

The little girl interrupted Alfredo's train of thought. She had come racing around the corner of the paddocks, braking hard at the obstacle of Alfredo. He backed the little girl out of the kennels, careful to obstruct any witness to the gross abomination that was being consummated by the dogs excited barks.

"The dogs are feeding now, we must leave them be". Alfredo noticed she wore a pretty little dress that had gotten dirty at the edges, a dress a mother would have forbidden.

"But Alfredo, Papa said!"

It annoyed him, his granddaughter calling him by his first name and The Caribe by his title.

"I must see! I must." The little girl stamping her foot.

"Later on I will show you."

"I must see now Alfredo, my Papa says..."

Again with this title at the mention of The Caribe, making the old man's sugar hot.

"The dogs are feeding, they are not very pretty when they feed little one, come I will show you where a hummingbird's nest is?"

"I do not want to see a stupid bird's nest, I wish to see the puppies so I can pick one."

"OK then, I know where a litter lies as we speak".

She was as impatient as her Mother at the same age, petulant, stubborn, beautiful - spoiled. A man had to play it cool with little girls; he knew this from Mauritza. Alfredo extended his hand as they walked to other dog paddocks away from the half devoured body. To his delight the little girl took it, holding it graciously. Alfredo enjoyed the brief contact,

Grandfather and unknowing grandchild. The little girl studied his empty eye.

"What happened to your eye Alfredo?"

Alfredo felt himself baffled for a moment.

"I lost it in a fight."

"Why were you fighting?"

"Men sometimes do, little one, but little girls must never."

"Is it sore Alfredo?"

The old man looked at his granddaughter and smiled softly.

"Sometimes."

"And can you see out of that eye?"

"No I can't, little one I see nothing but black from that eye".

"Is it all black?"

"All black."

The little girl closed one of her eyes tight and observed the world through the other; she turned her head right and left, and upside down staring all around.

"Not too bad."

"Not too bad is right little one".

Alfredo said amused by the little girl. She opened her eye again and looked up at Alfredo.

"Was the man a bad man that hurt your eye?"

Alfredo nodded his head slightly to confirm.

"Are you angry that you lost?"

Alfredo paused for a moment, thinking about the question, it was a good question, and an intelligent one that told him his Granddaughter had a bright mind.

"Not angry, sad."

"Sad because you have no eye?"

"Yes, and other things..."

"What things?"

"Things that a young pretty young girl like you should never have to worry about."

The little girl accepted this, knowing that to press any further would be disrespectful.

"Can I see the puppies now?"

Alfredo looked at the little girl, resplendent in her beauty, brimming with life, innocent of what the world was and what it could bring, and it occurred to him that life was about hope, and children, and doing what was right.

"Yes my love, come with me, what type of puppy would you like?"

"A black one?"

"Why a black one?"

"Because it's my favourite colour."

Alfredo looked at his little granddaughter worried that her choice of colour might be a genetic trait of her diabolic ancestry. The young and feminine should never favour that colour

Alfredo knew then he had to get her away from the ranch, before The Caribe's influence grew stronger.

Alfredo took her to the stables where the good brood bitches whelped their litters, beside The Caribe's prize Argentinean stallion. The young horse grateful for the company, the way horses like dogs. There were three litters of weaned pups, Alfredo took her to a good bitch he knew. A bitch with a fine temperament that could only be riled in battle

She picked, as she had said, a black puppy, with plenty of knuckle and a strong jaw.

Alfredo knew the puppy's parents and grandparents, and even their grandparents. They had deliberately mated line-bred relatives trapping the fiery, incestuous blood of champions.

The dog was good breeding, the puppy a wise choice, and it pleased him that the little girl had an eye for dogs.

"So what shall you call him my beauty queen?"

"I don't know, what do you think?"

The old man scratched his rough hair, making a sound like glass being scraped.

"How about Blackie?"

The little girl looked at him disparagingly.

"That's what everyone calls their dogs?"

"How about darkie?"

The little girl laughed, a mature and beautiful laugh for one so small, amused at the old man's lack of imagination and weary mind.

"Darkie, that's even worse." she said.

"You're hard to please, little one."

The little girl paused putting her hand comically on her chin the way she had seen the men at the ranch do. She sat on a stable stool, pondering, and then she spoke.

"I think I'll call him Midnight."

Alfredo nodded his head in slow approval, he rubbed the old growth on his chin mimicking his granddaughter, trying to imagine the dog being urged into battle, onto another unfortunate beast, hoping that she would never have to witness such barbarity.

"Midnight it is little one."

***

The Caribe went to Alfredo's hut late in the night; he had been there a long time before Alfredo awoke, roused by the strong scents of his citrus perfume, cigar and sweat.

The Caribe at the edge of bed, alert in the nocturne of night.

"Troubled sleep old man?"

Alfredo's voice cracked out the words half formed from an open mouth and with no spit.

"No, no - just sleeping." Disorientated.

"You talk in your sleep Alfredo?"

"I do?"

The Caribe was seated in Alfredo's old wicker chair, the great muscles moved like liquid in the weak light and Alfredo could see the man's eyes, live and wild in the night, the way predator's eyes were.

"You need me for something?"

"No I just came to thank you old man."

"Thank?"

"Yes thank you old man."

Alfredo cursed himself for he was as jumpy as a pig in a noose.

"What for?"

"Many things old man, years of service, your wisdom, the sins of your daughter - the puppy."

Alfredo felt his blood bubble, the flaming pain that scorched his legs. The Caribe mocking him again.

"The puppy?"

"The black puppy, it was a good choice."

"She chose it, she is a smart girl"

Alfredo prompted himself thinking about what would be acceptable and what would not be.

"Must get it from her Mother, eh old man?"

Alfredo did not answer.

"I have a few questions for you, you with the wisdom of age. About the tourist?"

"Senor the tourist?" Alfredo hesitating, the sleep and rising blood sugar making him jittery, unsure if his ruse was discovered, unable to match The Caribe's intellect.

"You did what I asked, you let the sun sting him, and fill him full of pus to tenderise for the dogs, and the heat take his life?"

Alfredo nodded an unconvincing yes.

"And then you put him to the dogs, the strong sapling pups?"

"I put him to the sapling pups, starved them the night before, and before that fed them only a little milk and bread, so their bodies would be singing for meat."

"The sapling pups?" The Caribe repeated the question leaning forward from the chair.

"And was he alive when he was put to the dogs?"

Alfredo paused, unsure if it was a trick question, his brain working fast in trying to work what The Caribe knew.

"Not for long, he wasn't."

"You lie Alfredo, you're too soft to put a man live to dogs."

"I don't lie."

Alfredo, for all his faults and obvious dislike of The Caribe, since he had known him had been always a man of honour, a man of his word.

"For the first time I don't believe you Alfredo."

"I can do nothing about that senor."

The Caribe read Alfredos' eyes seeking out cracks.

"Then why didn't you contact me?"

"I thought you would have more important things to do senor?"

"This gringo who came to my ranch, who killed my men, my dogs, my beloved dragon - and you deny me to witness his demise, because you thought that I would have more important things to do? The only thing more important than watching that shit die is if I was buried to the hilt in your daughter, but I am beginning to grow tired of that too..."

The Caribe's deep voice, growing louder.

Alfredo's world swam with the hot blood sugar, the room loomed and The Caribe closer.

Alfredo searched for the piece of dried out mango under the pillow to fend off hypoglycaemic attacks. It was gone. The Caribe extended the huge hand that revealed the piece of fruit. A petty morsel to most, but to Alfredo the cornucopia of life.

"She is nothing to do with this! Please my blood is too low."

The old man begged with his hands .The Caribe, enjoying the old man's desperation, he dropped the mango on the floor. Alfredo searched frantically for it, the way a beggar would spilled change. Alfredo crabbed the floor finding it and ate it in one swallow, grateful for some respite.

"Oh she has Alfredo."

"How?"

"I think your daughter, the whore, gave the tourist the knife."

The Caribe chose each word carefully; baiting each one hoping the old man would bite.

"That is not possible."

"Oh, and why is that old man?"

"Why would she do that? It is not within her interest to do that, she has nothing to gain."

"No?"

"No."

It had been a long time since Alfredo had stood up to the man. It was time.

"Maybe she sees something in the tourist that she cannot find in other men, maybe she thinks the lure of her sweet pussy can propel a man to do crazy shit, like kill my men, like kill my dogs, my dragon, maybe even try and kill me?" The Caribe said.

He was human Alfredo thought, he had mortal dreads and jealousy, his petty insults about his daughter revealed his frailty.

"A dragon is one thing, but what damage could he do to the mighty Caribe?"

Alfredo stared at the Caribe watching the dark eyes that glittered iron back in his direction. Alfredo knew that this was a question to be considered, that preyed on the Caribe's mind. Alfredo sensed danger now. He had to defuse it.

"He could have taken the knife from one of the men he killed, the way he took the rifle no?"

It was all Alfredo had, nothing else was believable, and nothing else would wash. Either that or throw his hands up, assume responsibility, feign to make coffee and pick up the machete on the stove and - no that wouldn't work, he would be dead from a thousand wounds, dead by being broke in half by those big arms.

The Caribe stared, quickly tilting his head from side to side trying gauge if the old man was lying, like a Pit Bull waiting for a rat to bolt from a hole, as if a different angle would reveal the truth. There was blank uniformity in the old man's face. The Caribe knew he had been an army man, a man educated in interrogation techniques.

"You look like you don't know the reason, it might be better for me to go to the source of my mistrust, old man?"

"Mauritza did nothing."

The Caribe foraged for more, with his hunting eyes. Alfredo continued on.

"What possible benefit, could she achieve, except certain death?" Alfredo finished.

"The only thing you have said right."

The Caribe got off the wicker chair, like a noctivagant before a hunt and left leaving the old man to mull, and mull he did.

Chapter 18

Alfredo awoke Mauritza in her house in the old city. He had driven there in the early hours at high speed. She brought him coffee fearing the worst.

"You must go Mauritza."

"I won't leave you Papa."

"You must."

"How does he know?" Mauritza asked.

"How do the family of butcher birds know where there is dead meat? Maybe in his consultation with the saints? He suspects us both, he just knows. You must listen to me Mauritza, tomorrow you must go. Jose will take you to a safe place in the country."

"I will not leave her Papa?"

"Then take her."

Mauritza looked at her father. She had never seen him more stern or worried. Alfredo matched her glance, with no words. The situation was critical she knew this by the fact that he told her to abduct her own daughter, from a man that would punish them beyond any concept of pain.

"Why now Papa?"

"Because my love, she is ready now, she must be saved from his world, she must be rescued, before, before she is polluted by him."

Mauritza paused a second deciphering.

"You don't think?"

Alfredo interrupted her "In her he sees you, she is just a child, he is her Papa but it will not be long until she becomes a girl, and then a woman. A woman as beautiful as you are today Mauritza, only without free will or judgement, moulded into whatever he wants her to be. Now she is at an age where he is an influence, and he should never be an influence..."

Maurtiza raised her hand to her mouth, the reality registering.

"I have told Jose to collect you at the old station. Today she rides with Beny, I will bring her to you."

"Then Papa?"

"Then I must try to do what I should done have a long time ago."

"Papa no!"

"Mauritza every one has got to die sometime. At least I will die the man I came into the world, as and not as I am now. It is only a matter of time anyway. Jose will take you to another friend of ours, and you must wait a while before you go to Pretan. Trinidad is a good place, Pretan a good man. Take care of the little girl. She will be afraid, win her trust, stay with the

Irishman and then hopefully he will repay the debt sealed in his blood and spit. He owes us both."

"Papa, oh dear Papa!"

She hugged her old man, and sobbed, tiny little laments that she was unable to keep in, and she wondered why life in Havana was so hard.

***

The Caribe kicked the dogs away from the fleshy skeleton, and all what was, supposedly, left of the tourist. He discovered the head buried in dirt, a dog trophy heavily bitten with the imprints of a thousand teeth. He lifted the grisly head that was still connected to a well-licked spinal column; he inspected part of the skull and found what he was looking for, a perfectly formed bullet hole at the back of the skull too perfect to be inflicted by a tooth.

"Live uh?"

Alfredo had lied. The Bogelio was right. He dropped the remnants of the skeleton among the skulking dogs and went looking Alfredo.

CHAPTER 19

Natalia rode well for someone her age, but then she had had the best tutors and most complacent horses. Her soda fawn pony trotted, swishing its tail from side to side and snorting from its velvet mouth. Beny was grumpy allocated to holding the pony whilst the little girl shot out demands.

The fucking thing had tried to bite him twice. He dreamt of two more fights before he would desert the camp. Beny had it all worked out, when he got his money, he would get up early in the morning and he would head to the mountains of Escambray. The Caribe would naturally suspect him of holing up in Havana. He would lie low a few weeks, then pay some fisherman the ludicrous amount to drop him as close to Florida as possible.

Natalia halted the horse as she saw the old man with one eye approach on a mule.

"Hello Alfredo." Natalia said.

"Hello little one how are you?"

"I'm good, how's your eye?"

"It is much better today Miss."

"Beny the big boss wants you back at the ranch. I have to take Miss on her riding lesson."

"What for?" Beny asked. The Caribe spooked Beny like a Devil. The less time spent in his company the better.

"How do I know, I am no babalawo."

Beny suspected physical labour of some kind. He hated it more than knife fighting, there was nothing worse than toiling in a hot sun, building dog paddocks or more pits, or slaughtering scrawny goats and old cattle to sell as beef to the restaurants in Havana.

Beny pressed a thumb in the direction of Natalia.

"This is what I do old man."

"Beny you think I come all the way out here on this old mule for nothing, man?

Beny looked at the snaggle-toothed mule, it reminded him of another old tourist girlfriend, old being the operative word.

"Look I tell you what - You take the mule back and I'll stay with Natalia."

Beny thought about it and agreed. He was tired of being bitten by the cantankerous pony and listening to the little girl talk. He could take his time and hopefully arrive there by the time they had finished whatever shitty job he had been assigned. He nodded to the old man and took the mule, and headed back towards the ranch, leaving the old man with the girl and the pony. Beny tapped the old mule with the flat end of his machete, not too hard as he wanted to make his way back as slowly as possible. Miami pussy and cold beers was what he was dreaming off, cold beers in the tyrannical sun. The last time he had a cold beer was with an old queer from England. Nigel was his name. Beny had let him suck his big cock for food favours and let him buy a cold beer in The Nacional. He sure did like the cold beer and sitting in the Nacional looking at the photographs of old movie stars, being served instead of serving.

Beny was following a path left by farm labourers that wound through a large sugar cane field when he noticed dust in the air. The dust approached him like a tiny cyclone. A lone rider, travelling at speed. Beny shielded his eyes from the evening sun and watched as the horse rider streaked towards him. There was only one horse that could move like that, The Caribe's Argentinian stallion, only one man who could ride like that. The Caribe jarred the reins, making the horse wheel and buck. Dressed all in white, but to Beny he was no knight in shining armor. For a second the Caribe looked like a normal sized man on the huge wild-eyed stallion, until up close the horse dwarfed the mule. The horse's withers swathed in a thick foam of sweat, panting heavily, and snorting madly. The Caribe ruled the horse with one brawny forearm, where he had entwined the reins like a catholic would rosary beads. In the other he had a leather switch.

"Where is the girl?" The Caribe shot the words at Beny.

"The old man told me –"

"Where?"

The conversation grew shorter quick.

"At the bottom, beside the old railway cars." Beny said fast.

The Caribe fired him a look and slashed the great horse with the thick switch, igniting it to speed. Beny watched, coughing at the dirt kicked up by the fiery man - beast that was the Caribe and his horse as they sped through the sugarcane. Beny worried now as the horse and rider disappeared through the cane, smashing through tearing it up worse than a hundred machetes. The time to go was now - no ifs, buts or whys he'd fucked up, within his experience a man didn't fuck up with the big boss. He slapped the old mule hard on the haunches and headed for the hills, hoping he would reach somewhere safe, before The Caribe returned, some clandestine area, where the man could never find him. And there and then Beny knew the only safe place would be Miami.

***

"Where are we going Alfredo?"

"To a special place my love. I am glad we have this chance to talk, there is something I would like to tell you Natalia, something I may never get the chance to again." Alfredo spoke softly wondering if this was the right thing he was doing.

"Do you know what a grandfather is?"

"A grandfather is an ancestor." Natalia replied.

"Excellent little legs." Alfredo said.

"My Papa told me my great ancestors were fearless warriors".

"Natalia, I am your grandfather."

"No, you are Alfredo the doggie man."

"My name is Alfredo Augustus Lopez, I was born on the 14th of the ninth nineteen forty six, your Grandmother was Telia Lopez, and she died many years ago. I am the Father of your Mother."

"My Mother died when I was very little."

"Your Mother is alive and well."

"I don't understand Alfredo."

"I know little legs, it is complicated, but it'll be explained, I just wanted to tell you that, before –"

"Before what?"

The old man stopped and bent down and kissed the little girl's head. He had said his piece.

"Not too far now little legs."

Alfredo dragged the stubborn pony through the cane. They were close to the pick up spot he could see the broken, rusting, ribs of the old railway tracks but no sign of Jose's pick up truck.

"Where are we going Alfredo?"

"We are close now."

"Why are we going?"

"Only you my love, and my daughter Mauritza, you're going there - for a little vacation."

Alfredo disliked lying to the girl, but he knew no other way, no other reason that could explain the reality to a six-year-old child.

He noticed she was uncomfortable with the change of events, sensing intuitively that there was something wrong.

"But my Papa."

"I will explain to your Papa".

"I do not want to go!"

The little girl stopped the pony, digging her heels into its barrel sides. The little horse responded by trying to nip Alfredo, he slapped the pony on its soft mouth.

"Little one it is for the best, this place you go to is beautiful, full of waterfalls, and places you can explore and you can meet my daughter, her name is Mauritza.

Alfredo noticed recognition on the little girls' face at the mention of the name.

"Is she Papa's friend?"

Alfredo felt anger come fast as spit on his tongue.

"No she is not a friend of your father's."

"I hear Papa talk to a woman called Mauritza, sometimes I see her, in his room. I am forbidden to speak to her."

"Well not no more little one. Now you will be able to speak to her as often as you want, I think you and her will get along just fine."

"I'm still not going. What about my puppy and my pony, and papa?"

Alfredo had anticipated this reaction, because of his own daughter, and because Natalia was Mauritza's daughter.

"Would you go if I told you, you could bring a little friend?"

The little girl read the old man's face, in her eyes shone the light of intelligence.

Alfredo with great care removed from the inside of his old cloth jacket, the black Pit Bull puppy, blinking bleary eyed from being roused from its drug induced sleep.

"Midnight!"

Alfredo handed her the little puppy, watching her, transfixed by her delight.

"Will you go now my love?"

"Just for a little while?"

"Just for a little while, little legs." Alfredo said.

***

Jose and Mauritza arrived a little while later. The old pick - up nearly overturning as it breached part of the dilapidated railway track at speed. Natalia watched the wrecked vehicle repulsed, used to the more luxurious transport her Father supplied in his Cadillac.

Jose and Mauritza exited the pick up Jose opening the front door for Mauritza and then standing guard with a rifle at the back of the vehicle scouring the horizon for inevitable enemies. The little girl eyed them both with suspicion. Alfredo noticed this and got to his knees, which creaked and cracked like branches in a storm, so that he was eye level with his granddaughter. He could see worry in her eyes, as he addressed her concerns.

"Little one, sometimes in life we have to do things that are wrong in order to help people that we care about." Alfredo said,

The little girl looked at him, the world to her now was a maze of confusion.

"But why?" Natalia asked.

"That is just the way of the world my love."

"What about my pony, the ranch, Papa?"

"Your pony will be ok, he is getting old, time to give his sore back a break."

"He is a she Alfredo"

The old man smiled gently at the little girl.

"Will you tell Papa where I am going?"

Alfredo paused aware of her fear and responded with a nod of his head. Instinctively he touched the little girl's face tenderly, old skin on the young skin.

"Personally little one". The intimate moment interrupted by Mauritza as she approached tentative and nervous.

"This is"-

The old man was momentarily caught out by how to introduce Mother to daughter in the best manner.

"Mauritza." Mauritza rescued him. The little girl smiled at her.

"You're pretty." Natalia said.

"So are you." Mauritza said.

"This is my puppy - Midnight is his name."

Mauritza tenderly shook the puppy's paw.

"Well Midnight, my name is Mauritza, I am very honoured to meet you."

The puppy yipped.

"He likes you Mauritza."

Snakes of lightning flashed in the distance and thunder grumbled from the sky, or was it the sound of a horse travelling at speed? Whichever, it alerted Alfredo and Jose to more pressing matters. Jose whistling shrilly like a monkey sentry up a tree, seeing a silhouette on the skyline.

"You must go - Now." Alfredo demanded.

Mauritza looked at her old man.

"Come with us Papa, there is nothing here for you now?"

"There is one thing Mauritza I have to do."

All she could conjure was a single "but". Alfredo stopped her with his old hand putting it on her silently wounded face, the way he had did with his granddaughter. Mauritza kissed the back of it, for the last time feeling the calluses and masculine hairs on her lips. They bear -hugged and Alfredo then ushered them both into the truck, driving them before him in a hurry. Mauritza sat in the front seat of the pick - up with the little girl. In her heart there was agony, in her mind truth. Jose punched this foot down on the stiff gas pedal and they took off fast, both Mauritza and Natalia waving goodbye through the back window their view, blotted by the, cancroid, mucous smears of dead bugs.

Alfredo stood at the side of the dirt road watching his daughter and granddaughter heading away towards a better life. A life he hoped would last longer than his. He watched the truck fade away, rocking perilously on the railway tracks until he could see nothing, except dust in the distance. The old man observed the skyline behind and planted his feet in the dirt in preparation. From the old army belt at the back of his trousers he took out his fighting knife, his army issue combat knife. A single long female hair from his daughter's hair streamed from the hole in the blade. He pointed the blade to the lightning streaked sky. The electric storm tinted the blade with light, and he extracted the long hair with care and kissed it, tying it around his right hand, and he waited, unafraid of the oncoming storm and his deadly enemy.

The Caribe arrived minutes later. He slowed the big horse down to a trot knowing that he was too late, and approached Alfredo. He dismounted from the horse, landing expertly and removed from his saddle the elaborate cigar box full of knives. Neither of them spoke. There was nothing to say Alfredo realised. Both parties had their own motivations, one an act of betrayal, the other an altruistic gift. The Caribe chose a combat knife, a nine-inch ATS steel blade with a serrated edge, a knife for a specific use. Alfredo tucked his own blade to his hip, and put his other arm up to guide his one good eye. Both waited, circling each other, two destined enemies, the storm their symphony and spooked horses their only witnesses. Alfredo knew what he was up against. The real difficulty would to match the mongoose speed of The Caribe and he did not want it to go any longer than it had too, fearing a diabetic episode, which would diminish his manly stance. Thunder sparked the horses to flight in equine solidarity, displaying none of the enmity of their bearers. But Alfredo had a plan. There was no shame in dying, Alfredo thought the only shame a man could suffer was in not fighting. His plan was audacious in its conception, but so far fetched he thought it might provide a chance.

The storm was on their backs, beside the hissing, swaying fields of cane, close enough for Alfredo to see the silent snakes of lightning dancing in the black steel retinas of The Caribe's eyes. Watching, waiting, like two dogs Alfredo thought. Alfredo took pride in the fact that The Caribe was affording him respect, he knew from military history and his own army experience the biggest failure in war and brawls was to underestimate the antagonist, something The Caribe never did. Alfredo was glad he had no fear, considering his predicament, as a man with a terminal illness will suddenly fear no more, accepting destiny for what it is. But, still, he was glad there was none.

The Caribe exploded forward like a sprinter from traps, a feigned rush, and one designed to lure a strike, Alfredo held his ground. The Caribe froze, slightly out of distance waiting for Alfredo's response. Alfredo crouched low and walked forward, The Caribe retreated slowly backwards with one arm held up guarding his chest and abdomen, the huge blade raised above his head, the metal shimmering in the lightning. He could tell from Alfredo's stance that the old man was willing to sacrifice his arm to achieve a sudden death, a kill strike. The older man felt the pops of sweat glide off his face, bile coating his throat. Men familiar with each other, with nothing but silence between them now. In the sky above them turkey vultures circled on storm thermals, their only emphatic witnesses.

The Caribe was calm, regulating his breathing, slow deep breaths, from his gut. The pinnacle of success, being the blade an extension of the hand, that's how the masters of the blade fought.

Alfredo thought of his daughter and of his granddaughter. He thought he had made the right choice in telling the little girl who he was, and what he was. Maybe life might be better for them both. Then he thought of the revolution and how great his country was, and how he regretted being a part of a criminal activity, where men fought to death for money. A man should only fight for causes, he thought, a man should fight for what was right, for socialism, for love, and this is what he fought for now. Spurred on by those righteous thoughts Alfredo lunged forward fast, momentarily surprising The Caribe with his desire for battle. He directed the blade to The Caribes' chest cavity. The Caribe slapped at the blade, his hand moving quicker than a hummingbird wing. He brought the other hand down rapidly, with such speed Alfredo knew himself lucky to evade the blade.

Both retreated back, to their battery positions. Alfredo could see caution on The Caribe's face and he was happy for this. The Caribe had not expected the old man to be fast, he had not thought that the old man would attempt a kill.

Alfredo had narrowly missed the vital organs, but The Caribe had moved even quicker, Alfredo looked at his arm and black blood slid in stria, from wounds. Alfredo knew there and then that these would kill him; the way they bled, he thought there wasn't that amount of blood in him. Desperately he rushed The Caribe, who leapt backwards, side stepping, and slashing

231

Alfredos' thigh. Alfredo felt this cut, stinging, like there was a hive of wasps in the wound. The Caribe could have killed him with shots to his organs, but this would not be his way, The Caribe wanted the blood, the gore, and the pain. As he had known he would. There were a few things a man could predict about The Caribe, but one was pain. Alfredo rushed again, limping gamely, but The Caribe merely backtracked elusive and out of range. His logic was simple, the more the old man moved the more he bled, the sooner he would be immobile. After ten minutes the world around Alfredo began to spin, images multiplied and rotated, he found it impossible to judge distance and The Caribe had moved out of view, insulting his older adversary by smoking a cigar, blowing the smoke towards Alfredo.

"Kill me, you son of whores." Alfredo coughed, the black blood no longer pouring but a solemn drip, the fading of life from his wounds, his feet and toes going cold in the fading storm's humidity.

"I'd rather be the son of whores, than the sire." The Caribe came closer to the dying old man.

"Old man I promise you this, your act of mercy was not mercy, your act was a curse. A curse that will afflict not only your daughter, but your granddaughter also?" The Caribe whispered it viciously close to the old man's ear.

"Your own daughter? You sick fuck. Know what I think ?"

"What do you think sire of whores?"

"I think you miss prison prick..."

And the old man smiled grateful for the last word as he felt nine inches of steel drive into his heart. That lifted him into the air and slightly above The Caribe. There he remained. He looked downwards to see The Caribe holding him like a flag, pig stuck on an invisible blade, invisible, hidden in his body. Closer than salsa, Alfredo thought. He stared into his killer's eyes. They reflected his tabescent agony in hellfire mirrors, he tried to issue more insults but it was as if the knife forbade language from his throat, denying him another ebbing luxury of cursing his killer.

"Where are they Alfredo? And it will be quicker, the blade blocks the haemorrhage. I remove it and the cold sleep will come."

Alfredo stared close into his assassin's eyes; he could taste the acidity of his own blood, metallic in his mouth and feel the blade cold in his body. He thought of happy things, chasing the gangsters from the Casinos as a boy, the first time Che and Fidel entered Havana, a picnic in Santiago he had with his wife the first time they became lovers, the birth of Mauritza, playing baseball with his daughter as a child, and lastly, picking the puppy with Natalia. Anything that took him away from the blade, and his dying. Alfredo looked over The Caribe's shoulder to the far off mountains where he knew his daughter and granddaughter were and smiled through black blood into his killer's face. The blood dripped onto The Caribe's face, and The Caribe lolled a thick tongue, tasting it, grotesquely unaffected. The Caribe whispered into the old man's ear.

"I want you to know one thing old man before you die - I am going to kill that bitch of a daughter slow."

And with that The Caribe, using his massive upper body strength levered the big blade from side to side in a sawing motion that tore the old man clean in half.

The Caribe sat for a long time, in rage, thinking hard, and nothing came, except vultures to feed.

Chapter 20

O'Neill had been now with Pretan three weeks. Growing stronger every day, his wounds had healed and with healthy nutrition and convalescence it had been a long time since O'Neill had felt better. They trained three times a day. The old man had insisted on him training in the sea, and with his strength increasing each day, O'Neill could definitely testify to the sea's medicinal and physical properties. Every morning they would go to the beach where Pretan would send him into the waves. The water not only treated his sores but O'Neill found its balmy temperature quite pleasurable compared to Ireland's freezing Atlantic. The physical regime came naturally to O'Neill from his time as a combatant.

After the initial physical difficulties had been surpassed, after a week or so, O'Neill found himself well adapted, and enjoying the early morning dips that seemed about solidifying his core strength. Pretan made him dig his feet in the sand and oppose the breaking waves. Other exercises consisted of treading water for as long as an hour, before they would break for breakfast. Diet was as important to the Pretan as exercise. He explaining to O'Neill the benefits of natural food - berries, nuts, seeds, the only protein he consumed was fish and shellfish, and in such close proximity to the sea there were copious amounts of both. With each passing day O'Neill grew more comfortable with his trainer. Indeed O'Neill liked the fact that a man in the twilight of his life had that much energy, for Pretan embraced all aspects of a life that somehow O'Neill thought would have been lost his peers. Often Pretan would make O'Neill burst out laughing with little jokes that not only revealed his infinite knowledge, but a fine sense of humour.

"Fishy good for memory, better for ball bag".

Both had laughed the joke.

After lunch Pretan would insist on him chopping firewood with a machete, for the upper body. In the evenings before dinner they would concentrate on close combat fighting with knives. O'Neill had never seen faster hands, it was incredible that a man of this age could have hands like that; it was the speed of light. O'Neill could only imagine what a force of nature Pretan must have been as a younger man, a terrible danger to those that defied him. The exercise and diet had boiled O'Neill down to his fighting weight, and he imagined possibly the best condition of his life. After training every evening they would share the evening sun, drinking herbal teas that Pretan had concocted from the local fauna.

"Tomorrow we go fishy me, not from beach in canoe." Pretan said.

O'Neill nodded, the old man had kept him right so far.

"Irelandes in training there are plateaus – a man needs new challenges, we fishy in the open water, and you row kayak, for stamina."

"For stamina." O'Neill said confirming.

Pretan giggled to himself, a girlish giggle that belied his age.

"Fishy good for ball bag".

Both burst out laughing, the joke crude in construction, but in repeat it never failed, like a schoolboy with a fart.

***

They had set out early that morning, Pretan insisting that O'Neill carry the kayak from the palm hut to the sea. Now they were a mile out, in the old wooden canoe that reeked of dead fish, with a low stern that caught a lot of the choppy surf. They passed into deeper water and angrier waves that licked at the side of the boat like rasping tongues. O'Neill didn't think the canoe would be strong enough to sustain a big wave, never mind several waves. He rowed strongly, pulling the oars fluidly through the sea. Three hours had passed and they were now in deep water; the deeper water confirmed by the absence of the lighter marine hues of water, and the darker sfumato of the deep. O'Neill kept looking behind glad to see land still visible. Working on the assumption that if he could see it he could swim to it. Water spumed into the canoe with each heavy pull of the oars, hitting O'Neill with every wave, dissolving magically in fizzing bubbles leaving him soaked.

"Pretan where are we going, Florida?" O'Neill asked.

Pretan, quiet now a little smile on his face hiding the true purpose.

"You want a big fishy, you go to deep water". Pretan replied.

"I thought it was for stamina Pretan?"

"Stamina comes from the big fishy, when Pretan was a little boy in the Philippines. Boy becomes a man when he brings a big fishy home."

Pretan wanted to show him something he had learnt in the Philippines, a trick his ancestors had shown him. O'Neill guessed it was some kind of bizarre ritual to do with catching fish, something Pretan was extremely good at, judging the amount of fish Pretan brought home. O'Neill thought it was for Marlin, for he knew from the holiday brochures, and from the old Spencer Tracy film he had seen, that Cuba was a mecca for Marlin. It was evening by the time Pretan motioned for him to stop paddling, O'Neill's arms now dense with fatigue. They were in real deep water, black and bottomless. They sat for half an hour, and O'Neill worried now he could no longer see any land. At regular intervals (O'Neill thought every fifteen minutes) the old man beat the water with the flat base of one of the oars, as if summoning something. The fact that they had no nets or rods puzzled O'Neill but the man was eccentric and O'Neill knew this was the kind of thing eccentric people did - weird things. Pretan's weird thing was fish. The old man beat the water again with the oar, more a rap than anything else, as if he was trying to rouse something under the water. The old man pivoted to face O'Neill sparks of excitement on his face as he pointed out beyond the waves to deeper and darker water, to something that was invisible to O'Neill's unseeing, uneducated eyes. The old man pointed again to the darker water.

"Big Fishy me." Pretan said.

O'Neill focused his eyes straining at the area Pretan pointed to, and blinked in disbelief for there, not twenty yards, scything through the water was the gun metal coloured dorsal fin of a shark.

"Fuck!" O'Neill said.

The old man rapped the water again and the dorsal fin actually turned, as if directed approaching the skimpy canoe, the man was calling the shark in.

"No, Pretan no."

The old Filipino put a dick sized finger to his mouth and blew an ssshh to O'Neill. O'Neill was nearing shock, rigid on his damp seat. The fin approached the vessel; horrified O'Neill glanced to the dorsal fin, which now began to slowly circle the boat.

O'Neill couldn't be sure but estimated the shark fin was at least two feet high jutting out of the water putting the shark as a big animal. Pretan banged the water harder on the proximity of the big fish and O'Neill watched in horror as the shark pulled alongside the boat. He dared not look, but the same morbid fascination that had plagued him for most of his life forced him, he peered over the side to see a shark that was longer than the boat!

The boat was seven feet long, O'Neill put the shark at least nine feet, relieved to see that it wasn't a Great White, which he thought he would have recognised from movies and documentaries. No, this shark was dark blue, bullet shaped slim and streamlined with another smaller parasitic fish attached to its white stomach. The shark moved alongside the boat torsional. Pretan patted the water harder on the opposite side, for some incredible reason this seemed to stupefy the fish. The shark raised its big head out from the water and Pretan patted the shark on the nose area, carefully avoiding the multiple rows of razor sharp, serrated teeth. Pretan almost sensuously rubbed the animal's nose in clockwise and anti clockwise motions and incredibly, like a cat getting it's belly petted it seemed to be put into a trance, mesmerised by the old man's spell the shark unconsciously rolled onto its back revealing the brilliant white belly. Pretan, confident now he had the shark under his spell, leaned over one side put a big right hand inside the fish's gills and urged O'Neill to do the same. O'Neill inserted his hand into the wet gills.

With one adroit movement both of them lifted the giant fish out of the water with one arm each into the boat. The water cascaded off it in a million tiny tears.

O'Neill saw the strain of the lift pull the thick sinews of the old arms taut, like a rope being pulled tight. Jesus the old man was strong. Out of the water, senses sharpened by the lack of its natural environment the fish writhed wildly. Pretan with his other free arm, clubbed it hard at the side of the head with the flat base of the oar, which seemed to stun the big fish momentarily, the tail thrashing less.

The old man moved fast, dropping the oar, and with his now free hand he removed a giant, glinting knife from within the lap of his kimono, and plunged it deep into the brain area of the shark. Blood ejaculated from the wound hitting the old man in the eye, this prompted more frantic desperate thrashing, the fish exercising it's right to death throes.

Pretan with his other hand still in the gills the old man rolled the shark onto it's back revealing the half moon crescent mouth, its' spikes of serrated teeth now biting furiously at invisible enemies in it's finality. O'Neill sat in disbelief as Pretan, patted the big fish's white underbelly that had nearly capsized the boat and now spilled precariously over the stern, content with the days catch and began to paddle, heading for home.

"Big Fishy good, veby good."

It took O'Neill a few minutes for what had happened to register and for him to join in paddling for home with their catch, and it occurred to him that in the great list of incredible things that he had seen in his life, this would be the most incredible. One story in an already bursting book that if he ever made it out of this incredible place, he would enthral strangers with. They rowed for home in the choppy surf, gulls their guides, the skies slung with tropical colours and cotton wool clouds. O'Neill noticed the knife on the seat beside the old man. It was sheathed in a tiger skin pouch, that looked and felt real, he removed the knife which seemed more a dagger than a knife, the blade at ten inches, the purest of steel. O'Neill dared not run a finger over its edges. Pretan spoke without turning knowing O'Neill had it in his hands.

"Illongo dagger," Pretan explained.

"That's a name for a knife."

"No knife – dagger. In Pretan family two hundred years."

"Good knife for killing sharks..." O'Neill said.

"Not knife, dagger." Pretan repeated

"Good dagger for killing sharks..." O'Neill corrected himself.

"Good dagger to kill anything." Pretan smiled softly to the Irishman.

CHAPTER 21

With the hastily agreed abduction and flight from The Caribe, there had been last minute changes to Mauritza and Natalia's route. This had involved Alfredo instructing Jose to take the women of his last remaining blood, to the Gramma province that had formerly been called Oriente. Jose had blood relations there among the old cowboys, who trusted no one but blood. They had been placed in a little hick town, a great distance from Havana and its provinces of sin. They took residence eight kms outside a little town called Bayamo, under the roof of a Guajiro peasant called Gerardo who had also served with Alfredo and Jose in Angola and who asked no questions and held nothing but a fierce loyalty to his blood and army buddies. It was a little palm-thatched cottage, with a huge TV aerial that zoomed bizarre like a unicorn horn from the roof, and a rocking chair and the clatter of chickens on the porch. And there, in this modest place Mother and daughter, strangers to each other, their appearances the only thing they had in common had eventually come to bond. It had been hard for the first three weeks, Mauritza unsure of what explanations to give and Natalia angry at the hardship she was unaccustomed to.

The jagged mountain ranges of the Sierra Maestra provided a scenic backdrop for Mother and daughter to try and understand each other's predicament. Mauritza thought it wily of her father to schedule their time in this historic place where the revolution was launched, far away from where The Caribe's presence was strong, and where the people were less corruptible. But Mauritza had avoided the clarity of truth for too long now, she felt it overcome her in her sleep, and in her heart, seeing the little girl burst into tears or push her plate of peasant food away, feeling persecuted, and not knowing the reason. The staggering reality was that the beautiful little girl, daughter by blood, denied to her by a man's desire – regarded her as her jailer.

Mauritza awoke early, the sun a furnace embossed in gold, the air rich with the scent of jasmine, the majestic mountain range at their front door almost close enough to touch.

Mauritza had decided that today in this truthful place she would no longer withhold the truth. She rapped gently on Natalia's makeshift door, and entered finding Natalia awake, her little brow still furrowed from the confusion of the last few weeks.

"I was thinking about a braid for your hair Natalia. When I was a little girl my Mother used to put one in mine, it would be cooler in this heat?"

The little girl sat up straight and beamed a look at Mauritza.

"Why am I here?" Natalia asked. The question an arrow to Mauritza.

"Because it is safer here than at the ranch Natalia".

"Why is it safer?"

Mauritza thought she would have asked the same questions, but being six years old was beyond anything her imagination could conjure up. Mauritza concentrated on the facts, the truth.

"The ranch is no place for a little girl." Mauritza reiterated.

"My papa is there, my pony, my dresses, my dolls." Natalia asserted.

"Those things, with the exception of your father are not important Natalia".

"Family is important, you hate Papa, this is why I am here in this stinky place!" Natalia said.

Mauritza could see this would be more difficult than she had imagined, she would have to be as clear as possible and not muddy the already murky waters.

"You are here in this place Natalia not because I hate your Papa, but because I love you!" Mauritza said, for once thinking the answer equal to the little girl's question.

"Why do you love me? You don't know me?" Natalia said.

Mauritza paused before telling, there was no other way, there could be no more lies or subterfuges. She had to tell her.

"I'm your Mother Natalia".

The words definite, leaving no room for Mauritza to shirk the responsibility. The little girl remained very quiet for the next few minutes, both robbed of conversation by the revelation. Mauritza could see the little girl's fierce intellect unravelling the truth working out the reality. Natalia, after a while of staring either into space or at the ground looked up at her

Mother's face. Tears had pooled in her almond, youthful eyes and she said.

"Papa told me my Mother is dead".

Mauritza could stand no more, she put her child's confused head into her bosom and kissed her forehead as if she was the most precious thing in the world, and she was.

"Not no more she is Natalia, not no more…"

Their private moment was interrupted by Gerardo, who entered the room without knocking wielding an old army revolver, gathering up their scant possessions in a impersonal, plastic bag.

"He is coming," was all he said.

***

The time in the country, in the company of Pretan had opened O'Neill's eyes to a new world, one of simple truths that he had been pleasantly surprised by. For O'Neill had discovered that he could survive and flourish without modern amenities, mobile phones and other Western technologies. There was something completely liberating without communication, billboards, and television, something pure.

They trained in a suntrap, beside the mangrove forest. Without a blade Pretan moved like a sloth climbing a tree, but the minute a blade entered his hand, it was a rejuvenation.

O'Neill's eyes never really adapted to the old man's speed. Pretan's life force energised the blade. O'Neill sensed the period of reaching a peak, regarding his physical and mental conditions. They trained for hours, then hours became days. O'Neill acquired knowledge the hard way, from Pretan's strikes. The blade master's tutelage inspiring. Pretan pulled elaborate feints, he accentuated the main arteries of man's body, by marking them with lime dust, directing O'Neill to the vital regions where a man could be killed quick, and how to sever the hamstrings. Pretan seemed glad to release the information, testament to the great carnage that he had inflicted, and that had been inflicted upon his person.

O'Neill sensed Pretan content, the information being transferred to a worthy, albeit a surrogate, heir. Pretan demonstrated the ranges, sleights of hands, and the positions that would immobilise, defend or execute a man, until the drills were their covenant in mind and movement. O'Neill thought his own affinity was connected to boxing; the training resembled boxing a lot in terms of footwork and defence, and rhythm, except a man in boxing could never die as quickly as in a knife fight. O'Neill paid attention, there was no margin for error. It was knowledge he could use; though he still felt no moral compulsion to fulfil the promise he had made to Alfredo and Mauritza. O'Neill memorised the ranges until they were as natural as walking, he learned about "de-fanging the snake" which meant taking the blade from a man. It was as much science as boxing. Knife fighting was about the centre of gravity, balance, feints and then wounds - slashing, stabbing, ripping, gouging, grips. O'Neill learned all about this from sparring and observation, from watching Pretan move, explanation was unnecessary. The old man showed him ancient methods, perfected in the Manila docks, and Thai mines methods that hadn't been seen or taught to another in a hundred years. O'Neill found it fascinating, empowering, like the first time he discovered he had a knock out punch, the weapon to stun another man, one shot, either hand left, or right, a gift it was, no matter who it was. The knock out ability that gave him a chance against any individual in the world. At night, he sometimes found it difficult to sleep, with the close heat and the insects from the swamp, but if truth were told, he was troubled by thoughts of Mauritza and Alfredo who had risked their lives, to free him. Ordinarily this would not have even been a question for his impervious conscience, but with his newfound lifestyle and healthy living he couldn't help dwell over the situation, and what was expected of him. And it was at this moral conjecture, in the dead of the tropical night, that he found himself outside the little palm, hut staring at the sea. He was still here O'Neill thought, of his own free will and volition. There was nothing to keep him here, he could walk into the night until he reached civilisation and go to the Irish embassy or go to the airport and be out of this shit once and for all, cut his losses on the cigars, put his conflict with the crime lord down to experience. What held him back? The questions began to answer themselves; he had sensed hope and some sort of misplaced faith that Alfredo and Mauritza had in him. It was more the old man than her, O'Neill thought. The bigger question he had for himself was what were the real reasons he trained so diligently with Pretan, when all others had failed in trying to save him. The banned organisations in Ireland, his old boxing trainers. Were they in some way connected to the promise that he would go to their rescue? Save her from the beast that was The Caribe, her and the little girl, her old man had mentioned. That hero notion again - how wrong they were. Or was it for his own selfish reasons, the desire to arm himself with another talent for destruction, more knowledge for havoc, more information to create ruin. O'Neill drank rain water from a coconut shell, out of a barrel beside a down pipe, and returned to sleep and when sleep didn't come, he resorted to the age old tactic man had employed to get to sleep and masturbated, careful not to disturb his mentor, and all he thought was of Mauritza coming in great gusts from his very marrow.

The very next morning after they had trained in the sea, O'Neill and Pretan breakfasted on tree ripened fresh mangoes, seated on an old Tamarind tree that had fallen and was covered with fragrant lichen, fending of the attentions of wasps and dragonflies.

"How did you know Alfredo, Pretan?" O'Neill said.

Pretan slurped on the lush wet flesh of the mango, before answering him.

"I know Alfredo from when I was a guerrilla fighter for Che and the boys, and then they reward me - to train the Cuban Special Forces in the way of the blade, to guard The Horse from CIA." Many a man would have dined out on this information for years, yet here he was, sucking windfall fruit.

"You were a rebel Pretan?"

"Now I am a rebel, in the beginning – a criminal, like you."

O'Neill listened, he had felt something kindred in the teacher the first time they had met.

He now knew what it was. The old man smiled mischievously sucking on the mango stone before spitting it out, his mouth a black tunnel without teeth, wry and insightful.

"I came to Cuba like many before me, to smuggle booze and tobacco, for the fast pussy and hot rum, and then I saw what happens here. The people like dogs on the street, whilst others - the rich, a tiny per cent, the poor a very many. The people, with The Horse and The Argentine they rise up, and I see a way, to undo all the criminal things in my life, by joining in the revolution."

O'Neill looked at Pretan, truth was the word that came into his head.

"Then I train for the army. The knife is man's claw, man strike man with blade, since time began – The oldest fight, toughest fight, blood and pain, much. You must sacrifice your own heart to kill your enemy with the blade, the blade is the closest of all the assassin's creeds, and until a man has offered his own heart for a righteous cause, not for swag nor loot, not for vengeance but the righteous cause of another – he is not a man, he just a criminal, a killer like all men." Pretan looked directly at O'Neill. O'Neill didn't know if it was a personal judgement on who O'Neill was and had been, but he was uncomfortable, uncomfortable because it had compartmentalised, mostly, what he had always thought he was.

It was obvious O'Neill was going to ask him, and O'Neill knew that Pretan would have the right answer; the assured counsel that he had given him every day.

"Pretan and how about you, you ever offer your heart?"

The old man smiled his rock breaking smile, and opened the old shirt with the formidable hands, revealing a creamy white scar that grooved deep into his ochre skin of his chest plate, above his heart scored, into the flesh, indelible, like a river on a mountain.

The old man laughed, wearing the scar as proudly as a victorious soldier carried a flag.

***

In the third week of searching all of Cuba, of rattling every cage at the ranch amongst the knife fighters, and shaking every tree in the old city amongst the rickshaw men and hustlers, he had discovered the hideout. Mauritza's old man had been meticulous about everything except one minor detail – the Army. Drawing blanks from the obvious sources, even his santeria Priest. The Caribe called in costly favours in from the two Army Generals he distributed cocaine for. They provided The Caribe with classified army files that revealed who Alfredo's military friends were. The men who had served with distinction with Alfredo in Africa, the men who would risk their lives for him. The process of elimination was simple then, for most that had served with and under Alfredo were dead. And then he read the file on Jose, and it had occurred to him that he had seen the diminutive man sometimes delivering fresh pineapples and mangoes to Alfredo in an old pick - up truck, no pesos being exchanged, both wearing easy smiles that seemed to come from the comfort of friendship. The Caribe remembered every one that came to his ranch, even the anonymous legions of tourists, that was his job. The

Caribe making a mental note at why the slight man he now knew by the name of Jose did not tip his straw hat, or flash the lights of his truck when he passed The Caribe in lieu the way of others he fed scraps to. He had dispatched minions, who had taken Alfredo's army comrade, half jaked on rum, from his malecon derelict residence and hung him upside down for the better part of a day to empty most of the cheap rum out. From there on in there was no let up in the ferocious interrogation. For three days Jose resisted, until the third day, and he had broken when The Caribe having lost patience instructed one of his knife fighter's to remove his genitals and as sure as the sun set, on the third day of his arrest, Jose screaming for a sudden death spilt the information out that The Caribe had demanded, like a cat coughed up a fur ball. The Caribe travelled to the country hideout with two others.

Gerardo was shooting the shit with Olivia the pretty cashier in the Government shop, trying to score a date in his cowboy hat, fine cotton shirt and his best Cuban boots, when he noticed the huge black Cadillac glide past the shop window, with the silver fishtail fins and he knew immediately it was the man he had been warned about. Whoever rode a car like that in a town full of shitty cars, was someone of power, and without a Government logo, it could only mean one thing. Gerardo hid in the secluded courtyard, which gave a good view of the street, morbidly curious at what his executioner looked like. Two men got out of the huge car, the first one taking a defensive position, standing guard, watching with what looked like a machine gun partially covered by a towel, the other opened the car's rear door subserviently, to a huge man dressed all in white, and who Gerardo thought moved elegantly from the car, unlike many big men that he had seen, finding it difficult to exit cars. Gerardo watched the group head towards the rickshaw men and knew the game was up there and then, knowing that the rickshaw men would sell their Grandmothers as prostitutes for the right price. Gerardo cocked his revolver and raced through the back streets to his battered vehicle, determined to get back to the bohio, to rescue the girls and keep his promise to his old army buddies, for in Gerardo's book if a man couldn't keep his word he no longer was a man.

The Caribe tapped the front door to Gerardo's home, but there was no answer, he shooed the dirty chickens from the porch with his nickel-plated cowboy boot. When there was no response the second time he rapped, he nodded to his two minions to enter first in case there was any gunplay, and then satisfied it was safe, he followed, entering the living room. He stood motionless in the peasant's cramped living room; as his two cohorts ran from room to room searching for the females. The Caribe monitored the interior, an old black and white TV that had a Castro repeat on, and the tepid coffee on the stove told him they weren't far. The Caribe switched off the cranky dictator banging a podium on the TV, the image being sucked into the vortex rapidly and checked out the interior of the room again, and a look of disdain on his face. His dead eyes took in peasant artefacts, and ornaments, that consisted mostly of little clay farmers with oxen on plough, on the tables and windowsills a black and white photograph of the arrested liberators of Cuba. Fidel and the boys, and even worse a bad painting of Jose Marti who stared cross eyed down at him from the wall. The Caribe cared nothing for this pathetic lifestyle, only for who was missing. He moved slightly to the centre of the room and inhaled deeply like a wolf wind scenting, drinking in the smells of the modest home. He could smell them, what he regarded as his. The mother and daughter, the hotel soap of Mauritza and a little perfume he had gave his daughter as a gift. One of his minions returned from the bedrooms with the Pit Bull puppy, abandoned during their haste for flight. He tentatively handed the puppy over to The Caribe, whimpering in the shoebox, a chiffon hair scarf keeping it company. The Caribe lifted the hair scarf out and put it to his nose, inhaling her essence.

He had given her the Italian silk scarf, three months before. He let the scarf go and watched it swoon to the floor. The Caribe then picked up the bewildered pup, which yelped excitedly at this new attention. The Caribe tenderly placed a finger under its jaw and sat it down in the centre of the peasant house, on the cool floor tiles of the living room, inserting the shoe box lid back on the box gently squeezing the puppy back into it, careful not to get it's paws caught as the box closed. The puppy's whimpering increased, scared in the darkness of the box, and in a motion that surprised and even abhorred his two minions, he stamped hard on the box with his cruel Cuban heel, making a squelching noise that silenced the whimpering. Blood leaked from the corners of the now silent box, in the middle of the room on the cool tiles, pooling out dominating the centre of the room with the colour. He left first, the others followed.

Gerardo knew where to go. The Zapata peninsula, beside the beach. The information drilled into his head many times by Jose. Gerardo expected him to be dead now, and wondered about his own fate. After three days they arrived, and after a few hours consulting with other poor farmers like himself, he had discovered the old man and then place. Fearful at how things had turned out, he had said his goodbyes quickly as he had hellos and left to try and find an existence far away from the powerful people who he suspected killed Jose and were hunting him and the women.

O'Neill liked the little girl Natalia; she had balls, metaphorically speaking. Accepting where she was now, no tears, with an adult sensibility of the need to survive. He wondered what the real story was? Trying to really figure it out. It was clear she was Mauritza's daughter, clear as the noses on their faces, but there was a distance between the two. He had been caught unawares by their arrival, caught out by feelings that he had thought he was close to erasing, and by the look of desperation on Mauritza's face.

Pretan seemed strangely at ease with it all, showering one and all with Grandfatherly attention, separating the room with palm fronds to secure the privacy of the girls.

O'Neill hadn't counted on them coming to him. Guilt chided him; it was an unspoken certainty that she would be cashing in the big favour. She knew as her old man had known, what the deal was. O'Neill's life for hers, and now it seemed, including the little girl's. Mauritza had said very little to him. He thought she was playing him creating more sympathy for herself with the silence. Remaining quiet about their personal debt but letting him know through her mannerisms and expressions, that it was the all-consuming reason, with her melancholy eyes and telepathic pleas. The situation was bizarre, a fucked up nuclear family consisting of him nothing more than a mercenary and assassin, a decrepit Grandfatherly knife master who did nothing but eat, from shark to shell from mango to mice, the Doctor who was a hooker, and the young girl! O'Neill, uncomfortable with all of this, could sense expectations, the hopes of all, even Pretan, that he feared would soon become obligations, responsibilities, and if time could tell anything, it was O'Neill didn't do responsibilities.

O'Neill paced the beach, walking and thinking. The old man had spoken of a hurricane, O'Neill did not know how he had come to that conclusion, but he doubted very little the old man said after the shark scenario. The skies had been black for a few days now, the sea rolling vast breakers, with the winds picking up. O'Neill marched up the beach, occasionally doing wind sprints to outrun the conflicts in his head. After an hour of running and thinking he decided he would have to go, to get away. Get away from these people's hopes and renege on the deal that was done. Alfredo had been wrong to entrust the futures of others to O'Neill. How could a dying man give his word to fulfil the livings' wish? Typical Cuba, they had got everything fucked up again; a dying man gave his wish, a living man accepted, like "Tony Montana". But hadn't Alfredo always been a dying man? Dying from the minute he crossed The Caribe, dead the minute he gave him the knife to kill the lizard.

O'Neill knew there was a small town, not far away. He had noticed it on the drive in with Jose. If he got to there it would be simple, take some two bit, shitty anachronistic truck, hi-jack it if necessary, fill it up with whatever fuel he could find, if not take a fucking horse.

He had but one thing to do that he thought would give him some sort of karmic peace in all of this, and that was to give Tony Montana's unlucky spouse the bunch of crumpled, blood streaked hundred bills he'd entrusted him with. There was only one way he was going to get in a knife fight - and that was if he had a gun!

Fuck her - Fuck Alfredo with one eye, fuck the kid. All that mattered was living, surviving, the way it always did, the way it had kept him alive his thirty nine years of his life, through the war in Ireland, through the feuds, through every shitty situation he had ever been in his still smoking lucky life!

He still had feelings for her, but he convinced himself they were just feelings, feelings that would dissipate with distance. The woman was hard, tough, intelligent and cunning - a combination that could bring the downfall of any man, on top of being a great lay. The only person he had to thank was Pretan, he thought, as he headed back to the beach shack. Tired from the wind sprints, he lay on the hammock on the porch pushing off the wall of the beach hut with a languid leg in the mid morning humidity, seeking the rocking motion that would put him to sleep and alleviate the thoughts that left him fatigued. He was awoken later by her voice.

"All you do is lie around."

O'Neill looked through a splayed hand that splintered the sunlight to see Mauritza with a pine pail of water, noticing that some of the water had splashed on her soiled shirt, making her breasts partially diaphanous. He could make out the caramel aureole around her nipples, which had been tagged to heads by the cool water, ruddy country dirt striped her face, making her even more beautiful.

"What is your contribution to the camp tourist?"

"I do my bit - firewood, fish."

Mauritza opened her eyes wide, as blatant as a question mark.

"Last I remember I'm out of jail right?"

Mauritza spooked her eyebrows to the top of her head; he had noticed the little girl Natalia do the same.

"You're just like a Cuban man, you know with the macho bullshit."

"And you're just like an Irishwoman, a ball buster!" O'Neill retaliated

"Have a look around, you think this is the fockin" hotel Nacional!"

He loved the way she swore, it made the age-old profanities sound new and erotic.

O'Neill looked around him, nothing but sea, jungle and mountains.

"Listen…" O'Neill said

"No you listen - you owe us your life, comprehende"?"

O'Neill knew that was the undercurrent of the argument, his debt being cast up to him under an innocuous non sequitur. It was the way women got to subjects, never direct, in a roundabout manner.

"Fuck me!"

It was an exclamation to himself, of the gravity of her demand.

"I already did, so don't flatter yourself!" Mauritza said.

"Well it fucking cost enough!"

"You get what you pay for!" Mauritza spat back matching him in vitriol.

"I owe you nothing, Mauritza."

"No fock" you, you have short memory, not too long ago, you were lying with dead dogs. My Father died saving you, O'Neill, you understand? Murdered. He did that because he thought you could help us, you gave him your word as a man, sealed with spit."

"Well I guess he was wrong about me Mauritza".

O'Neill looked away, hoping she would leave him with his shame, all she did was stare.

"We helped you?" Mauritza's mood changing with the rejection.

O'Neill returned the stare.

"For a reason - for me to return to fucking kill count fucking Dracula back there. That's not the way the story is going to go Mauritza, see that's fucking Disneyworld, you know what Disneyworld is don't you? It's not ninety miles from here as the crow flies, only it might as well be a million."

She said nothing, but her different coloured eyes told all.

"Don't look so shocked about people. Don't be so disappointed Mauritza. You're not some teenage girl, it's in the nature of men to let people down. Especially bad men."

"So you're a bad man now?"

"I know I'm no hero. A piece of advice? There is no such thing."

"You are wrong O'Neill, my Father was a hero."

"Your Father organised men to gut each other for tourists."

"My Father was a socialist!"

"Is that what it's called? And tell me this Mauritza, when did you become a socialist?

Did this drop upon you when you were lying fucking some tourist, or sucking some old man's dick!"

"In Habana you do what you do to survive, you should know that."

"Believe me I do".

"It's OK. You think what you think about me, but I know, O'Neill, in my heart what I am, and you know something tourist? That is a much more enriching experience than the person who never knows who they really are."

Mauritza jabbed a finger, condemning his right arm, pricking at the image of Che engraved on his arm.

"Like you, how dare you wear his image!"

"That was when I young, punchy from boxing and punchy with stupid ideals inserted there by stupid fucking people."

"Still fockin punchy."

"The sooner you get this through your head, it'll be easier. People don't give a fuck about people, Mauritza, they don't give a fuck about world poverty and sewer systems, people give a fuck about things - like money, and big cars and satellite TV and fucking over the less fortunate. Societies don't give a fuck, in fact societies they'll kill you if you do - like they did Che Guevara. This tattoo on my arm used to mean something else. You know what it means now? Nothing but another bad tattoo, an anchor on a sailor or a football team I used to support. You know what a martyr is Mauritza? A martyr is a dead man, and I'm no fucking martyr."

O'Neill paused he could see his words were taking effect.

He could see her close to tears, they had filled her big eyes, he felt guilty not at what he had said but at the ferocious way he had said it, like some cynical adult telling a child Santa didn't exist with spite. Mauritza absorbed the hard words and for a second he had thought she had had enough until she wheeled and faced him, her tears gone.

"There was only one Che!"

She slung the pail of water so fast it engulfed him, hitting him in a liquid pane, freezing him, making his balls retreat into the sanctuary of his stomach.

"Shit, Jesus Christ!" O'Neill said gasping for air.

Mauritza stormed into the hut, leaving him saturated, stealing quick shocked breaths that after a while strangely refreshed him. Pretan approached from a clump of mangroves with two dead flamingos slung over his shoulder, and a necklace of multi coloured flowers, Natalia following in his wake wearing wristbands of the same exotic flowers around her wrists fashioning a new one. Pretan made a fine dandy with the flowers and the dead flamingos that reminded O'Neill of a cabaret transvestite. The old man was laughing.

"Chikka" wet me?"

O'Neill looked at the old man, laughing with his black mouth open and no sound.

"She's crazy!" O'Neill said.

Pretan laughed hard now, like a comedian in a silent film. His whole face a complex network of lines. Natalia seemed amused at his state. The old man passed him, into the shack. Natalia sat beside O'Neill, watching him in his drenched state, she handed him a bracelet of exotic flowers. O'Neill accepted sheepishly.

"For you." Natalia said.

"Thanks."

"Irelandes all Chikka"s crazy!" The words came from Pretan from the interior of the hut and O'Neill was getting tired of him always being right.

O'Neill awoke late the next day. It had been a difficult sleep with the arguments of the previous day visiting him in the groggy torpor of disjointed dreams. He found it strange that he had overslept with the nightmares after so much restful sleep in the spartan conditions. When he got up he was the only one left in the hut. He thought about a few things; one was to leave without a word, disappear, and ghost away like he had done to so many people. But the fact remained, he owed her something more than damnation as his final words.

He found her cutting up coconuts with a machete not far from the shack. He stepped on a stick, which cracked like a rifle shot, startling her. She wheeled around with the machete fixed in her hand ready to strike.

"Whoa Mauritza. "

"Yes?"

"Look, about yesterday".

Before he could continue she cut him short.

"What's said is said, and you were wrong."

These Cuban women were something else O'Neill thought, centuries of machismo had imbued them invincible, apologies were not acceptable, unless you accepted ridicule as well.

"Now I wouldn't say that."

"Well I would and I did."

Mauritza continued back hacking hitting the coconuts with heavy cracks. O'Neill couldn't help being reminded of human heads.

"Look Mauritza I'm trying here, is everything a confrontation?"

"Yes in Cuba it normally is."

"I mean why are so you, so…" O'Neill struggled to find words that would not inflame.

"So what?"

"So fucking difficult!" Fuck it O'Neill had pussy footed around the issue too long.

She flashed an angry look at him, he felt uncomfortable arguing with her now, especially with a machete in her hand, even with all his newly acquired knowledge of the blade. He countered quickly, trying to defuse the situation.

"Look I only came to say I was sorry about the way I spoke to you yesterday, I know the risks your father took for me, I appreciate it…"

Mauritza stopped, now she was outraged.

"Appreciate! Appreciate! Che can rest in his grave knowing that. My Father can rest in heaven too. You come here to Cuba, to Habana and you take, take take?"

Mauritza used her hand to mimic a greedy bird.

"What do you give O'Neill?"

The question was banked, demanding. She already knew the answer, he didn't. You had to be sharp with this one, sharp because there were obstacles and difficulties.

"I give you my admiration, because you have passion and ideals, and heart, and there's very few people I can say have that now."

Mauritza could tell it was genuine that the Irishman had meant it. For without those assets they both knew he wouldn't be breathing this day.

"It's a start." Mauritza said, and put the machete down, removing one barrier. Jasmine drifted, magical, all around them. She fixed her differently coloured eyes on O'Neill. He felt the connection. Her anger dissipated. Now it seemed the real issue was live between them, as if they were the last two people on the earth in this arcipluvian place amongst the descending blossom and hovering hummingbirds.

"That was a nice thing to say..." Mauritza said.

"Don't worry I won't do it again."

She laughed, real, enjoying it.

Something was happening, something that hadn't occurred in a long time for the both of them. Removed from the stifle of Havana, and the city agendas imposed by their own vested interests and The Caribe's sanctions. Out in the beautiful, simple, countryside, jungle and mountains their only witnesses, they were but two people discovering who each other really was.

"You know, I knew you were some stamp of woman from the moment I kissed you?"

O'Neill said.

"Wow, how romantic, what is it they say in the Yankee movies? You knock my socks off." Mauritza said with playful sarcasm. O'Neill wanted to stride across and take her, kiss her, love her, but he was cautious of the intensity of his feelings and the repercussions. Was he taking advantage of her vulnerable status as some hunted prize?

She was hardly helpless but there was something lost about her . O'Neill's firewall screamed intrusion at the first recognition of emotion.

Mauritza did not know why she approached the Irishman; some invisible force, some invincible tractor beam. For once she was in charge of her own sexual future, beyond the constraints of others, her whole being craved some emotional intensity that wasn't directed or dictated to her, and possibly, she knew he was not brave enough to go to her.

Mauritza met him with a kiss, even more beautiful, through the haze of jasmine. Their teeth colliding too eager for the kiss. For the first time, in a long time, he was unsure what to do. Her mouth found his first in the kiss, his mouth responded too quickly, mashing his teeth against hers. She slowed down the kiss dictating the pace, sucking on his tongue in that sexy Cuban way. O'Neill found his rhythm, and he matched her mouth full and open, allowing her tongue to dominate his. They fell to the ground stripping each other hungrily, amongst moist tree lichen and pink hibiscus flowers, while the perpetual Jasmine descended dreamlike around them, like surreal summer snowflakes. There they enmeshed into each other's bodies, clenching like a perfect fist, wild and real, amidst dragonflies and hummingbirds. Afterwards, they lay contented in the clearing, her naked in his big arms.

"Promise me one thing O'Neill?"

"What Mauritza?"

"If he takes me, you will help Natalia get off this Island?"

"He won't take you, Mauritza – how would he find you, here, at the back end of nowhere?"

"As long as he is alive, he will find me. And in Cuba he is everywhere. Promise me O'Neill?"

"I promise you Mauritza". He lied.

***

It was late at night as he gathered up what little he had, old flip-flops the mangled Guinness T shirt, and a jug of water. He checked the inside of his shorts for the blood soaked money Tony Montana had given him, flicking through the notes to find the one hundred dollar bill with the dead man's address on it. O'Neill checked on the other three occupants – Pretan snoring soundly and the palm frond barrier that gave the girls privacy. O'Neill got to his feet and tip toed barefoot, heading towards the front door. As he passed the area where Mauritza and Natalia slept he sneaked a peek to see what he was leaving. Both Mother and daughter lay slightly apart from each other, each other's feet at their faces. O'Neill looked at Mauritza, incoherent and in deep sleep she still seemed wounded, in a restless sleep. And then at little Natalia, her miniature clone of her beautiful Mother, but with a richer more chocolate finish to her skin that reminded him who her Father was.

O'Neill proceeded, walking on his toes, following the well-beaten jungle path to the beach. Until he was stopped mid stride, by a little girl's voice.

"Where are you going?"

O'Neill turned to see Natalia on the porch of the beach hut, her eyes bright and alert untroubled by the disorientation of newly roused sleep.

"Go back to sleep my love."

The little girl hid her face, he could hear her begin to sob. O'Neill cursed his luck and went to her eager for her, not to alert the others of their abandonment.

"What's wrong Natalia?"

Still there was no answer, just a vacant stare, from the hidden depths of her eyes. Finally, as her sobs subsided she spoke.

"You're not coming back are you?"

O'Neill didn't answer. He had nothing to say.

"I don't want Papa to hurt Mauritza or Pretan?"

"No not here, you're safe here Natalia, in the country."

The girl grew quiet again staring at him; he felt shame all around him, compromised.

Natalia spoke, beyond her years.

"Sometimes he comes to my room late at night now, I hear him breathing outside, sometimes the door will crack open a little, and then close again."

"Maybe he's just checking to see if you're asleep?"

He knew it sounded trite, but what did a man say? It was all he had to reassure her, what was he supposed to say, do? The girl shook her head, and there and then an image filled his head of the huge man waiting outside her door, the only barrier between him and the little girl, a breeze blowing the muslin curtains across his person, partially veiling the huge, dark, man, waiting for the little girl to come of age, with those dead Sonny Liston eyes.

"At the start when I first came on my, my vacation? I got homesick and I wanted to go back, but now? I never want to go back there." Natalia said. And neither did O'Neill.

CHAPTER 22

The black Fleetwood glided gracefully down the malecon, the steel tail fins sharp as knuckle blades and blinding chrome wheel trims spinning warped reflections of the old city. It's big wheels splatted the translucent ghostly jellyfish that lay on the road like spectral road kills, cast from the black sea onto the road by the nightly white manes of angry surf. The ruined buildings facing the sea were caked with salt, and the light from the normally searing sky was grey, de-saturating the bright pastel colours of the houses of the Malecon. The Caribe sat in the back cleaning his knives with a hard granite stone from the cigar box as Beny drove. Fresh white cotton dressing filled the orbit where he was now missing an eye. A big wave crashed onto the black shiny bonnet of the car making Beny swerve a little. He checked nervously in the mirror to see The Caribe's reaction, there was none at all, nothing but a set mask of determination. They pulled off at Miramar and headed to Vedado to the Casa de Particulars. It had once belonged to a rich man. There were still traces of elegance; it had a garden full of Royal Palms, and an ornate black iron gate that clanged in the wind.

"Wait here Beny."

Beny nodded respectfully in the mirror, as the man placed the blades back into his cigar box and exited the car, carrying the cigar box in one arm. Beny watched as the Caribe entered the residence without knocking. Beny had been there five times, but never in the daytime. It was a reward for winning a fight. If a man won a fight, The Caribe gave him a girl, or a boy, in this Casa de Particulars. One night you would stay, fucking, and sucking.

The little woman, Grace he thought was her name, would bring you some nice rum free of charge although marijuana you had to pay for. He liked the little woman; she had once been a great freedom fighter with Che and Castro. Beny remembered a photograph of her on the wall, and she had been at one time a hot chikka. Beny lamented the good times a little drinky, a little pussy, and two good eyes. He could never think of going to Miami now. It was impossible to fight with one eye in a knife fight. He had once fancied himself, had a swagger, had thought he had been a bad boy with Oggun his saint, and his greedy blade. But all the fight seemed to be gone from him; his pride, ego, even his big prick failed him now, taken by The Caribe as punishment for losing the little girl. Shame flocked to his heart, thinking about how weak he had been, how his fight deserted him when confronted by him. The Caribe had caught up with him soon after he headed for the hills. He remembered the look on The Caribe's face as he dismounted from the wild eyed horse, and took his eye out, as easy as that.

"An eye for an eye," he had said and Beny had let him, without ever moving for his own blade. Still a man had to be positive about things; one eye was better than no eyes, and no eyes better than death, which was all he had to look forward to now. Worry came upon him again thinking, of what terrible thing the man was up to in the Casa de Particulars.

For once Havana seemed silent, without music. Beny expected this with the storm warnings; people normally hibernated, waiting for the storms to pass.

Then screaming jerked him from his wondering, for there was a lot of it. Beny turned to see two beautiful naked girls rush out from the residence, followed by a panicking fat German tourist, naked, his clothes in one hand, the other hiding his inchy prick. The German had bigger tits than the girls, panic and shock on his face at having witnessed violence. The first girl had a linen sheet wrapped around herself. Blood streaked through the sheet in a lot of places. The other girl, a statuesque mulatto in her early twenties, seemed to be in an extreme state of shock. There was so much blood that Beny could not tell where she was cut - probably everywhere.

Beny started to rise from his seat when he remembered The Caribe's last words; "Stay here". He looked at the other girl. In the sheet black as a panther, holding her ear, or a place where her ear had once been. Inside the Casa de Particulars The Caribe held Grace over the chair, well distanced from her antique revolver, his cigar box opened picking at the selection of knives the way an aristocrat might select chocolates.

"Grace, you are her lady in waiting. You must know something?"

Grace held her ground, her chin high, refusing to be intimidated by the shivering reflections of the blades.

"The house of cards is falling old woman. The old man is gone, his driver the hick Jose, and it's only a matter of time before we locate the cowboy, and then Miss Smarty Pants, and her little piggy too, and it will be all in vain".

"Even if I knew I would not tell you, Son of the Devil." Grace said.

"I have legions Grace, legions every day all over the country. They come to me from the provinces to fight, to be my soldiers. Those that defy me, will not survive I promise you that." The Caribe said.

"We met legions of soldiers before, and we paid them no heed, a few good men and women is all a country needs to rinse the scum from our streets." Grace said.

"You, a whore runner, profess gallant deeds?"

"I am no whore monger, the girls pay me for my rooms and dresses. Their money is their own, now do what you come to do, or have you not the balls for that either?" Grace spat at him, knowing his vanity would be offended meeting his eyes, not distracted by him or the fear of being cut by the blade before her eyes.

"Now you see Grace, that's where you got it all wrong, their money is my money."

The Caribe drove the blade through her mouth puncturing the palate and into the bottom part of her brain. The Caribe emerged from the casa de particulars striding dominantly to the black Fleetwood, oblivious to the girls who, on sighting him again grew more hysterical. The Caribe entered the car. Beny dared not look around for fear of reprisal.

He glanced in the rear view. On The Caribe's white suit he could make out a dusting of blood, speckling the brilliant white of the suit.

"These women are cunts. Beny, yak' yak' yak' and still their tongue never stops."

Beny shrugged his shoulders afraid to offer an opinion.

"So much you sometimes have to take it off..."

Beny glanced in the mirror to see The Caribe with a pink and blue veined mess in his great fleshy palm. It was only when The Caribe placed it close to his face, it was only then, Beny realised it was a human tongue, The Caribe enjoying his repulsion.

"Take me home".

Beny locked the wheel and pushed the great black car down the old street, past palms bent by the high winds, and levitating debris. He glided down the street, and they cruised around a corner, sliding by one of the still running girls, her bloody footprints staining the street in a fresh spoor of fear. Beny glanced in the rear view mirror to see The Caribe lower down the car window and hurl the severed tongue at the woman he had terrorised.

The tongue hit the girl direct on her face, and she stopped running froze on the spot as if impaled. She crumpled to the ground in hysterics, frantically fanning her face at the tongue's contact and the second sighting of the man in the white suit, and Beny knew how she felt...

CHAPTER 23

O'Neill arrived in the small town. Quiet and rural, a few people milling about the deserted streets. A young farmer in an ancient tractor rumbled through the main thoroughfare, salsa music sizzling from a radio in the back. O'Neill had arrived in the evening as a salmon sun fastened its rays to the old buildings in a pink half-light, which spread an ethereal glow over the old buildings. After the past few days he was glad to see a sun in the sky, and it bounced nicely off the pretty town streets. The little town was beautiful. O'Neill imagined that the town hadn't changed much in centuries. The buildings were pastel coloured with red tiled roofs, the streets were cobbled, very different from the filth of Havana. He walked along the cobbles, looking for a car he could hire, or steal if he had to. And bizarrely, and for the first time since he had arrived in Cuba he truly felt like a real tourist taking in the sights. People stared and pointed, his arrival was subject of much attention. O'Neill thought the town hadn't seen many tourists in a while. He turned a corner and headed up a side street, becoming cautious at the attention his blonde hair and fair skin was attracting. In the side street there wasn't much going on either. An old woman guided a lazy ox up a street with a bamboo cane, and kids on homemade bikes skidded into street kerbs enjoying the rubber collisions. Further up he passed two old men playing dominoes, who paid him no heed. It was undoubtedly one of the most beautiful places O'Neill had seen in his life. He headed two hundred yards on down, past painted mahogany balustrades that ran alongside shady colonnades, revealing leafy green courtyards, and bright flowers, not paying no attention to the green stately car that started it's engine as he crossed the street, a hundred yards behind him, tracing his movement at three miles per hour, it's engine purring. In the quiet streets the engine alerted him to their presence. O'Neill didn't turn around, deciding to stay out on the street amongst the public. At the top of the street he walked into a black cat with a bat fixed in its mouth. He stepped out of the way and let the cat pass, checking in the reflection of a window that the green stately car was still behind him – it was. O'Neill stepped up the pace and quickly took a left and then a sharp right, where he thought it too narrow for a car to follow. O'Neill cut through another side street, wary of getting lost himself, where he passed a house with a large open reja door. He entered uninvited, closing the door behind him, startling the resident – a bullet headed black man who said something unintelligible in Spanish. O'Neill placated him opening his hands and apologising, placing a U.S five dollar bill on a cabinet table. The man sat back down, sensing a bigger picture. O'Neill headed into the kitchen and searched through the cutlery drawer, selecting the only sharp knife from it. He strode into the back room of the house. The back wall was plastered in Cuban revolutionary posters, beneath them was an altar with the effigy of a black Madonna, and a cauldron covered with lace. On closer inspection O'Neill could see that the whole room was cocooned in lace, fine antique lace, like a huge spider web. O'Neill peeked through the curtains of the back window that gave a panoramic view of the main street he had just left. There, the green tailing car cruised at two miles per hour up the cobbled street, only now one of its occupants, a beanpole of a man in peasant vest, shorts and sandals, on foot carrying a shotgun at his hip escorted the hunting vehicle, banging on doors, questioning occupants. Mauritza's words came to O'Neill in an echo; "In Cuba he is everywhere". O'Neill realised just how much of a fool he had been wandering into the little village with his blonde hair, fair skin and tourist characteristics. O'Neill grabbed a peasant straw hat from the kitchen and exited the back door of the old house, breaking into a light jog, blade at his hip hunting his hunters.

The beanpole with the shotgun became aware of O'Neill's presence much too late, O'Neill driving the blade directly between his carthoid artery and collarbone killing him, instantly. The man dropped to the cobbled street, discharging a blast of shotgun, spitting a rain of buckshot that shredded an old colonial balustrade on the opposite side of the street, which O'Neill attributed to a hair trigger on the gun. The green car accelerated on the shotgun blast, out of range, rocking heavily on the uneven surface to turn at the top of the narrow street. O'Neill lifted the up – and - under shotgun in a fluid motion, and broke the weapon down to ensure there was another charge up the spout. There was. O'Neill snapped it back and lifted it to his shoulder. The huge car gunned towards him down the street, revving madly, bobbling unsteadily on the cobblestones. An Aztec looking accomplice hung precariously from the passenger side, discharging bursts of indiscriminate, and inaccurate, automatic gunfire from his perch. O'Neill kneeled and sighted the shotgun at the car's windscreen. As the bullets pinged from the cobblestones ricocheting everywhere O'Neill felt their slipstreams of heat scorch past him. As the car came within rage O'Neill let the charge go kibbling the windscreen and driver. The car fishtailed out of control, broadsliding, revs roaring and then going slack, as now unmanned, it smashed recklessly into some unfortunate's house on the opposite side of the street. O'Neill sprinted to the vehicle, aware that he had a small response time to drive home his advantage. O'Neill dragged the dead driver out, his head a pulpy mash, most of his right hand missing. In the opposite passenger seat, he could hear the accomplice moan in shock, holding his mangled face studded with buck shot. O'Neill dragged him to the kerb, contemplating killing him with the knife or the butt of the shotgun. He decided neither, feeling more pity than hate at the sight of his tattered face.

O'Neill reversed the car at speed, taking out a lot of masonry and plaster on the bonnet from the unfortunate's house, and gunned it out of the town.

O'Neill reached the old city four hours later. At gunpoint he had siphoned petrol from three other vehicles, for the journey to Havana.

The city was in darkness, as he tooled the car at 5mph around the streets. The big lamp lights of the Ford caught the red eyes of groups of young men standing at corners, in the middle of the night, like devils, O'Neill thought, unafraid, staring with venom back into the light although they knew not what was behind the wheel. O'Neill pulled up tight beside the kerb where he had first met Tony Montana, knowing he would not have to travel far to find his address. An hour later he found himself outside the address that was etched on the blood stained hundred-dollar bill Tony had given him. O'Neill entered the building, which had no lights, fumbling up a cracked stone stairwell that reeked of shit, guiding himself using the damp walls. After banging on three or four doors, and being chastised by angry residents, he finally reached the right number.

A woman answered the graffiti scarred door, but she kept the lock on, revealing only to O'Neill her sad eyes. She, from the little he had to go on, was prettier than he anticipated. He hadn't expected the little Cuban to have a woman with such handsome eyes.

"Who are you?" Berta asked.

O'Neill took his time to answer conjuring up his softest voice.

"Are you Berta?"

She didn't answer, but it confirmed to him that she was.

"I am a friend of your husband."

She looked him up and down a wicked look, anger flashing in her eyes. O'Neill thought it was resentment that the harbinger of such bad news was a stranger. She brought him into the hall and pushed open a desiccated door and they entered the damp living quarters room.

The room was filled with toys and kid clothes, which were stretched out to dry like the pelts of dead animals at every available opening where light could penetrate. A soggy photograph of the family complete with a happy Tony Montana took centre stage on a condensation stained wall.

Berta gave him some rum as Tony Montana's kids watched a baseball game on an ancient black and white Television. Berta counted the blood stained money O'Neill had gave her. The old TV glowed, the only light in the room as O'Neill struggled for words to tell her what she already knew. He told her lies about his murder, concocting a yarn that he thought believable. Telling her Tony had crashed into the sea on a motorbike, after robbing cigars from a ranch on the outskirts of Havana. O'Neill thought the woman bright enough to identify a lie.

"Twelve years we were married, in twelve years Victor was always been there to make breakfast, he was the worst cook, but he could make good coffee, one thing..."

O'Neill smiled, he felt invoked to an elegy, an oration of some sorts; all that came paled.

"He told me to tell you - he tried."

Berta fired him a look that was almost ungrateful.

"This place stinks".

O'Neill didn't want to be rude but it did. Faecal.

"It does, you know why? Fourteen people have to shit in the one toilet, fourteen people.

When the toilet blocks up, no one admits to it, so no one cleans it. In a way it is like all of this country no one admits to the shit, no one likes to speak of what is wrong here, because of the neighbourhood watches, because of the Government, Castro, the cops, and The Caribe. My husband was a good man; you know he was a qualified dentist? What use is there being a dentist when there is no toothpaste. A dentist who had to become a hustler, a thief to feed us all."

O'Neill said nothing. It wasn't his time, he was there only in the capacity of portent.

"And now I have to cater to that as well."

"I'm sorry Berta."

"So am I senor, so am I." Berta said, the words drifting off, faint, as she contemplated her future.

"I hate to trouble you Berta, but I need somewhere to stay just for tonight, the journey has been long".

"You can stay here."

Berta made a bed for him on the floor. Soon he drifted off to sleep only to be awoken in the middle of the night by the fluttering nebulous flame of a candle. He blinked hard, waking his eyes up. Berta stood naked in front of him holding a rotund molten candle that cried waxy tears, which plopped onto the old stone floor. She helped him to his feet and led him by his fingers into her bed without speaking. The only language they spoke was in their tender sex. He awoke early to find himself alone in bed and feeling guilty. The first image that came into view was a photograph of Tony Montana on the wall.

He discovered Berta in her babies' bed, asleep curled around her children. He contemplated waking her, but thought it might lead to another uncomfortable situation.

For some reason he thought he should apologise, but then he remembered that it was her that had roused him. It made sense now, people sought solace in intimacy, and mourning rendered people vulnerable. O'Neill had had a part to play, but it was very minor. Berta had wanted contact, he had provided a service, nothing more, nothing less, the act a consecration of the contact between two maimed people.

He dressed and left, making his way out into the busy street, extra cautious in The Caribe's true domain. Construction workers lazed on the back of an ancient lorry eating pineapples and green bananas. Kids on roller-skates sped past him playing tag. O'Neill headed up through Chinatown and into the wide streets. He passed a sign that said

"AEROPORT". O'Neill stopped and studied the sign.

For the first time in a while he had options. He could go to one of embassies, or he could use what little bucks he had left and go to the airport. Get one of his contacts in the States to wire him money, cut his losses and say adios to this place where he had very nearly lost his life. O'Neill had to accept that the machinations and everyday hardships of the citizens of Havana was no concern of his. It annoyed him that suddenly, after all these years of near scrapes, and living on the edge, that a conscience was beginning to rear its ugly, moral head. He didn't know what it was, until he looked at the wall facing him.

Another mural of Che, above it a slogan "Socialismo o Muerte." On an electric yellow wall, pulverised by sea salt and what looked like giant bites, that had taken large parts of the concrete away. O'Neill knew what it meant from jail. An old inmate used to quote it to him. "Socialism or death". He looked at the mural again, at the huge iconic face of Che, then to the same identical image on his right arm.

O'Neill approached a young man coughing as dust flumed out from construction site. The man was standing beside an Oldsmobile, roughly painted black in house paint, ignoring the taunts of the macho construction workers. The young man had his eyebrows plucked, a queer, wearing polyester hot pants and smelling of cheap women's perfume. The young man looked at O'Neill the way a woman would. O'Neill fetched the last fifty dollars he thought he would ever possess and spoke to the young queer.

"Take me to Trinidad."

Soon they were heading out of Havana again, back into the mire. O'Neill did not know why. Maybe it was guilt, maybe it was what Mauritza said to him, or the night he had spent with Berta, or the little girl afraid of going back to The Caribe, or even Che on the wall and on his arm. Whatever it was it had, something to do with Cuba and the fact that he had confronted a truth in his heart that had been long buried under avarice, and the selfish need to survive. The truth was that the tattoo on his arm did mean something after all.

They sped past fields of tall green cane, and white cattle egrets that sat on wooden fences like angelic sentinels. The radio blared out traffic reports from Miami, making O'Neill aware of just how close they were to the States.

"What type of car is this?" O'Neill asked

The young man looked at him.

"I don't know." The younger man's voice was a throaty rasp, one octave more and he would have been a girl.

O'Neill thought about what the young man had said, and looked at him again. The young man answered his question.

"It's not my car."

O'Neill shook his head, smiling, and hoped he got to Trinidad before The Caribe.

Chapter 24

Gerardo had finally given up, tired of being haunted by the apparitions and evil spectres of The Caribe and his minions that had shadowed him from province to province, ever since they had discovered his identity, and that he had harboured Mauritza and Natalia. It had only been a matter of time before they captured him. And now on the fourth day of his incarceration at the ranch, and the systematic torture, he had decided he had had enough, realising there was only so much pain a human body could take. The pain had been so bad he had thought he was in Angola again. Nineteen seventy-seven. The first time he had met Alfredo, in the army with his cousin Jose. Gerardo liked Alfredo, liked the fact that he didn't poke fun at his country ways the way the other guys from Havana did, and how Alfredo would encourage him to sing the old Jose Marti songs to raise their morale on military drills. And indeed Alfredo had saved his life, saved him in a firefight with UNITA Guerrillas. He remembered the bullet's impact - a tracer, a shooting nimbus star of blue light that flared through the African jungle, smashing through his right arm and finding a home in the fleshy part of Alfredos' right thigh; their experiences of an exquisite pain shared like the same girlfriend, and if it hadn't been for Alfredo and his return of fire both would have been dead.

Alfredo was a better soldier than Gerardo, a fact not only confirmed by rank but also in the field. A man who refused to allow Gerardo to give up. He remembered stumbling in agony with his broken arm and shoulder, and Alfredo limping heavily, jumpy, and shooting at shadows until their company rescued them. That's what Gerardo thought about now -

Angola. It wasn't often in life that a Cuban considered himself lucky to be Cuban, but after Africa he did. At least they had food rations in Cuba, no matter how meagre, at least they had education, and the best doctors in the world, even if they had no medicine.

Gerardo recalled living underground, in the subterranean camps. He remembered how unhealthy the men would get without sunlight and good food, fresh water. The drumming of 80mm mortars thudding above their heads every second night. The constant bombardment took a toll on men. Just the way what was happening now. Gerardo did not know how he came to be in a well. He knew he wouldn't have been hard to find after a while, the fear of what hunted him, driving him to drink and to spit eternal curses of The Caribe. And in the shadows of the old city it was only a matter of time before the voice of dissent reached the big boss and his whereabouts. He was a simple man, like Jose his cousin, country people who all their days sought to be led. Gerardo remembered little of being knocked unconscious by The Caribe, one vicious uppercut that had broken his jaw in many places, all he knew now was that every three to four hours, a hail of shit and piss came from above, and the morning before they had set dogs on him. He took a little comfort that at least now he could see the stars in the night sky from the well. Gerardo was beyond cold now; he imagined that the numbness he felt all over his body was how life in the arctic wastes must be. The night before he had sung his guarjira ballad, before they poured more waste over him. The songs failed him tonight, he hadn't got much left.

Gerardo thought a lot about what happened to his comrades Alfredo and his cousin Jose. He wondered how macho he had been in comparison to them. His entire body was a host to pain. He had been in the well for days now, and the punishment seemed to be increasing. He had no other choice, it was either die slow or die fast, a simple choice and he had grown weary of the suffering. Gerardo did not want to die; he had a little grandchild, and maybe even a new senorita; with Olivia in the Government shop a younger black woman who made him feel grateful for life. But he knew that with Alfredo and Jose gone, death was an inevitability. Gerardo had given him up, part of the lethal chain of events that had been unleashed trying to help the woman and her daughter.

Gerardo had fulfilled his part of the bargain, more than his part. What were they thinking, daring to cross the big boss of all Cuba? And so it was with a heavy heart that he shouted from the bottom of the well to the guards on top.

"Senor? Senor? I wish to speak to The Caribe?"

The two knife fighters that stood guard over the well looked at each other, it was late.

None wanted to disturb him.

"Tell him I know where the woman and the little girl are?"

One of the knife fighters spat into the well. The second addressed him solemnly.

"Amigo you better not be lying?"

"And the tourist."

The words wafted from the well, slow and deliberate. And the knife fighters drew straws, for they had no coins.

CHAPTER 25

Pretan awoke again, this time not disturbed by a nightmare but by real thunder and female screams; in the night with a knife deep in his old chest, and life creeping away from him in violent gasps. There had been a time when no man could have killed him in his sleep, but he had to accept that, that time had passed in the dark, close to a man with the eyes of the Devil, black dirty eyes that Pretan wished he had never seen as life left him. Pretan remained calm, he had seen so many men die without dignity. It was important that he did not. Pretan looked at The Caribe and the ebony eels he had for eyes, and smiled, mocking the kill. The world began to mist over, and he could hear his ancestors call him home as he drifted back to the coal mine and his unseen opponent, and a blistering white light that approached him like a fireball. And he was glad for this, instead of the last thing he had seen.

O'Neill reached Pretan's shack early in the morning. He could tell by the fresh tire tracks that had ploughed through the muddy road that he was too late. He left the road, instructing the young man to wait. Seeking the sanctuary of cover, he stalked through the shrubbery at the back of the beach hut, cautious of an ambush in case they were waiting on him, planning every step as if his life depended on it, and it did. He emerged peeking from heavy foliage at the back of the shack, listening intently for any sounds other than insects and birds, as cagey as an animal sensing the vicinity of a trap. After a while, when he was as sure as he could be that there was no one in shack, he entered into the busted up shack.

The palm frond door spilled light on a scene of carnage. Pretan, azoic. As if nailed to his mat. Rigor mortis had left his huge hands hooked and hard. Blood surrounded him. On closer inspection O'Neill could see the huge gash inflicted by a blade as long as a macabre letterbox, in his chest. O'Neill chased the beetles and flies off the old man, and closed his tiny eyes, sorry for the horror they had witnessed, engraved in the ingravescent cataracts. He touched the cold face that had given him solace and good advice.

O'Neill searched the rest of the shack, worried about Mauritza and Natalia. The entire interior torn asunder. O'Neill discovered blood that spotted the slight walls as if sprinkled there, and the long dark female hair that lay in clumps.

Outside he found Gerardo and the explanation of the discovery of Pretan's domicile was complete. There were signs of torture on Gerardo's body; his torso blistered with the blunt stubs of cigars and dog bites, his once brown skin now white from blood loss. Dice cuts laced his arms and legs, criss crossing through major arteries, and this had been the cause of death. Gerardo's blood trail swirled from the front porch, elucidating even for O'Neill's unforensic eyes a reconstruction of events. O'Neill backtracked the man's mazy trail, from the porch, where he had been struck first to the location where he had rushed to in a panic, before deflating into the white cadaver he was now. The man had made thirty yards before massive blood loss had taken its toll.

O'Neill buried Pretan in the mangrove swamp where he had trained O'Neill in the ways of the blade, leaving the traitor Gerardo to the family of butcher birds that ruled the Cuban skies. Carrying Pretan, he discovered the Ilongo dagger in the

Tiger skin pouch, which had tumbled out from the silk kimono like an omen. O'Neill withdrew the blade, ten inches of antique steel that shone in the afternoon sun like a beacon, and he remembered one of the old man's anecdotes of advice, "Never fight fair."

***

The Caribe pondered over his next move on the marble chess set. Mauritza beside him, as they sat on the veranda overlooking the ranch. The Caribe sipped rum. She had a full glass but it remained untouched. Dusk had clad the country in coral hues, the sound of Rumba drums filled the air like the background noise of a radio. Black streaking bows of swallows swirling through the evening air, snatching insects on the wing. On Mauritza's cheek bore angry red wound, the length of a good cigar. It still smarted from when he had stroked a slim blade across her face the day before, after taking her from Pretan.

"Your move?" The Caribe said.

Mauritza stared beyond him, seeing nothing but the coral horizon, ignoring him.

"First you betray me, now you defy me Mauritza. Why do you so? You have clothes, rum, make up, perfume, sex, a full belly, all the good things."

As if he didn't exist, her eyes glass.

"Are you angry about your little nick? You are lucky. I had some fine acid. I have a colleague who works for Havana sewers, this acid eats away all the sewer blockages – uh, and you can imagine what that does to a pretty face?"

The Caribe his own face, the same place where Mauritza was marked.

"But I am getting soft in my old age. Mauritza you know for one and all there is consequences."

She flicked her eyes at him angrily, away from the distant place where they had focused.

"That is true, for one and all." Maurtiza said.

"Yeah?"

She retreated to that place in her mind where he couldn't penetrate.

"Oh, you await your Knight, your dragon killer. The tourist, you think he will come eh? I think so too - maybe with Fidel, Che even?"

The Caribe laughed alone.

"Oh you wonder how I know all this? Like I told you before Mauritza, here I am the dragonfly, here I am the sun. Jose, and then Gerardo, told me all about Alfredo's grand designs for you, how he would rescue you, you see him? Hello tourist? Hello Bobby Sands? The tourist is gone, Mauritza, think about it Mauritza if you were him, if you had seen what he had seen, felt what he had felt, and what would you do? Risk your life for a common whore? There is nothing here for him, no more cigars, no more money, no more sweet pussy – nothing but death".

She ignored him trying to blot out the cruel words; she needed something to believe in, that there was a way out.

"Like I say, your move". The Caribe smiling, the smile forming unnaturally on his face.

"I won't play your fockin" game!" Mauritza retorted.

The Caribe's dead eyes bored into her at her insolence, and this was the first time she had ever answered back, with venom in her words.

"Well maybe my daughter will then?" The Caribe said.

The words jerked her back to reality. She had to think beyond her hate, protect Natalia.

"Little girls like little games, and you know the thing about that is, the adult sets the rules." The Caribe spoke slowly, delivering each word with an absence of malice.

"You should be proud Mauritza, she will blossom into a beautiful woman eh?"

The Caribe spoke as if he had no connection with Natalia, as was his intention, complimenting her looks, not as a father, but as an admirer. Mauritza knew this tone of voice, it was how he spoke about her or one of his exotic pets. The Caribe's words diminished his responsibility as Natalia's biological father in order to create another mindset, the mindset of a man. Mauritza felt her blood slow to ice in her veins.

"She is your daughter also." Mauritza, complying, moved a soldier on the marble chess table. Trying to earn a reprieve for her daughter.

"You know my ancestry Mauritza, you know I am a Caribe, you know Mauritza that the Caribe tribes were cannibals?"

"I am educated also in our history."

"You know that they said that they declared the flesh of man, or woman, so good that nothing could compare with it in the world?"

"No I didn't know this, but thank you for that."

"You know what they also said Mauritza? They said the flesh of the young was such a delicacy, that the men, the fathers, had to be banished from the villages, when the women gave birth - for they used to eat their own children as the mothers bore them. For years in the villages, the women would gather around their infants, never allowing the fathers to be alone with them, until they were of a mature age, and by then it wasn't their appetite to eat that was their fear, it was other appetites..."

Mauritza met his gaze, her terror scolding her for her insolence, she picked up a marble chess queen, and moved it a across the table facing his king. The Caribe pondered his next move. He studied the table, cracking his big knuckles, enjoying the verbal as well as the mental jousts, the unnatural smile on his face again. It was an intelligent move, a direct threat to his game; he countered quickly, taking her queen.

"Checkmate."

Mauritza looked across the table at the man who had sired her daughter, at the man who had murdered her father; and no doubt when he had tired of her, he would soon kill her, and she prayed that there was a God or a black saint in this world, and it didn't matter which one, that would liberate her from this horror.

***

O'Neill woke early, the sun a torch that fried his eyes through the shack door. The pong of death still haunted the interior, reminding him of his own mortality. He left and headed down the dirt track making for the main road (just a bigger dirt track) and a whole new realm of trouble he seemed hell bent on fashioning for himself.

The young gay guy long gone, with his pruned eyebrows, bambi eyelashes, and stolen car. He had been impressed by the young queer, O'Neill thinking that being queer in Havana would be harder than being queer in most other places, and thought that somewhere down the line in life that you had to make a stand, like Pretan had said, and offer your heart. O'Neill thought it was about time he offered his.

He had always been the underdog and now it was no different. When a man was the underdog there was less pressure, and between two men there would always be a moment, an opportunity. Which was all he could ask for, a fair crack of the whip, one on one. He remembered, as a young man, boxing in the world youth championships.

Ironically, a very good Cuban, who had shot his liver and kidneys to pieces from long range with wicked hooks. They were in the third and final round, O'Neill way behind on points, when the Cuban dropped his hands, for the slightest moment, and O'Neill knocked him into the midnight of unconsciousness with one shot, a booming overhand right - not even his best shot. That's all a man needed in a fight, one lucky shot and it went his way. And that's all O'Neill believed he had now, one shot and love in his heart.

O'Neill had thought himself incapable of caring for anybody after Meabh. Ireland was as distant as childhood to him now, with all what had happened to him over those past few months in Havana. There was nowhere else to go. The only thing he regarded and worth fighting for was on the ruddy muck he stood. O'Neill dropped to his knees and picked the red earth up in his hands. Rich pabulum, and bloody, not brown or black like Irish soil.

Red, red with the blood of patriot and peasant.

O'Neill knew now that he cared, he knew that by what he had felt with Mauritza, he knew it from being with Pretan, from leaving Natalia, and it no longer terrified him, because there was no longer a reason to run, everything reverted back to the same thing that had been such a dirty word to him for so many years - a cause. And the cause was the right to address a wrong, to oppose evil, evil that preyed on the vulnerable, that fed men to lizards and dogs, that made men fight to the death for the sake of money, that killed old men in their sleep, and deprived a mother of her child.

He was proud of how he felt, an epiphany had occurred, a reality that made O'Neill think he was a better man, a man who could care, who could love, and who would defend what was right. It wasn't long before the dirt track became a hot main road. O'Neill stopped, stretching out his hamstrings, and rotated his back on his hips. Each step he took rasped with the rubber of his cheap white trainers, clinging and melting on the surface, the hot tar coming alive in the morning sun. He started inhaling through his nose, getting the breathing right, for breathing was everything in a fight breathing was everything in life. He rocked his neck from shoulder to shoulder loosening up his neck muscles, sounding out cracks of tension, just the way he used to before a fight. He packed the great dagger in its sheath and fixed it firmly to the back of his shorts and broke into a brisk walk, heading in the direction where he knew the ranch to be, and to the biggest fight he would ever have.

Two hours later, and a few pounds lighter from dehydration, he discovered a farm workers big old pick up truck at the side of the road. The truck was nearly as big as a lorry, with a steering wheel that looked like it could guide a ship in heavy seas. On the other side of the road was a ripe cane, field where he could see countrymen in baggy shirts and floppy hats chopping the giant cane. He got in the truck on the passenger side, away from the view of the men, relieved to see the keys in the ignition; another sign of good luck he thought. He started the huge vehicle up, it came alive. A mechanical behemoth disturbed jolting forward in gear. He punched the gas and he was away at speed, to the shocked stares of the men in the field, chugging smoke from the tired engine like a locomotive, thundering past a broken sign that displayed no destination.

Chapter 26

The Caribe now had eighty seven fighters. Eighty-seven bad boys. Men had came from all over Cuba, desperation their guide. They had heard about the ranch. Black, white, cinnamon, chocolate, olive, young, middle-aged, and even the old. The only thing they had in common other than crippling poverty, were scars and tattoos. They trained in the corrals, in the courtyard; some grappled in the earth, others used sticks as substitutes for knives; The Caribe disliked them using knives in training. The combination of testosterone and competition had in the past resulted in fatalities; if any dying was to be done The Caribe liked it to be in front of a baying, paying mess of tourists. Some sparred, others trained on their upper bodies, tugging useless car parts and engine blocks into the air on frayed pulley ropes in impressive exhibitions of brute strength. The Caribe liked this in the morning, the industry of blood and guts and him the factory boss. He liked to see the men hungry, eager to kill or be killed. That was the way of the world, that was why men had war, that was why men fought, to perpetuate their strength, that was why his ancestors devoured the hearts of other men. As long as The Caribe had men like this, and rich tourists, he had a business. And no matter what happened in the world, Cuba always had rich tourists. The Caribe knew that people possessed carnal desires and sacred lusts, and that they would always watch men kill each other, and pay handsomely to do so. There was no crookedness in his fights, no fights could be thrown like with boxers and crime syndicates, no horses slowed up before the finishing line; in his executive game it was winner or loser, it was to the death - truth. Soon, when Cuba came to its senses and he no longer had to worry about decrepit Castro and his senile brother and their archaic Government, The Caribe would have bigger business, better than the bulls in Spain he thought. Turn the ranch into a hotel; build a swimming pool like the five star Hotel Melia Cohiba, with bars, and brothels, casinos and cabarets. The Caribbean Las Vegas, entire factories of sin.

The Caribe walked amongst them. All nodded to him, and bid him good morning. They knew him by myth, from the barrios, from the jails, from the legends spun in old city bars, from the dark places in their hearts, and the hellfires in his dead eyes. The Caribe stalked proudly through the training men, he wore his white suit and white straw hat and carried the cigar box in one hand. A young fighter walked towards him, slim and lithe. As the young man passed in a lightning fast movement The Caribe pricked him in his kidneys with an unseen blade.

"Senor?" The Caribe said.

The young man wheeled around obedient.

"Yes?"

"It is polite to wish good morning to one's boss?"

"Si senor - Good morning."

"Gracias senor."

The young man continued on, blood streaking from a cut so delicate he was oblivious to it. The Caribe walked to another villa where he had segregated Natalia.

"Better than bulls." He spoke to no one but himself.

The Caribe entered the quarters where Natalia was staying under armed guard. She sat on the edge of the bed with another new white puppy and hand fed it some chicken. She barely looked at him, staring out into the horizon the way her mother did. He sat on the edge of the small wooden bed, making it creak with his bulk, and extended a huge hand to her cheek. She shied away from him as he tried to touch her face. The Caribe pushed the puppy away from its food with the heel of his boot. The little dog yelped and snapped at the heels. The Caribe shot a hand out and seized the pup by the folds of skin around the scruff, and held it aloft, pulling the skin so taut that the little puppy eyes near popped out of its head.

"Put him down!" Natalia demanded. The Caribe looked at the girl, noticing the change in demeanour and tone of voice since her short vacation with her Mother.

"Excuse me?"

"Please put him down!"

"Dog's must be disciplined, especially one that bites the hand that feeds it Natalia."

"Please."

The Caribe looked at the little girl, close to tears now, her lip shivering.

"You would never bite the hand that feeds you would you Natalia?"

Natalia shook her head slowly. Almost simultaneously as he dropped the puppy, which landed ungainly and screaming on the cold tiles, Natalia collected it, quickly soothing it with her petting hands.

"Not like your mother Natalia. You know what a whore is, Natalia?"

The little girl shook her head, terrified. Danger seemed to be all around as he stood up, swallowing what little space there was in the room.

"Well you want to be more careful, or soon you will find out."

The Caribe approached, her extending a huge hand to her face, when the air around them was suddenly filled with the sound of metal carnage, and the roaring revving of a vehicle, the angry shouts of men and the infuriated barking of pit bulls. The Caribe distracted from his dark intentions responded immediately, heading out of Natalia's room and towards the source, of the noise came from. Natalia petted her little dog soothing his whimpers with soft words, and even though her puppy was neither black in colour, or the puppy she had left behind in Gerardo's, she spoke to it as if it was.

"It's going to be OK Midnight, it's going to be OK."

And in her heart, she prayed it would.

O'Neill smashed through the Ranch's big metal gates at seventy-four miles per hour. His foot jammed to the floor. He gunned the leviathan vehicle down the dusty road and straight into the middle of the courtyard scattering the fighters. O'Neill jumped out of the vehicle, hands raised high and shouting calling out to The Caribe in his loudest voice.

The fighters in the yard approached, some circled like hyenas a lion. The bravest ones moved forward mouthing Spanish obscenities at his dramatic arrival. O'Neill hit the closest one to him, a straight jab, earning some well deserved space, fearing he would be swarmed and mangled by the group. A second man loaded up an arm with a knife and came in fast from the rear. O'Neill sucked in his body in the way Pretan had taught him and hit him a ferocious right hook. The man's eyes dimmed, and he staggered, legs tottering like an infant gazelle. O'Neill was surprised he didn't go down immediately; the man had a serious chin. O'Neill followed up, hitting him with a right cross that rocked the man's head back onto his neck, and down to one knee and then he dropped horizontal, the job complete. This served a warning to the others who stepped back, half in shock at who and what O'Neill was. O'Neill reassured them, that he meant them no harm, if they would afford him the same respect.

"I'm not here to fight you, I am here to fight the killer of babies, women and old men. You have my respect, he is nothing but shit, a son of puta The Caribe motherfucker comprehende?"

O'Neill could see the wicked faces of the bad boys; he knew probably none of them had much English but the most likely words they would be able to decipher would be

"Motherfucker" and "Caribe". He repeated them again only in a scream that dominated all other sounds of the ranch. O'Neill pulled the dagger from his sleeve the way Pretan had shown him.

"Mano o mano, with the knife." O'Neill pointing to the dagger.

The bad boys stood back at the sight of the great dagger, iridescent in the blazing sun, understanding and now fearful of the challenge. Some whispered to each other, and made circle signs at their temples, the universal indication that someone was crazy.

"Where are you motherfucker! Son of a puta. Brave with an army, how brave is he on his own?"

He roared to the ranch's eaves, sparking birds to flight. A voice answered his challenge, a smoky hiss from close range. Deep and dominant.

"Here tourist."

O'Neill pivoted to his left to see the bad boys split obediently to reveal The Caribe. The muscular man moved through them, the men almost bowing in reverence. There was no further need for insults now. O'Neill felt slightly shamed, caught out talking behind someone's back, then realising they've been listening all the time.

"You want to fight with a knife – You want to fight me?" The Caribe asked, pointing a finger first at O'Neill and then at his own person, as if O'Neill was insane.

"That's right I want to fight you, motherfucker."

The Caribe laughed like some evil caricature from a bad movie. Some of the fighters joined in, sycophantic, as they had never seen the big boss laugh.

O'Neill nodded his head in affirmation, eyeballing The Caribe hoping that the biggest risk he had ever taken in his life wasn't as insane as it looked. O'Neill gesticulated, slow, pointing at the dagger in his hand, accentuating every movement so as to articulate to one and all what his intentions were. This was vital, seeking the edge. He remembered what Mauritza had told him "ego, dick, machismo."

O'Neill was calling him out in front of his flock, in a blasphemous liturgy, a direct confrontation calling upon The Caribe to act with dignity as a man in the time honoured tradition, that had endured for centuries. The knife fighters read both men's reactions, but because O'Neill had asked the vital question launched in his own indomitable style, most of their eyes turned to The Caribe.

The Caribe was as calm as a man fishing; O'Neill could feel his own heart beating in a lot of places.

"Ok. Hey I know this gringo, this is The Terminator."

O'Neill noticed some of the bad boy fighters snigger.

"But I am busy now, tomorrow when I am not so busy". The Caribe said. Dismissive of O'Neill's entrance, dismissive of his challenge and threat, belittling him.

"Now motherfucker!" O'Neill trying to maintain the tempo.

This wiped the smiles of a few faces.

"But senor, I am unarmed?"

The Caribe opened his big arms wide, revealing nothing but muscles.

"Get fucking armed." O'Neill spat at him, feeling the moment and adrenaline being quashed by The Caribe's derision. O'Neill had come prepared, but he hadn't counted on The Caribe not being. And even though he was on home ground, in front of all his bad boys, that preparation was vital for the fight. He was earning himself time to work the fight out, to discover who his opponent was and what really was at stake. He was cerebral as well as physical.

"OK, OK, how about this tourist? Tonight you stay as my guest, and tomorrow morning in front of all the bad boys, we fight?"

O'Neill stared in disbelief at The Caribe; this was without doubt the biggest anti- climax of his life.

"I don't trust you. Motherfucker."

O'Neill spat out the expletive one last time, it's currency had dropped with the casual and insouciant response of The Caribe. He drove it home with venom, he needed to rattle this fuckers' cage, and this time he did. Anger flitted across The Caribes' face like a lizard on a wall. The Caribe spoke to the bad boys in Spanish, with authority. The men responded with nods and chatter, some with laughter.

"What did you say?" O'Neill disliking not understanding.

"I told them that tomorrow morning, before breakfast, that if you are not here and we do not have a duel in front of all these witnesses, then I am truly a Motherfucker and have no business leading men. Now I cannot be any fairer than that tourist?"

O'Neill, identifying the insults in each phrase.

O'Neill read his face, his instinct expertly detecting there was more.

"What else did you say?"

The Caribe smiled his unnatural smile.

"I told them to be up early to see you die..."

Mauritza looked through the reja bars. The view was muddy with blood from the burst capillaries in her eyes, she couldn't make out exactly but she knew it was him, knew by his accent, the defiant tone. He had come, O'Neill had come.

***

O'Neill stood in the large airy room of the ranch, experiencing probably the most surreal situation of his life, drinking good red wine and chugging on a fine cigar. The Caribe's men had taken the dagger from him, but The Caribe had promised to return it for their duel. He had waited in the room for the most of the day, watched by three knife fighters standing guard with AK 47s. Strangely, he did not feel like a prisoner. Mambo music blared in the background, O'Neill watched the cutlery jig across the thick wooden table in a jerky rhythm, as he sat waiting on a meal. Rhythm, that's what Cuba was, non-stop music and rhythm. Everywhere, the music sizzled, from the city to the country, and it played now. The pungent fine smells of chicken and lobster filled the room. O'Neill felt like he was being seduced, an uncomfortable sensation, smoking and drinking with your potential killer.

The chef, an old black man brought them fried chicken cooked with pineapples, and lobsters with ketchup. The Caribe seemed proud, that he had tomato ketchup at the table, a talisman of wealth in this poor country. O'Neill had been hesitant about the food, until hunger overtook him, like a fighter after a weigh in demanding protein for fuel. Everyone he had met in Cuba, held a conversation with, had intelligence, gifts that betrayed their situations, that if applied in different circumstances might have brought them success.

But what was success in life? To most it was money, to some love. The Caribe was smart, smart in his operations, smart in his cunning, in his ferocity. The Caribe sat at the opposite end of the big pine table. The interior of the spacious room was Moorish in design, complete with columns and Arabesque iron grills that guarded the tall open windows, reminding O'Neill of jail. Antiquities cluttered the room in the form of art and ornaments, the place was history.

A pale wooden cabinet one metre to his left, held many knives, of every shape and size, from four inch knuckle blades to ten inch bowies. O'Neill read the names on the steel, "Gerber", "Fairbairn", "Loveless", knives of every shape and design. Blades that became strangely luminescent in the errant rays of the golden evening that strayed through the reja windows into the room. The blades roosted in the cabinet like the fossil incisors and fangs of some mystical terrible beast.

"A man needs an enemy to truly test himself," The Caribe said.

He had a voice that belonged to an orator. Deep and rich it fluctuated between spiritual exhortation and authoritative schoolteacher. O'Neill glared at The Caribe. He was sure this man had many enemies, but all with fear in their hearts, and none that had confronted him like O'Neill.

"I'm sure after your adventures, tourist, you wish you never left the green of your homeland?"

"We make our own beds." O'Neill said.

"Tell me why you come to my home tourist?"

"A lot of things."

"The woman?" The Caribe asked. O'Neill suspected that The Caribe didn't use her name for fear of personalising her worth to him. A paradox, considering what lengths The Caribe had gone to retrieve her, bind her. You can try to be too clever sometimes O'Neill thought, enjoying The Caribe revealing a chink in his armour.

"As I said, a lot of things."

And there were, starting with Tony Montana, getting beaten half to death; his cigars, his money; being thrown to a fucking lizard; Alfredo, Mauritza, Natalia, Pretan, He could go on, tell the bastard what he really thought, but that would too much, that would allow The Caribe to know what he cared about, what area to target.

"But mostly I don't like bullies, and people trying to kill me."

"In the circumstances, as I do recall, you could have walked away with a lot of money and your life…"

"Like I said, we make our own beds…"

"As a tribute, I could have a young girl brought to you tonight, a young boy even whatever your inclination?"

O'Neill smirked at the big Cuban, it was intentional.

"I'm fine here, but don't let me stop you with the little boys…"

O'Neill watched a little fire grow in the black eyes.

"Motherfucker is not a nice name to call anyone tourist."

"Better than Tourist."

"But I don't know your name?"

O'Neill paused a second; he thought about it; he had a good name, a name that meant something, in a world where most names didn't.

"O'Neill is my name."

"O'Neill; that's an old name in Hirish history yeah? I know a lot about history hizepecially Irelandes."

"And why is that?" O'Neill enquired.

"We are Island people, colonised, and oppressed; warriors - fighters."

"Do you box?" O'Neill asked.

"I'm Cuban, every man has boxed here." The Caribe answered.

There could be only weight for a man like this.

"Super heavy?" O'Neill probed.

The Caribe nodded, closing his hooded eyes momentarily. It was the first time O'Neill had noticed him.

"You too, tourist? Don't tell me - middle?

There it was, the insult slipped into the conversation. O'Neill nodded his head, the insult with a non-response.

"A super heavyweight versus middleweight, there can only be one winner." The Caribe said.

O'Neill nodded slowly, happier now with the trash talk, the hype, standard head fuck, psychological games, cerebral gymnastics that pre-empted almost every fight.

"Yeah but you forgot about the knife, and the fact that the middleweight is faster, you got yourself a fight there..." O'Neill said.

The Caribe grinned.

"Touche, here's to the Hirish."

The Caribe raised his glass of blood red wine, O'Neill thought about refraining from joining him in the toast, but he decided the time for blood would come soon enough, and raised his glass, and toasted.

"Slainte"

The Caribe laughed out loud, deep and belling, it was good there could be humour before death.

"If I am right the O'Neill's fought Cromwell?"

The Caribe was right, the O'Neills' were the only Irish clan that Cromwell couldn't conquer. O'Neill was impressed - the man had history as well as bad intentions.

"Oliver Cromwell; now there was an enemy. I am Caribe - my ancestors were the only opponents to the Spanish, they too had great enemies; Diego Velazquez, Cortes, even the acclaimed Colombus. Men as ferocious as your Oliver

Cromwell, men who were commended for their genocide, immortalised in history for their conquests and sins..."

"The way you think you will?" O'Neill said.

The Caribe met his question with a dead eyed stare.

"In the words of one great Cuban dictator - 'History will absolve me'."

O'Neill shook his head slowly as The Caribe walked to the back wall of the room, towards an oil painting.

"Look at this".

O'Neill didn't respond.

"Please".

With hesitation he approached where the bigger man stood, O'Neill barely reaching The Caribe's shoulder. The painting depicted a ship being attacked by ferocious looking Indians wielding hatchets and knives.

"My people could swim for many hours unaided. These are my people and this is the crew of a Spanish ship in 1546, two hundred and forty five men were slain, two hundred and forty five Spanish oppressors. The Caribes ate every one of them, apparently the Spanish were extremely hard to digest."

The Caribe smiled that unnatural smile at his own joke, believing that it would amuse, the mood had become loaded and coiled.

"Then, they ate the crew of a French ship in 1596, one hundred and eighty eight men, whose flesh was so good that they considered the French a delicacy."

"Fascinating." O'Neill said in a mocking tone, sensing that The Cuban was seeking the edge.

It was a comment filled with sarcasm. The Caribe turned towering over O'Neill, O'Neill recognised the anger flitting across his face again.

"And your point is?"

"The point is tomorrow morning, after I kill you, in honour of my ancestors I want you to know I will gorge on your heart - Motherfucker..."

The moment exploded on O'Neill, catching him completely unawares. For a split second O'Neill thought The Caribe would make his move but the moment passed as quickly as it had detonated. The Caribe walked away from him towards the door. And it then occurred to O'Neill that the man had anger, which meant he had fear, no different to O'Neill, no different to any man. As the Caribe reached the door he turned slowly.

"You also have your wish, for tonight you are staying at our presidential suite, with an old friend, although, it maybe a little hard to recognise her."

Two guards took him to an outhouse on the ranch, beside where Alfredo had hid him in the aviary. They locked him in a rank room where he discovered Mauritza, naked and beaten, her face scarred and her body covered in copper and purple bruises.

O'Neill was afraid to touch her, for fearing of hurting her. Mauritza guarding her private place with a rag.

"Mauritza?"

"I knew you would come O'Neill, I knew."

"Jesus Christ." O'Neill said as he went to her on his knees, noticing her maimed face, her hair torn from her head in large clumps, her broken nose and a thin stream of serous fluid that skeined from her thigh to her calf.

"Will you ever want me again?" Mauritza asked.

The words came wispy and light, he nodded his head yes.

"Always and forever," O'Neill said and held her. On her breasts and arms there were bite marks, scratches.

"He said you would not come, but I knew you would, I knew you would."

O'Neill comforted her gently.

"Have you seen Natalia?" Mauritza said.

"No I haven't Mauritza."

She began to sob; he cradled her once again in his arms.

"He's going to ruin her, ruin her the way he ruined me." Mauritza said.

"You are not ruined my love, just unbreakable". They were the right words that she needed to hear.

"He sent knife fighters to me, I have lost count – animals, but I fought, O'Neill, I fought everyone of those fucks, until I could fight no more.

And O'Neill knew she had. She was unable to speak anymore, she crumpled, crying, sucking on her thumb like the child she had become. O'Neill consoled her as best a man could, with the embarrassed ignorance of a man, unable to speak for fear of not knowing.

As she slept he removed bits of straw from her matted hair, anger knotting in his stomach, rushing through his body, making his muscles hard as stone with lactic acid. Mauritza fended off assailants in her dreams. O'Neill gave her his Guinness T-shirt and did not move when his arm cramped up ashamed to wake her. He wished sleep would come, but he was too angry to sleep. All he could think about was plunging the big dagger into The Caribe's chest, and watching those Sonny Liston eyes dim, and the hellfires flicker out, and nothing else mattered, nothing except Mauritza.

***

Morning came and with it drums, startling him just as fatigue had made his eyes close.

He removed himself from Mauritza, still in a heavy sleep, no doubt induced by her injuries and the stress, careful not to disturb her. His right arm where she had rested for the night, felt as if it wasn't there. He placed a kiss on her head and walked to the door, waiting.

Two men came to the door, men with dirty eyes. One had a big pistol, a silver pistol O'Neill recognised as Tony Montana's. It was a good sign, before a fight O'Neill thought, men who fought against the odds needed such signs. O'Neill glared at them, his own eyes pouring shame on them at what had occurred in the cell with Mauritza, making their dirty eyes lower. He walked in front of them, through the kennels and out past the paddocks, where pit bulls smashed off the wire snarling with rage, making the guards flinch, but not O'Neill, who now regarded them as old friends.

The sun was an igneous ball of heat that dominated the sky. Knife fighters were everywhere, sitting on the corrals, slung across the bonnets of the old cars some eating pig feet, some smoking cigars eager for the show to begin. If he ever made it out cigars and scars were all that he would remember about these men. O'Neill walked past them.

He could detect begrudged respect in their dirty hard eyes. One nodded, a small token of solidarity between doomed strangers, warriors with no way out. Or was it something for them to remember when they met in the next world?

He focused and thought, he needed to be less tense, or he felt he would spontaneously combust. He'd heard about that before, people who generated so much electricity that they literally exploded. It was one of those unexplained things, like ghosts. Ghosts, O'Neill thought, there was a word. He tried to remember all the peoples' lives he had taken, all the people he had seen killed, through feuds, political assassinations, bar room brawls, in foreign countries. Death, the only thing a man could be sure of. O'Neill reckoned he thought like this because it was in the proximity and so close to it. It was in the air as they marched him to the centre of the ranch, to the emptied swimming pool tattooed with mulled stains of shit, blood and piss, smelling of shit, blood and piss. The stains of life and death and survival O'Neill thought, the fluids we all had to sustain and void that kept the human heart beating, because that's all we were, human beings, simple human beings. That's all this man monster The Caribe was, a human being, no more no less.

The Caribe lifted the ancient artefacts, from the chest he kept them in. The precious items looted from an archaeological burial site that had belonged to his ancestors. The necklace, with the tools of predatory animals all but myths in the current zeitgeist. Of giant shark, Jaguar, alligator, the tusks of huge boars, and the hoary clasp of eagle talons, and placed it around his neck. The Caribe dipped his fingers, into the crimson red of the war paint, concocted from the bloody tannins of his dead fighting dogs, and the ground that had borne him. He painted chevrons on his face, like those before him had, he assumed their mantel, the daubing of disaster. And finally he donned the armour of a murdered Spanish Conquistador, a spear hole in the breastplate, the sole attestation now.

Wearing the rank thorax in tribute, he left the domain.

The beating of drums reaching a crescendo. O'Neill turned to see The Caribe enter at the opposite end of the swimming pool, the sun on his back, in the grotesque costume and make up of ancient heathen, a monster, clown fiend, haloed by a crown of flies attracted to the festered filigree of war paint on his face to the triumphant cheers, whistles and the Cuban hisses from the knife fighters. Like fighting a Mexican in Mexico, O'Neill thought.

A man had to knock his opponent out to win in places like this. Only this contest didn't have that option. At the end of it there would be no hand held high, no bumping of fists. At the end of this contest there would be a man violently dead, eviscerated. The Caribe stretched, the dark supple skin pulling tight over the rack of muscles, so tight it looked if the skin would crack and reveal them, raw. Oblique muscles that rigged in little number three shapes, and pectoral, protected by the ancient breast plate. O'Neill pointed at the breastplate, aggrieved at what he thought was an abuse of the rules, and unfair advantage.

He needn't have worried as The Caribe, dropped the breastplate to the ground, much to audible laughter of the fighters, it only an ornament of the slain. In his bare torso, the muscles flashed with every movement, muscles that slipped and slid, buffed by special oil rubbed over his big body to make them shine. Man was dense with it. Muscles never impressed O'Neill. A fighter needed elasticity, quickness as well as power; O'Neill would just have to avoid any sort of clinches, where upper body strength would be an advantage. The Caribe removed his blade from behind his back, and held it aloft to catch the sun. A huge knife, with a persimmon black handle that resembled the shape of a coffin. O'Neill put it at ten inches. The blade shone, phosphorescent, casting beams of light that blinded the watchers, including O'Neill.

"Where is my dagger?"

The Caribe put the blade down allowing him to see again the dull dead Sonny Liston eyes, strangely enhanced by the blood paint. O'Neill could see the hell fires start to light.

Two men in a ring where nothing else mattered except the dismantling and destruction of your opponent.

"My dagger?" O'Neill repeated.

Magically the dagger dropped at his feet with a clang, thrown there by one of The Caribes' minions. O'Neill picked it up and fixed it in his hand, the way a man would carry a hammer. It was a simple ploy; inexperienced knife fighters did this, and this was exactly what he wanted The Caribe to think. The bait Pretan had taught him, to lure his opponent into the thinking that he was fighting a novice. O'Neill stared back, returning his own dead eyed stare.

***

The Caribe breathed through his nose, gently inhaling and exhaling, testing the regularity with the rising of his diaphragm. He could feel the sun on his back, the oil on his body making every motion fluid, and battle heat, the slick electric that made the blade an extension of his hand. It was as if the blade was joined to his hand, his every touch - death, and death it would be. The destruction of the tourist would anchor the thoughts of every one of his knife fighter bulls watching, alerting each of them to what they had to face if they dared to compete against him. There will be no dogs for you Irishman, The Caribe thought, take you to my pot, just like my grandfathers' grandfathers' did, make her cook the heart and then share it heart at the dinner table. The Caribe thought about Mauritza, about what she had proclaimed.

"I love him"! The words still infuriated him. How could she love? That was the reason he had sent the knife fighters to her. Love what? What will there be left to love? Blood and guts, no heart, no mind, no soul, no cock, just meat in my pot bitch, treacherous fucking bitch! I am the man, champion, slayer of men, six foot five, two hundred and eighty pounds of muscle, no fat, bigger than Savon, the champion boxer, triple gold medal winner of all of Cuba, stronger than Savon, badder than Savon, from the places no one has seen, from a world of flame and steel, with the cannibal warrior's blood coursing through my veins - I am the dragonfly, I am the sun.

***

O'Neill documented his reasons; for Mauritza, for Natalia, for Tony Montana, for Berta, for Alfredo, for Pretan, for Che, for Cuba… The men circled, wide legged like crabs, feet planted, both with their own tolls to pay.

O'Neill made the first move towards The Caribe, the gaudy face, unfunny and macabre, in this Cuban Grand Guignol. Who stood motionless, aiming his blade low to his hip training it on O'Neill as if it were a loaded gun.

The Caribe was trying to direct sunlight from the blade into O'Neill's eyes, like a child in school with a new watch O'Neill thought. Pretan's words came back to him, like a distant echo in a labyrinth of caves.

"Never fight fair."

O'Neill spat at the big man's face and tried to manoeuvre away, but still the blinding light followed him, like a fly under a magnifying glass, burning and blinding. O'Neill lunged towards The Caribe, deliberate, well out of range. The movement was futile, to get the light out of his eyes and establish that he was unafraid of territory and the man. The Caribe did nothing, apt treatment for O'Neills' disrespect. O'Neill shifted his feet back, moving quickly. He had always had good feet, unusual for a seemingly one-dimensional fighter who led with his face, and they served him well now. Now, The Caribe advanced, the big blade slung low at his hip, the other meaty arm, shielding his vital organs. O'Neill moved back, raising his blade above his head like an ice pick. The Caribe relentless, tracking O'Neill no emotion on his face, cutting off the swimming pool the way a brawler would the ring. For the first time in his life O'Neill felt like the fighters who had faced him, the artistes who shot jabs, and ran and backtracked fearful of him trapping them on the ropes and corners. O'Neill fixed a snarl on his face to veil his fear.

The point about fear was not to give in to it, to use it. The Caribe exploded forward. The speed was beyond anything O'Neill had ever encountered, not in the boxing ring, not in life. It was supernatural speed, like the skirmish of tigers. O'Neill was unsure if there had been contact, until a ligature of blood skeined from his forearm. He was lucky. If he hadn't feinted, and shrugged his organs into a shell, he would have been bleeding from a lot more wounds. The Caribe returned to his battery position and waited. O'Neill was in awe. A man that close, of that size and weight might have decided to use his power, in a direct assault. The Caribe had not. It took intelligence and control to do that. The reward was first blood and he had achieved that.

"De- fang the snake".

The words came from the archives of his head Pretan guiding him from the grave. The Caribe approached from another angle, both hands in a blur of motion, trying to lure a strike, The Caribe drove forward on one knee, the blade speared with power towards O'Neill's groin. O'Neill brought the dagger down fast as he had been shown. The Caribe's hand and blade returned quickly to shield his big body. Like a snake retreating into coils O'Neill thought. He did not know if his own dagger had made contact, but the speed at which the Caribe's hand traced back gave him encouragement. The blade returned as, The Caribe feinted; O'Neill parried the blade with his dagger, creating supernova flashes from the colliding steel.

The Irishman was good, The Caribe now aware that the old man had taught him well. It was an unusual style but effective, made apparent in the way the Irishman moved, and combined with an impressive hand speed, it had kept him alive so far. The man had boxed, The Caribe could tell, the type of man who had natural fitness too.

O'Neill had noticed something about The Caribe. He kept his right elbow tight to his stomach, using the bone to shield his stomach but leaving his liver momentarily exposed. A man's liver was the key to his life. Hook hard to the liver and all the men he had ever hit went to their knees. Going to your knees would reveal all the areas Pretan had shown him, in which to kill a man with one blow. The only bad thing was his arm. His great arm, the arm that had felled men, like a chainsaw trees, the arm with Che on it, would be exposed and indefensible.

"De fang the snake". Pretan's words getting louder as the battle raged harder.

Pretan was beside him again, speaking logic, opposing his big plans. O'Neill bulled forward after him, backing the big man up, bobbing and feinting from distance, trying to get the bigger man to come into the range where he could get to that big hand and the blade.

The Caribe stopped and sprang forward kicking him hard at his wrist. O'Neill completely caught unawares at the new tactic. O'Neill stared in horror as the great dagger sailed from his hand, and ten yards behind The Caribe and into the pit. Ten yards might have as well been ten miles. The garish face in front of him with the necklace of animal talons and fangs revealed a slight smile, O'Neill's vulnerability current, the obstacle insurmountable. O'Neill now the de fanged. The Caribe toyed with him, mimicking his movement, shifting left and right, blocking both ways. Knowing that the Irishman had to pass him, that when he did, he would drive the blade to the colon, where he would unspool the great coils of viscera from the gut, and watch the final demise of his nemesis, and take another eye to add to his collection.

"Run." Was what Pretan said when a man was de-fanged, only where did a man run to a pit? O'Neill looked to the ground, his eyes attracted to the mirrored shimmer of the ancient Spanish, dented, breastplate, The Caribe had cast to the ground in tribute to his ancestors. It was five yards to his left. Five yards was better than ten, O'Neill feinted right to break for the knife, and launched himself left to the breast plate, seizing it just in time, bringing it up to fend of a full frontal attack. The Caribe's blade punched into the breast plate, causing a second fissure, the impact caused O'Neill to miscue his feet and lose his footing. With two strikes, The Caribe had severed his Achilles tendon and hamstring on separate legs. O'Neill stood like a bull that had just been administered the coup de grace at a slaughterhouse, legs akimbo, slowly spreading. Legs unable to follow the brain's commands. He tried to remain on his feet as The Caribe slashed at his throat, he moved his head three inches to the right, out of sheer instinct saving the vital organs, but drawing significant amounts of blood from his upper face. The wounds vespiary. The Caribe retreated, back into battery position, unscathed, waiting, conserving energy, and gathering his wind. O'Neill felt the world leaving him now, clouds scudding spectacularly fast across the sky blotting out the sun, the eclipse symbolic and impending of his plight. His right leg, the one that was hamstrung, slumped useless to the ground at a forty five degree angle, his other leg, shivered and shook unable to compensate the loss, and accommodate the unnatural stance. The blood hot on his face, aware of long strips of skin curling from his brow to his cheek like wood shavings, obscuring his view. Half crippled and near blind. Curtains of blood flooded his vision and all he could hear now was his heartbeat, above everything, the rumble of salsa, above the shouts of the crowd, above the yelping of dogs that smelt his blood, rapid and jolting. O'Neill stared into the dead eyes, banded by the crimson colour, the hellfires now glittering livid in the imminence of victory.

"Into the eyes of the Devil".

The voice of Mohammad Ali now reverberating in his head. That's what Mohammed Ali had said about Sonny Liston. It was time, when there was no time left, his blood saturating the ground, touching up the old stains. Four critical wounds he thought, each one, seemingly competing for dominance. The wound on his arm was worse than he suspected, dominant now, ringing up and down his arm with pain. The Caribe, thriving on his subsiding, prolonging the end, and the agony. But it wasn't over yet, as long as O'Neill held breath. The scudding of clouds passed, releasing the sun, and the breast plate as a powerful, natural mirror. O'Neill raised the ancient breast plate to the sun, sutured by implements now fossils capturing it's full reflection and directed it's blinding force full into The Caribe's face blitzing the foul greasepaint, and for once closing momentarily, those pagan eyes. As if the effigy - spirit of murdered Conquistador who that it once played host to, rally in one last glorious mutiny. The moment was all it took, O'Neill scrambled forward hopping, more than any other locomotion, like a line struck bird confined to the ground outlasting predatorily conquest only by fluke. He reached the great dagger, and clenched it tightly in his hand, now it could only be acquired when he was dead. But still the odds outweighed him. O'Neill hobbled backwards, until he felt his back touch the wall, where he braced himself. At least he was upright now, but cornered.

He put his least stricken leg forward, from the position he had now, he could at least torque defence with his hips. The Caribe seemed slightly thrown by the missed opportunity. O'Neill beckoned to him with his bloodied fingers, to come forward, opening his arms to expose the chest area, the dropping of the vital guard to now reveal the tantalising swag of his heart, not a metre from The Caribe's blade. "Offer your heart," again Pretan's disembodied and long gone voice screaming through O'Neill's mind. The Caribe, hesitated, cautious of being intoxicated by the bait and immediacy of victory. The brutal colours on his face now wept sweat in kitschy streaks. Some knife fighters urged The Caribe forward in hisses, one man even booed. The Caribe stared to the frieze of unseen faces, and no other dared. Silence fell upon them all. The Caribe read O'Neill's vital signs; blood plopped on the ground between his feet, the eyes glassy, the transition transmogrifying to a taxidermist's trophy. O'Neill wiped blood from his eyes, with each passing second, the Irishman seemed to diminish against the wall. His head growing heavier, squatting onto the neck for support. The Caribe concentrated on his opponent's dagger hand, noticing the hand falter below his hip, long gone as guardian of the heart. The Caribe detonated forward aiming the huge blade for the central target of the cardiac area. O'Neill blocked the attacking blade with his own blade, and torqued from his hip, using the wall as leverage feinted and whipped all he had into his right hook The Caribe anticipated a strike, but not a punch. O'Neill felt the punch hammer home, slamming it as hard as he could into the liver of The Caribe. The motherfucker tottered a little, halted for a millionth of a second, trying to suck in the wicked pain and transfer it somewhere else, still standing, still retaining enough to dice every major artery on O'Neill's right arm, scarring Che's salient gaze forever.

"Offer your heart…"

Pretan, for the last time, from the ruddy red earth of Cuba. It was the opportunity O'Neill had been waiting for and he drove the Illongo dagger home, shearing through the big fingers raised in desperate defence, The Caribe aware that the angle created to hit the chest and heart was O'Neill's and not his. O'Neill's blade went slow, but definite, sinking through the mass of meat and muscle. He withdrew it and pumped it in again, desperate, again and again until he saw the hellfires dim in the black eyes, made clearer by the gory make up. They rolled once, like a shark feeding, the face more barbarous, than hilarious still unfunny in it's clown grimace then back to their gloomy black.

O'Neill retreated in disbelief as the huge man still stood, blood gushing from the gaping cavity left in his chest. The Caribe began to fall, slow and heavy like a building being demolished, down to the dirt, and the bloody quag, for which he had been responsible.

O'Neill slumped down the wall beside the dying man, and the music stopped; even the dogs barking too, as if one and all were supernaturally connected to the black heart of the Caribe. An epic engine of sin that was conking out. The blood loss was making The Caribe cold, cold in the oppressive heat. The Caribe now knew what a hundred others before him had known, and what had been his only envy of the dead; that as life leaves a man, what special secrets flutter fast through the mind's eye like a book's pages in a wind. The answers came quick to him. The people he killed mobbed him all at once, men, women, and children who gloated at his demise, a baying legion of screams that terrorised him in their mob. Their many images like footprints in sand. Then further regression, as he was revisited by the reprehensible acts committed on him, as a child in dungeons by evil men that he thought should now bear some responsibility for his actions as a man. The Caribe appealed for sanctuary to the black Saints and his Carib ancestors, clasping onto the artefact around his neck. They came, to escort him out of his mortal coils, to a savage place where the battering of jungle drums and the torment of life deafened his ears and the taste of the sweetest meat prominent on his tongue.

The regression accelerated, transmigrating beyond his natural form, until he was a great bird of prey from the family of butchers gliding tranquil on thermal winds patrolling the sky, and then plunging to deep water, where he became a huge shark probing the depths for prey. The images and experiences were fearful but not unpleasant to one that had interest in such matters, to one who embraced the dark, to one who had owned the night. But the last image that remained with The Caribe returning him to the blood blistered earth of Cuba, was of Mauritza. The unnatural smile formed on his war face, as the image eroded in his dying brain. Mauritza before him in a simple cotton dress, with her different coloured eyes, on the diamond white sand beach. With her beautiful smile, twenty years before, a seashell in her hand. Just a girl and he just a young man, before his sins and diabolical influences took over. And this is what he took with him, as a last image, to his eternal new kingdom of night.

***

O'Neill looked to the fighters above him their faces open in shock at the outcome, silent, and he fell to his knees beside The Caribe, dying also, hearing the sounds of the world going low, the spit in his mouth turning dry. O'Neill felt as if he was underwater for a long time. He watched as his own blood streamed from his wounds, flowing to merge and congregate with The Caribe's, in a bloody isthmus, who lay not two feet from him. Just his luck he thought. They'd probably share the same cell in hell he thought; now that was punishment.

"Motherfucker."

Was all he said before he went to his own dark places.

Chapter 77

O'Neill awoke a month later with no left arm, and no Che. Awoke in a clinic in downtown Havana. He felt as weak as a child and was whiter than the sheets he lay in with his suppurating stump. The Doctors told him that they had to send for blood, from all over the Island to keep him alive. It made O'Neill happy that he had the blood of all the good Cuban people running through his veins now; that somehow the scarlet blood of the revolt had rinsed all his bad traits away. In the evenings he would walk with Mauritza in the clinic gardens, overrun with dragonflies. Her face had healed up, all except the inflamed scar that ran from her cheek to her mouth, fresh testament to their shared history. His n' Her scars. They were the members of some secret sect. Mauritza had told him strange things - that the knife fighters all left the ranch after The Caribe's death, that the corpse burned for a full day, and that the dagger was so deeply embedded in his heart that it couldn't be removed. O'Neill was glad to hear that they burned him, he couldn't rest easy with a motherfucker buried in the ground, too afraid of his being resurrected by some local witch doctor.

They sat alone in the gardens on one fine summer evening.

"How's Natalia?" O'Neill asked

"Good, we've moved into a nice home in Miramar, she calls me "Mother" now. I got a good swap for the ranch. He left the ranch to me. Can you believe that?"

O'Neill could. He had always sensed that under the surface The Caribe had more than just a sexual attraction to her, he had sensed it bubble like lava in an active volcano. Why else would he have scarred and beaten her? It would have been simpler just to kill her.

"You'll be getting discharged soon." Mauritza said inspecting his wounds.

"I hope so."

She touched her pretty nose, smiling surreptitiously.

"I have friends in high places."

"What about that confidentiality thing?"

"Not amongst the doctors in Habana." Mauritza said.

She winked at him with her green eye, and fetched a dragonfly with care that had landed magically on his head, and ushered it into the air.

"They said it was a miracle that I lived." O'Neill said.

"Not miracle, Cuba, best health system in the world."

O'Neill looked at her. She was still the most beautiful woman he had ever seen, the scars just made her merely mortal.

"Stay with me O'Neill."

He looked at her, the beautiful different coloured eyes.

"Me with one arm?"

"I don't care if you had no arms, no legs, O'Neill."

He kissed her, and then he broke off.

"On one condition."

"What?"

"You know where I could get a tattoo done around here?"

She nodded her head affirming.

"What type of tattoo?"

"Che, some motherfucker stole the other one."

She smiled at him. She could see hope in his face, and love. She was grateful it was for her.

"I love you O'Neill". She said.

O'Neill sensed she had travelled every day through her life to reach this point; he knew that he had.

"And I you Mauritza", he said. Mauritza placed her hand by mistake to where his right arm used to be. She looked sad to have done so. O'Neill dismissed it by offering his other arm. She gratefully took it.

"I know a place in Salem."

"Well let's go then –"

Mauritza helped him to his feet and kissed him. They hit the street, and the sounds of the sizzling salsa, with the sun sinking over the Malecon into the calm sea, where children bobbed on inner tubes that looked like big black donuts, fishing for lobster. They passed a new mural being painted on an old wall in the street by a group of young people; it was of Che. The image was nearly finished, O'Neill stopped and looked into its eyes, eyes staring off to far away places, foraging for new countries to liberate, and new peasants to train.

"There is only one Che." Mauritza said.

O'Neill turned to her. She smiled gently, like a child getting the last word in. O'Neill laughed and looked to the mural and saluted the new image with his only arm.

"Gracias companero." was all he had to say.

About The Author

Originally from Belfast, Northern Ireland with a career that spans over two decades Pearse Elliott is a recognised award-winning playwright and screenplay writer.

He created and wrote the Number 1 hit TV series Pulling Moves (BBCNI 2004) and was the writer behind one of the most successful independent Irish Films to date Man About Dog (2004) which subsequently became a Number 1 Box Office hit.

Pearse was also the writer and director behind the critically acclaimed film The Mighty Celt (2005) for which former X-Files star Gillian Anderson went on to win Best International Actress for her part as Kate at the IFTAs (Irish Film & TV Awards) in the same year.

The commercial success of Irish horror film Shrooms in 2007 cemented Pearse's growing reputation as a much sought-after screenplay writer.

His stage play Man In The Moon (2013) went on to show across the UK and Ireland as well as a four week run at the

Irish Theatre Festival in New York (2014). Man In The Moon was also nominated for best play, best director and best actor at the Origin's First Irish Theatre Festival (2014).

Pearse's play The Holy Holy Bus (2014) sold out Belfast's Waterfront Hall, Lyric Theatre and the Grand Opera House (2016) before returning to The Lyric (2017). It was also a winner of the Audience Award at The Belfast Festival the year it opened and has been commissioned as a screenplay by BFI.

Pearse was the winner of the prestigious BBC First Bite Young Playwrights competition in 1996, received an Aisling Award for Outstanding Contribution in Arts and Culture in 2005, was nominated for a Radio Sony award (1996) and recognised as a Top 40 Under 40 Artist in 2008.

To date Pearse has written over 20 critically acclaimed stage plays and has been nominated over 15 times at the Irish Film and Television Awards for his work.

Man In The Moon will show at The Mac theatre, Belfast in May 2018 and Pearse's latest play The Sword And The Sand premieres at The Lyric Theatre, Belfast also in May 2018.

Pearse's debut fiction novel The Executive Game (released April 2018), published by Excalibur Press, is set in Cuba and follows the story of Irish smuggler O'Neill in what is a bloody and violent visit to Havana.

Pic by Debbie Deboo Photography

Pearse Elliott

Printed by Amazon Italia Logistica S.r.l.
Torrazza Piemonte (TO), Italy

59319309R00191